Nick Tyrone is a journalist who writes regularly for *The Spectator*. He is also a policy specialist who has worked with several leading UK think tanks. He is the author of both non-fiction and fiction books and lives in London with his family.

www.nicktyrone.com

 @NicholasTyrone

THE PATIENT

Nick Tyrone

ACCENT

First published in 2021 by
HEADLINE PUBLISHING GROUP

1

Cataloguing in Publication Data is available from the British Library

ISBN 978 1 4722 8779 3

Typeset in 11.5/14.75pt Bembo Std by Jouve (UK), Milton Keynes

Printed and bound in Great Britain by Clays Ltd, Elcograf S.p.A.

HEADLINE PUBLISHING GROUP
An Hachette UK Company
Carmelite House
50 Victoria Embankment
London
EC4Y 0DZ

www.headline.co.uk
www.hachette.co.uk

To my daughter Constance who gave me the
inspiration for this story.

Chapter One

Mammary Monthly

The Big Day has come two weeks late. As a result of this delay, Mrs Sincope is booked in for an induction at the hospital this morning. With any luck, she will soon be in labour and her daughter will be born in a few hours' time.

The Sincopes exit their flat using their building's old, frightening lift. Standing there together beside each other as they descend, Mrs Sincope wearing the tracksuit ensemble that had unconsciously become her late-pregnancy fashion, Mr Sincope dressed as always in a perfectly presentable yet clearly cheap and slightly ill-fitting suit and tie with a much nicer bluish-grey overcoat on top, one could take a photograph of them face on and get a perfect sense of both their respective personalities. Mr Sincope looks bored and slightly put out; Mrs Sincope appears nervous yet strong at the same time; both of them stare straight ahead and give no outward sign of even being aware of their spouse's presence in any meaningful sense.

Once outside, the couple walk towards and then climb into their Skoda Felicia, a cheap used car they had bought six months back.

'Felicia. That's what we should have called our daughter instead!' Mr Sincope shouts mostly to himself as he starts the vehicle. This is precisely the sort of insensitive, passive-aggressive comment that is essential to understanding his personality. He had conceded ground unhappily prior to departing the flat in a semi-argument with his wife about what they should name their as yet unborn daughter; while the logical and honest thing to do would have been to extend the conversation, at least as far as him revealing to his wife how much naming their daughter Dorothy meant to him, even if they went with Mrs Sincope's choice of Faith in the end, he had already decided instead to simply be lightly bitchy about the name of his daughter for the rest of his life.

'I thought we had reached an agreement on this, dear. Unless you'd like to talk it about it further?' Mrs Sincope asks in a take-no-shit sort of a voice. This shuts Mr Sincope up for a bit. Ten minutes go by without a further word between them as the Skoda slowly proceeds in the direction of the hospital.

'Traffic is bad. We should have left earlier,' Mrs Sincope says to break the silence. The comment is inspired by her recollection of her husband's telephone conversation of the previous day, to arrange for the induction she is now on her way to face. He had seemed extremely stressed throughout the call and relayed to her afterwards that the man on the other end of the line – who, Mr Sincope felt the need to stress, spoke with a *northern accent* – had really gone overboard in insisting that the Sincopes not be late for the induction, but by the same token, that they not arrive *too* early either. It had left Mr Sincope confused and scared about what was expected of him.

'Please be prompt,' the man on the other end of the line had said to Mr Sincope.

'I was intending to be precisely on time,' Mr Sincope had sharply responded with after this slant on his punctuality.

'If you were to arrive even two or three minutes late, I can't be liable for what might happen.'

'We'll arrive early then.'

'Good. But not too early, if you please.'

'All right then. My wife and I will arrive fifteen minutes before the appointment is due to start, have no fear.'

'Oh no, no, fifteen minutes is far too early, sir! If everyone turned up that promptly I'd have a right mess on my hands here,' the northern man on the phone had said with panic in his voice.

'Ten minutes then?'

'We wouldn't want your poor wife to have to be sat there for ten minutes waiting about, sir.'

Mr Sincope, a patient man when it comes to coping with mundanity, had at last begun to get genuinely annoyed with the pedantic detail involved in the conversation.

'Fine then, I'll get there six minutes and forty seconds early!'

'I'll leave that sort of detail to you, sir,' the receptionist had said, as though the strangeness of the conversation had all flowed from the other end of the line.

Mr Sincope had been wound up before he'd made this call and afterwards his blood pressure sky-rocketed. His stress relating to this conversation with the hospital receptionist even disturbed his sleep that night, something which was a rare occurrence for him. He could snooze through almost anything in the normal run of things. The insomnia that night was, to be fair, at least partly down to the toll the month leading up to the Big Day had taken, what with his wife's constant complaining about her late-term aches and pains and all of his work colleagues chivvying him about his flat ('I've heard small flats like those, particularly ones in buildings with dodgy lifts like yours, can be death traps for infants. Surely the order of operations goes, house first, baby second.'). The worst thing for him about all this work-based badgering had been the fact that the Sincopes could actually afford to buy a house, easily if they sold the flat. But Mrs Sincope was deeply averse to the idea. She hoped for a while to give her husband the hint by lightly pushing against the plan, always finding something not to like in every house they viewed.

'Look at these curtains. I couldn't live in a place with these curtains.'

'We'll replace the curtains, dear.'

'I don't like the way the hallway is decorated.'

'We'll get it redone.'

'I don't like the neighbourhood.'

'It's two blocks away from where we live now!'

'I think if we're going to buy a house we ought to move up in the world, don't you think?'

Mr Sincope was always terribly embarrassed when his wife would mutter what he would consider uncouth things in public, such as the line about 'moving up in the world'. For him they were a demonstration of the gulf in upbringing between them. Both of his parents were stockbrokers and he grew up in a large detached house in North London where he was raised by an English nanny, something in which as a child he took immense pride (no foreigners raising the stockbroker Sincope's boy, thank you kindly). Meanwhile, Mrs Sincope's family was mostly still a mystery to her husband due to her reticence in talking about them in much detail. She was from the north, mostly Manchester although there was some moving about that had been done, her father being a drunk whom Mr Sincope had met on precisely one occasion and who hadn't even bothered to turn up at their wedding. He was dead now; her mother had died when she was a child. She had a sister named Lucille whom he had never even spoken to on the phone, much less met in person. Although she had of course been invited, Lucille hadn't turned up at the wedding either, although at least her absence was partly expected as she lived in South America.

That was almost the sum total of what Mr Sincope knew about his wife's family. Luckily, Mr Sincope wasn't actually interested in knowing a whole lot more about his wife's relations despite being a little suspicious now and then about her obfuscation on the matter. What she had filled him in on already sounded ghastly enough. All those secrets; all that familial dysfunction; all that 'northern-ness' (Mr Sincope, as we have learned, was not a fan of northerners in general, a fact which oddly hadn't prevented him from marrying one). Mrs Sincope doesn't speak with a northern accent, adding an even stranger layer to everything. Her speaking voice is a nondescript, middle-class sounding RP, something which rubs up against her upbringing, at least as her husband understands it.

Traffic is bad in West London on this Big Day Thursday. Mr Sincope honks the Skoda's horn and flings a four-letter word in the direction of a white van as it cuts him off.

'What did we say about swearing in the car, dear?' Mrs Sincope says, patting her husband patronisingly on the arm as she often does when he loses his temper. They had made an agreement a few weeks back not to use profanity while riding in the Skoda. This pact was made in the hope that it would help them prevent using bad language in front of their daughter after she had arrived. Using the vehicle as a sort of training ground for not f-ing and blinding, as it were.

'If the traffic is like this the whole way, we'll be late for the appointment,' Mr Sincope says matter-of-factly. As luck would have it, right at that moment the traffic starts to clear and as a result the Sincopes arrive at the hospital *fourteen* minutes early. *I'm so glad we have this car,* Mr Sincope thinks to himself as he pulls the cheap, rusting machine into a parking spot. Mr Sincope was initially against owning a vehicle. He had always felt it was wasteful to own a car in London. But his workmates had bullied him into the purchase ('You have to have a car if you're going to have a kid, right? How are you going to get your wife to the hospital when she's in labour – wait for a bus to turn up?'). The crucial difference to the house-moving situation and the lack of momentum there came down to the fact that Mrs Sincope was all for the car idea. Mr Sincope only had to mention it and the next weekend Mrs Sincope had bought the Skoda Felicia from an Egyptian man who had advertised it on the internet. Mr Sincope was initially appalled at the purchase of such an inexpensive vehicle and yet he grew to appreciate it. He was nothing if not exceedingly cheap.

'Can you believe it,' she says. 'Later on today we'll take little Faith home in that car seat back there.'

Mr Sincope smiles in a slightly patronising manner while placing his hand on his wife's knee.

'Please don't get your hopes up too high, dear. We could well be in the hospital overnight. Perhaps even two.'

'I know,' Mrs Sincope says, looking down at her hands as she unconsciously folds them into a miniature cradle. 'I just can't wait for our baby to come.'

'Me neither. But let's stay realistic. We may have a tough day or two ahead of us so we should be mentally prepared for it.'

Being 'mentally prepared' is a phrase used so often by Mr Sincope it would be high on a list of traits to use should one wish to caricature the man.

'Of course, you're right,' Mrs Sincope says as she breaks the hand-cradle, her determination to stay strong in the face of whatever was ahead obliterating the tenderness to which she had succumbed. Mr Sincope exits the car and walks over to the ticket machine to examine how much it will cost to park. This leaves Mrs Sincope to struggle her way out of the Skoda all by herself. It had annoyed her greatly as her pregnancy had proceeded that despite male strangers constantly giving up their seats on public transport for her sake, her own husband had never once thought to aid her in getting out of that tiny car, an undertaking she found an ever-increasing challenge after the seventh month.

'Jesus Christ, it's three pounds a shitting hour!' Mr Sincope exclaims as he discovers the tariff.

'Remember what we discussed about swearing, dear,' his wife says. 'Faith can hear you now.'

She points at her rotund belly as she shouts this to her husband. Mr Sincope hates when she does this; a dramatic gesturing to her uterus which had become ubiquitous at some point he'd lost track of within the third trimester. In his mind, to indicate to one's lower abdomen in and of itself was barbaric and uncivilised, something belonging to a lower class of people. He also felt that to point at one's offspring like that in any circumstance would be unacceptable as well. To compound his annoyance, the deal they had made was to avoid using profanity in the car solely, and he was clearly not sitting in the Skoda at that moment.

'What should we do then?' Mr Sincope snaps at her. 'I'm not paying three quid an hour to park here.'

'What else are we going to do? If we move the car, we'll be late.'

His wife is correct in this assertion. And although Mr Sincope loathes feeling like he is being ripped off, the thought of getting their arrival time wrong after yesterday's phone conversation scares him much more. Looking at his watch and realising they only had a little over four and a half minutes until they would only be ten minutes early, Mr Sincope, having decided that being between ten and five minutes early would be optimal given what he said on the phone yesterday, flies into a sudden panic.

'You're right, we must hurry!' he bellows. Mr Sincope pays for the parking, runs to put the ticket in the car window, slams the door shut and then grabs Mrs Sincope's hand a little too violently and begins to run into the hospital with her trailing behind, trying to keep pace.

'Slow down, would you!' she shouts at her husband while rubbing her bump ostentatiously with her free hand. She knows now that she has lost him to one of his frequent quasi-panic attacks, and so she behaves as she always does when she finds herself in this situation: she thinks about something pleasant instead. Like how she had, for the most part, enjoyed being pregnant. In the early days she was amazed at how little affected by morning sickness she had been, particularly as it had hit her neighbour, Sarah, who lived in a flat on the same floor, hard with her first-born.

'It will be hell, trust me,' Sarah had told Mrs Sincope over tea when Mrs Sincope first announced she was pregnant. 'You'll be throwing up over bloody everything.'

Mrs Sincope was terrified as she didn't tend to have any sort of gastronomic difficulties in the normal run of things and didn't know how she would cope with such an inelegant change. She is secretly proud of the fact that she hadn't vomited once since she was fourteen. As it turned out, she didn't become physically ill one single morning during her entire pregnancy. And until the final two months, she hadn't felt particularly tired either. Having said all of that, the last couple months of the pregnancy had come with some downsides, like her aching lower back alongside the inability to find a single position that felt truly comfortable, either sitting or standing. Yet all of these were minor compared to the joyous sense of having her child inside of her, growing every moment. Thinking about this gives Mrs Sincope respite, particularly in moments like her husband yanking her by the arm at superhuman speed down hospital corridors on the day she is due to give birth to their child.

Mr and Mrs Sincope step off the hospital lift and enter the fifth floor. Mr Sincope approaches the reception desk still panting from the exertion of the mad dash from the car park. There sits a homely woman who looks to be around fifty years of age – but is in actual fact much younger than that – who brandishes a name tag that reads 'Jill'.

'Hello, we have a two p.m. appointment with Dr Blots,' Mr Sincope says to Jill as he recovers his breath. The receptionist looks up extremely slowly from the copy of *Gamers Bi-Weekly* she is reading. Jill is the type of gal who doesn't get out much. Her best friend in the world is her cat, Mittens. She speaks fluent Klingon. Her interests include blogging about her pet feline, electoral reform, and role-playing games. Her noted lack of general bodily swiftness on the Sincopes' Big Day is down to the fact that she had swallowed three barbiturate tablets twenty-five minutes prior to their arrival in Dr Blots' reception area, in doing so enacting what was perhaps the most half-hearted suicide attempt in the history of the human race. Jill is depressed because her girlfriend of eighteen months, Doreen, has finally left her. She was dumped the evening prior via a note which simply read:

I've met a bloke. See ya – D

Doreen had been Jill's lifeline, one of the few close human companions she'd had in the course of her sad, lonely, cat-filled existence.

'Have a seat,' the depressed receptionist says to the Sincopes in her high-pitched, squeaky voice that takes both of them slightly aback. Mr Sincope quickly recovers from the surprise and leans in closer to Jill.

'You might wish to make note of the time: we're six minutes and forty seconds early exactly,' he says. Jill looks at Mr Sincope as if he were completely mad, staring at him in bewildered silence. The downers in the receptionist's bloodstream make the situation even more awkward, as to Jill it doesn't seem like as much time is passing as is actually the case, her eyes focused on the strange man standing across the desk from her for several agonising seconds. Mr Sincope feels the need to try and explain his comment after Jill's reaction.

'You see, I had got the idea that showing up that sort of time before the appointment would be smiled upon here. I got that from the phone call with, um . . .'

Mr Sincope can't remember for the life of him the name of the northern man with whom he had made the appointment the previous day – logically, as he hadn't asked and the information hadn't been otherwise voluntarily given out. Jill continues staring at him soundless, looking like a sedated frog.

'Six minutes. Forty seconds. Early. That was what I worked out as being pretty much perfect. Anyhow, here we are,' Mr Sincope finally says after another long silence, all as awkwardly as humanly possible. Following a further awkward juncture, Jill at last breaks out of her semi-coma and mercifully ends the standoff.

'Have a seat. The doctor will be with you shortly,' she says.

The Sincopes sit down in the most remote corner of the three-sided waiting area. Straight ahead and to their right a sign on a door reads: 'DR BLOTS – OBSTRETICS'.

'Obstetrics is misspelled on that door insignia,' Mrs Sincope says in excited intrigue to her husband while nudging him in the side with her elbow.

'And?' he replies with a shrug, not understanding why this fact is so interesting to his wife. With anything non-arithmetical, he is not what one might describe as a 'details man'. He often marvelled internally at what his wife was able to glean from the slightest of glances at things; the amount of information she could absorb from a conversation of which she had only heard a tiny fragment, for instance. Mr Sincope could have sat in that waiting room for the rest of eternity and not noticed that the word 'obstetrics' was not spelled correctly on the door from which he sat opposite. Not out of a poor grasp of orthography on his part but simply due to the way his powers of observation functioned. Meanwhile, it had taken his wife less than five seconds to note the dodgy door sign.

Seeing that her husband is not in the slightest bit interested in the error, Mrs Sincope doesn't answer his one-word question but instead simply watches him as he scans the magazines sat on the see-through waiting room coffee table. *Golf Digest* is the only one he can bear to pick up and flip through; the rest of them are all directly related to child-rearing. *Mammary Monthly* is a title sat on the table that he recognises. Copies of it had been given out at the last of the NCT sessions he had managed to survive, that ultimate session being the one on breastfeeding.

'We love our breasts, don't we?' the mad woman running the seminar had intoned, looking as if she had drunk one cup of coffee too many that morning. 'When they become milk receptacles some of us start to feel like we are big fat cows. But we do not have to think like that! We can think of ourselves as tigers! As mummy tigers!'

Mr Sincope could barely stand to be in the room with the

11

mad mammary obsessive. He had wanted to duck and hide under the pile of knitted, breast-shaped pillows that she had sitting in the back of the room in their hundreds. Even with his rather limited powers of observation, Mr Sincope couldn't help but note that he was the only bloke in attendance at that final, boob-focused session. He and his wife had discussed whether or not he should go at all, he obviously arguing for his own omission and only submitting to tag along after his wife had slowly, over several days, whittled away at his obstinacy.

His initial bullheadedness on the topic of attendance was part of a larger debate he was having, mostly with himself but also occasionally involving his workmates, around whether he was going to be required to be present at the hospital for his daughter's birth itself when the Big Day arrived. Mr Sincope had only got as far as admitting internally that he needed to drive his wife to the hospital on that Biggest of Days – even then, he only came to this conclusion when a bloke at work, a particularly blokey bloke at that so noteworthy in this regard, insisted that this was the least he was contractually obligated to do in this day and age. What he hadn't yet decided as the Big Day dawned, and certainly hadn't talked about with his wife whatsoever, was exactly how long he was going to stick around for after he had got her safely to the hospital. This unmade decision and question left unasked to his wife hung around his neck like a dreadful weight, but his fear of confrontation kept him from resolving the issue.

'You don't even like golf,' Mrs Sincope says snidely as she ostentatiously picks up the copy of *Mammary Monthly* from the transparent table. She is actually completely uninterested in the magazine as she had noticed within seconds of sitting down that it's a copy that is eighteen months old. Breasts have come a long way in that year and a half, she thinks to herself, and giggles and what she perceives as her own wit. Yet she had spotted the opportunity to make her husband feel guilty and leapt upon it.

'It's a shame, as this magazine has a lot of good information about child-rearing in it,' she continues, trying to keep as stern a face as she can manage while she waves the magazine in his direction. The phony guilt trip isn't well pulled off on her part but it is done with enough earnestness to fool an emotionally tone-deaf individual such as her husband.

'I'll read up on things when she's born, promise. I want to think about something else right now.'

As he says this, the dramatic introduction into the waiting room of a man who resembles an ageing former male model comes about via the door with the misspelling upon it opening suddenly. He is tall and slender but muscular, with a strong jawline and well-coiffured hair. This is the Dr Blots of dodgy door sign infamy.

'Mr and Mrs Sincope, I presume?' the handsome obstetrician asks the magazine-wielding couple in a voice that verges on camp.

'Yes?' Mrs Sincope says more doubtfully than the uncontroversial nature of the query would have suggested. She is a little bit stunned by the good looks of the man in front of her. She even hopes he isn't the obstetrician as seems likely; perhaps the gorgeous man in front of her is simply a nurse. For reasons she chooses not to examine at this particular time, she finds the idea of being induced by an attractive man uncomfortable.

'I'm Dr Blots. Step into my office, please.'

The Sincopes get up from their reception area chairs and follow the doctor into the room behind the lexically challenged door, Mrs Sincope trailing behind her husband mostly as a way to sneak a close-up look at the spelling error that had so engrossed her, using her other half as camouflage.

Chapter Two

The Porless Implant

'We are gathered here today, we three, we humble three, for an induction,' Dr Blots says to the Sincopes, standing before taking a seat behind his mahogany desk. His speech has the air of a bad audition for a part as the slightly wacky yet implausibly fantastic-looking English doctor in some ghastly American television hospital drama.

'My understanding is that the procedure is fairly routine,' Mr Sincope says, mostly to the doctor but partly to his wife as well. This is typical of the man; trying to take charge of something he hasn't the foggiest about. 'But all the same, we all want to be mentally prepared for what's ahead.'

'The procedure is indeed routine, have no fear. But in light of your comment on preparedness, I should disclose at this juncture that the procedure also comes with some risks attached,' Dr Blots replies in a downbeat manner that immediately panics Mrs Sincope a little.

'What sort of risks are we talking about, Doctor?' she asks. Dr Blots then gets up and begins pacing back and forth in the short space between his desk and the back wall, taking comically short strides due to space limitations as he does so.

'Inductions, like all things related to one's pregnancy, are never as simple as they first appear,' Dr Blots says as he paces. 'Things can sometimes get complicated when having an induction process initiated.'

'Complicated?' Mrs Sincope asks, desperate to hide the panic in her voice. A week prior, Sarah had told her a story about her own induction that had mostly put Mrs Sincope's mind at ease about the whole thing.

'It's simple as. I went in, they stuck a thingo inside of me and wham! I was in labour within the hour.'

In light of Sarah's information, Mrs Sincope is now baffled about the pessimistic tone the doctor has adopted.

'It's nothing to get *too* alarmed about, Mrs Sincope,' the doctor responds with, finally affecting a reassuring timbre. 'I just think it wise to warn you that sometimes induction doesn't work. If that should happen – and let us hope that it does work – we then have to explore all of the remaining *options*.'

The final word is bizarrely emphasised, accompanied by a raised eyebrow from the doctor. This worries Mrs Sincope further.

'I assume you mean we need to go with a more drastic solution if that's the case?' Mr Sincope says, again trying to assert control over a situation that is never going to fall under his jurisdiction.

'Yes, that is one avenue we could explore,' the doctor says, sounding acutely tentative about this possibility for some reason. 'There are others. But all of this is academic; first, let us hope the induction all goes swimmingly, yes?'

'But you mentioned things getting complicated,' Mrs Sincope says, unable to shake her terror and needing her calm to be triggered by some further reassurance from the obstetrician. Dr Blots responds by laughing out loud in what comes across to his patient as a cruelly mocking manner but isn't meant as such, it's simply bad acting on his part as usual. This makes Mrs Sincope feel foolish, like she is being unreasonably thick regarding the whole affair.

'Such a worrywart! I shall repeat what I said again for you, Mrs Sincope. Induction might not work and so I need you to be prepared for the disappointment that might entail. You are not going to die, I can promise you that. Though having said that, of course, one never knows. Death is always hanging there, waiting for each and every one of us, isn't it?'

Having delivered this baroque speech, the doctor then laughs some more, this time more genuinely and obviously to himself. He is in fact chuckling about something entirely unrelated to the current situation, having suddenly recalled a rather stupid joke that one of the nurses had told him earlier that morning. Dr Blots giggles childishly for around ten seconds after he remembers the gag, after which he stares off into the middle distance for several seconds.

While the doctor is wrapped up in his thoughts, Mr Sincope makes up his own mind about the obstetrician and decides that what he feels for the doctor is extreme dislike bordering on hatred. This strong, sudden feeling shocks Mr Sincope, who is normally neutral towards everyone he comes across. He dismisses these feelings of animosity as being a by-product of the stress of the situation.

At last, Dr Blots snaps out of his daydream and ambles over to the examination table sat in the far corner of the room, one which is directly to the right of where the Sincopes are parked for the moment.

'Let us prop you up here,' says Blots to Mrs Sincope as he bangs his open palm on the onion-papered top of the table. She does as he requests, getting up out of the uncomfortable plastic chair she was sat in with some difficulty – again, and definitely noted by

Mrs Sincope herself, without any thought whatsoever from her husband around helping her up. She then walks the short distance to the examination table and proceeds to hoist herself slowly up and onto the corner – and noted as well, without any help from Dr Blots this time, despite him being in close proximity. The disappointment over the lack of the obstetrician's chivalry hits Mrs Sincope strangely hard, although you would never be able to tell this by looking at her in the moment. She has resolved to appear calm and collected and succeeds in this endeavour.

'I'm going to need you to remove all of your clothing now,' Dr Blots says to her once she has regained her breath. She looks at him, confused.

'Excuse me?' Mrs Sincope says almost by instinct. She flushes a little, embarrassed by being slightly aroused by Dr Blots' instruction to her. The doctor laughs out loud again, a chortle that has the effect of deepening further the hatred that Mr Sincope is brewing for him, as the father-to-be still sits in his own uncomfortable plastic chair.

'Pardon me,' Blots says, waving his hands overdramatically at Mrs Sincope in apology. 'What I meant was I'm going to need you to remove your trousers and knickers and get into one of these.'

He lifts up a white hospital gown that he seemingly produces out of thin air like a magic trick as he says the word 'these'.

'Your husband and I will of course wait outside while you get changed,' the doctor continues. He then makes a camp hand gesture inviting Mr Sincope to leave his office before him. Mr Sincope looks to his wife for direction, and with her offering none, Mr Sincope follows Blots out the door.

He is actually extremely pleased that the doctor has casually insisted on them both leaving the office. Mr Sincope had been uncomfortable being in the room during any procedure that involved his wife's genitals throughout the pregnancy and had dreaded the prospect of having to be next to her during the induction. Now he has an excuse to abscond from the whole thing. All he has to do is nip to the toilet and not be back in time.

'And where are you off to?' Dr Blots asks him as soon as they are both beyond the confines of the waiting room and Mr Sincope tries immediately to enact his quickly assembled plan.

'Need the loo,' Mr Sincope replies simply. Dr Blots laughs aloud again, his dreadful, fake-sounding, camp laugh, and walking right up to him, slaps Mr Sincope a touch too hard on the back, making a loud *whapping* sound that reverberates eerily through the hospital corridor in which they are both now standing.

'That old chestnut. I am afraid that you are not getting away that easily. I need you in the room when I perform the induction. Legal requirement,' the doctor says. Mr Sincope now feels deeply ashamed. It is abundantly clear that the doctor sees this sort of thing all the time and had read his intentions precisely. He had been caught like a schoolboy trying to fool the head teacher. The shame quickly subsiding, Mr Sincope then feels annoyed, his distaste for the obstetrician returning with a vengeance. He would now be forced to go through with being by his wife's side during the induction process, something that seemed all the worse now given he had for a moment thought he'd escaped the chore successfully.

The two men stand in the hallway in silence, neither looking at the other. After around thirty seconds of this, Dr Blots breaks the deadlock.

'I'm an actor, you know.'

'What, you're not actually a real doctor?'

Mr Sincope means this question sincerely but Dr Blots reads it as hilariously amusing sarcasm and laughs.

'Good one. What I meant was, I act in my spare time. You know, in plays and things.'

'Right, I see. Local stuff, in the community?'

Mr Sincope has no idea what he means by 'in the community' but thinks it sounds appropriately condescending.

'I was the lead in a toothpaste ad a few years ago. You must have seen it.'

Looking at the doctor again in light of this new information, Mr Sincope does sort of recognise him; possibly from the television, he supposes. Given passive aggressive attack is his only available weapon, Mr Sincope decides to use the opportunity to try and burst the doctor's bubble.

'No, I'm sorry, I definitely don't recognise you from the television.'

Dr Blots smiles confidently back.

'Trust me, you do. It's that ad where the annoying man with the white teeth follows an anthropomorphic tooth cavity around a large house furnished in 1970s fashion.'

Blots smiles even wider and points to his grinning mouth.

'I was the annoying man,' he says. Mr Sincope suddenly does distinctly remember the ad. It was on for months and while he rarely pays attention to television advertisements, that one did stand out as being notably irritating. The ad in question was in fact the real reason for Mr Sincope's intense dislike of the doctor; a subconscious remembrance of the televisual image that had so grated against his nerves. While this all comes back to Mr Sincope, he ponders whether it would be more hurtful to the doctor to now admit that he had remembered the ad and how much he had hated it, or if it was better to double down on denying any knowledge. Dr Blots renders such a tricky decision moot for the time being by attempting to call time on their corridor sojourn.

19

'She will be ready by now, I would have thought,' Dr Blots says. Mr Sincope is about to offer his thoughts on the matter when Dr Blots simply walks forward and bursts back into his office. Luckily for all involved, Mrs Sincope is already fully covered by the white gown. Mr Sincope wants to tell the doctor off for not having knocked first but realises that it is in fact the doctor's own office, which he feels nullifies his attack. Mr Sincope is a classic case of the boorish individual who has no tolerance for his own kind: men who are equally ill-mannered and mildly socially awkward, Dr Blots being a prime example of such a figure.

'And thus it begins,' Dr Blots says in a wide-eyed manner that would have suited a primary school teacher introducing a film about the Big Bang to his students on a day trip to the planetarium. He dashes over to his work counter and – as if to counterbalance this sudden haste – proceeds to slowly and methodically don a pair of rubber gloves.

'Aren't you supposed to wash your hands first?' Mrs Sincope asks, incredibly indignant about this lapse in hygiene.

'Nah,' Dr Blots says casually, as if he'd just finished off his second G&T of the afternoon. 'Because where I am about to venture is dirty as hell.'

Both of the Sincopes are so thrown off by this bizarre reply from Blots that neither has time to gather their thoughts before the next existential crisis rears its head. The doctor simply proceeds to the examination without any further discussion or preamble. Blots shakes his head dismissively seconds after having examined Mrs Sincope without warning.

'No dilation whatsoever,' the obstetrician says. Mrs Sincope is angered by this news. Right before they had launched into the ultimate Dorothy vs. Faith debate that morning, Mrs Sincope had insisted to her husband that she could feel her cervix widening.

Mr Sincope had replied at the time that this was a medical impossibility but she was adamant. It had now been shown that medical science was on her husband's side. She hated losing any dispute with her husband, but particularly one that involved her own body.

'What does that mean now then?' Mrs Sincope asks, trying to keep her irritation at the whole situation in check. Dr Blots smiles broadly at him, going back into cheesy hospital drama doctor mode.

'We cleave to the same path, forge the identical byway. The key difference is that I will now have to account for your, shall we call them for lack of a better term, disabilities.'

Mrs Sincope bites her lip, this insult by the doctor being one too many. She doesn't want to get angry with the obstetrician this early in the game, yet she is beginning to lose patience with his bedside manner. Mr Sincope, noticing his wife's distress for once, is almost overcome by an overwhelming instinct to punch Dr Blots square in the jaw, an urge he manages to resist.

'This is not the set of a toothpaste advert here, I hope you realise, Doctor,' Mr Sincope says to the obstetrician instead of thumping him. This comment completely baffles the doctor.

'I know. What a shame,' Blots replies with a real twinge of disappointment in his voice before sauntering over to his countertop and grabbing something sitting on top of it that resembles a tampon. He holds it aloft as if he were an air steward doing the safety routine at the start of a flight, as if the object in his hand was a floatation device.

'This is a Porless implant,' the doctor says to the Sincopes. 'Obviously you will have heard about this in your NCT classes or from your midwife.'

Mr and Mrs Sincope nod their heads in the affirmative. They had been well briefed from various sources on Porless implantation as a means of induction over the past couple of months; so much so, even Mr Sincope could regurgitate most of the information were it necessary.

'I insert this into your wife's cervix and hopefully and within an hour or two, it will be dilation city,' Dr Blots continues, reverting again to the bizarrely flippant persona of the 'dirty as hell' comment. Mr Sincope thinks to say something further to the doctor about his bedside manner, but this is replaced by the alarm that accompanies the suddenness with which Blots plants his right index and middle fingers into his wife's body while holding the implant. As quickly as he has put his fingers in, Dr Blots pulls his digits back out of Mrs Sincope, now sans Porless implant.

'Done. I suggest you two go for a walk. There is a park across the road which is lovely,' the doctor says, turning away from the couple back towards his countertop where he quickly removes his rubber gloves.

'Take a walk?' a befuddled Mr Sincope says. He is trying to remember why he'd been so alarmed only a moment ago but feels dazed; stoned almost. The doctor then turns towards Mr Sincope and addresses the following information directly to him.

'Yes. Get gravity on your side. Within the hour your wife should be feeling the contractions coming on. When that happens, return here to my office.'

Mrs Sincope is intensely disturbed by the fact that Dr Blots directs all this information through her husband. The whole thing feels to her like a time warp back to the 1960s. She is even pondering saying something to the doctor when, strangely, Dr Blots promptly departs his own office without another word, leaving the Sincopes alone.

'I suppose we should go to this park then,' Mr Sincope says, handing his wife all of her clothes back in a pile.

Chapter Three

The Missing Cat

Once Mrs Sincope is fully dressed again, she and her husband walk out into a colder than usual March afternoon to take a stroll in the park that sits across the road from the hospital's main entrance. As Dr Blots had opined, it is a pleasant public patch of green, triangular in shape with a fountain situated at every corner. What is odd is that the name of it is Four Fountains Park despite clearly only containing three fountains. A great deal of speculation surrounds this nomenclature amongst the local population. Perhaps the park had been a square at one point and then cut in half only for its title to remain the same? Or conceivably it was some sort of Dadaist joke – the park had been built in 1913 – that had long since ceased to be humorous? Whatever the explanation for the nomenclature, Mr and Mrs Sincope enter Four Fountains Park in high spirits. Mrs Sincope had now been induced and in her mind they were only one small stroll around a public park away from labour and the arrival of little Faith.

'Feeling anything yet?' Mr Sincope asks his wife.

'It hurts a bit. Could mean something, I suppose. Then again, I thought I could feel my cervix dilating this morning and you told me I was being silly. Turned out you were right on that count.'

23

'I only said that it was highly unlikely.'

'You are an expert on the functioning of the female body, dear,' Mrs Sincope says, loading enough sarcasm into her tone of voice to ensure that even her husband could not possibly misconstrue her intent. He does so anyhow.

'Thank you, dear,' he says sincerely. Mr Sincope does in fact fancy himself a bit of a crackerjack when it comes to the feminine form. He had been through many relationships with women before meeting Mrs Sincope; what could only, from an objective point of view, be described as a Herculean number of sexual liaisons given how boring and physically unattractive the man is. His penultimate girlfriend had been an Argentinean firebrand named Aleida. They met at his local one winter's evening only a few weeks into her time living in Britain. Their first proper conversation was an argument about the Falklands. Midway through this discourse, Aleida became so het up about Las Malvinas that Mr Sincope figured he might end up with a slap in the face and perhaps even a drink thrown in his lap.

'The islands were never at any point inhabited by Latins,' Mr Sincope stated during this maiden conversation. 'I mean, you might as well say the Falklands belong to the Incas.'

'Las Malvinas are three hundred miles from Argentina,' Aleida spat in her incredibly thickly accented English. 'They are eight thousand miles from Great Britain.'

'Self-determination is about geographical distance, is it?'

The argument went on in this interminable vein for hours until both of them were too drunk to be able to soldier on with the debate. Instead, they simply resorted to snogging one another. Convincing Aleida to come back to his place turned out to be rather easy; she was well oiled, and it was either Mr

Sincope's flat or the refugee camp-style hostel she was staying at which was all the way out in Earl's Court. Mr Sincope lived in North London at the time, Islington, a short walk from where the drinks had taken place. Aleida had wandered up there because she was a football fan and wanted to walk around Arsenal FC's stadium.

It should be mentioned at this point that the story of Aleida the Argentinean and the Islington snog is a great example of Mr Sincope's counter-intuitive luck with women. Whenever he had met an attractive girl, he automatically assumed he had no chance whatsoever of seducing her and so had a habit of saying whatever happened to pop into his head. Many women mistook his don't-give-a-shit attitude for confidence.

After the initial, Falklands-heavy encounter, Mr Sincope dated Aleida for almost five months. They broke up when she had to return to Buenos Aires owing to her visa being about to expire due to a mix-up at the company she worked for at the time. She wanted to technically stay together, have a stab at a long-distance relationship, but Mr Sincope responded to this idea with his typical candour.

'I don't think that sounds like a good idea at all,' he said drily to Aleida the day before her Aerolineas flight home. Following that final encounter, the two broke contact with each other completely. A couple of months later, Mr Sincope met his future wife.

Mr and Mrs Sincope walk towards the fountain that sits at the right-angle corner of Four Fountains Park. It is a miniature knock-off of the Fontaine der Mers in Paris. Something about its simulacrum nature riles Mr Sincope a little.

'Why couldn't they have thought of something original to put here instead of copying something, you know, something . . .'

'Foreign?' Mrs Sincope asks with a cruel smile. She found his xenophobia annoying when they first met but over time came to see it in a humorous light.

'I was searching for another word but foreign will do, dear. You getting a niggle or anything yet?'

'You asked me almost the same thing two minutes ago,' she says with irritation in her voice.

'Trying to stay mentally prepared for whatever is coming my way, that's all.'

'It hurts a little more than it did a half hour ago. I suppose that's a good sign, isn't it?'

'Probably one of the few times in life when you can take increased pain as a positive omen,' he says as though he's stumbled upon something profound here. 'You know something, I never thought about it quite that way until now.'

Both of their attentions are then diverted by a traffic accident that occurs on the road that runs between the park and the hospital. A silver Honda has slammed into the side of a blue Citroën whilst changing lanes ill-advisedly. Mediterranean-looking men are behind the wheels of both vehicles. The silver Honda has a striking-looking woman, who appears to Mr Sincope to be Italian, in the passenger's seat. In the back of the Honda are two small children, both of them between the ages of three and six. None of them appear to have been hurt by the accident. By contrast, there is a woman in the passenger's seat of the blue Citroën who is clutching what appears to be a handkerchief to her forehead, the hanky drenched in blood. Her head wound seems to be pretty bad from Mr Sincope's perspective. Seemingly oblivious to his passenger's injury, the driver of the blue Citroën gets out of his car and storms angrily towards the silver Honda. The driver of the Honda takes this manoeuvre for unwarranted aggression and steps out of his vehicle as well. The two men come together almost exactly where their automobiles had met less than twenty seconds earlier and begin arguing ferociously with one another. The Honda driver is Spanish and is yelling in his native tongue; the Citroën driver yells back in Portuguese. The argument between the two men escalates and amplifies further. It begins to seem impossible for them to avoid coming to blows, at least to Mrs Sincope.

'They aren't going to start punching each other, are they? Oh, Jesus,' she says, clutching at her husband's elbow. He responds by simply laughing at the idea.

'I know these Mediterranean types. They're all mouth and no trousers. They'll shout theatrically at one another until the police turn up and then they'll settle right down again immediately, you'll see.'

Mr Sincope's prediction could not have been more incorrect, for in the next moment the Spaniard takes his right fist and slams it into the face of his Portuguese partner in accident. In the immediate aftermath of this, the Spanish man appears stunned by his own harsh action and seems to immediately regret it as the Portuguese falls backwards while clutching at his face. Blood flows between the victim's fingers. The Spaniard looks ready to walk towards his sparring mate in a conciliatory manner – until the driver of the blue Citroën launches himself at the Honda owner, tackling him to the street. Once there, the two men start to viscerally scrap, each one's arms flailing wildly as they both attempt to land as many blows as possible on their opposing number. Blood is everywhere within seconds.

'Oh Christ, what a display,' Mrs Sincope says, notably upset by the whole thing. She loathes violence. She cannot even bear to watch it in a cinema. This is yet another area of profound disagreement between the Sincopes. Mr Sincope loves violent movies. In fact, it is the only reason he watches any sort of visual entertainment, if he was being completely honest. Like most things, this isn't something he has ever shared with his wife. Violence on screen is another victim of political correctness, Mr Sincope would often lament internally. As a result, he suffers endless rom-coms through gritted teeth, bored to tears, wishing they were watching a particularly unwholesome video nasty or at least an offensively malevolent American action flick.

Mrs Sincope's acute aversion to violence stems from a particular childhood incident that she has subsequently repressed. One evening when she was eleven years of age, her father took her to the local pub, just she and him. She was incredibly excited about this outing; the pub had always seemed the essence of the strong, off limits, mysterious masculinity that she had so adored in her father. The boozer in question was a real males-only zone as well, the sort of place that hosted punch-ups between rival football hooligans on a Saturday late afternoon. Why Mrs Sincope's father had decided to take his young daughter to the pub that evening was down simply to a gap in childcare; his wife had left him at home with their daughter as a way of ensuring he wouldn't go to the pub that evening. It backfired spectacularly and there her little daughter had found herself, in amongst a room full of sweaty, drunk, working class men. As often happened when he visited the pub, her father got alarmingly pissed very quickly and soon found himself in an argument with another man over something trivial. Mrs Sincope's father had picked on the wrong individual that night however, as the other chap involved in this argument broke a beer bottle on the bar and slashed her father's face with the jagged edge of it. Blood shot from his wound across the bar and Mrs Sincope's injured dad collapsed in a heap to the pub floor directly in front of her.

He was hospitalised for the evening and the incident was never mentioned again between father and daughter. Despite her dad bearing a nasty scar on his cheek for the rest of his days, Mrs Sincope impressively managed to bury the memory of being there when it was created. The only thing she retained was a subconscious horror of the savage, a terror of any outward expression of testosterone.

'You should step in now, I think; try and break them up,' Mrs Sincope says nervously to her husband, gripping his elbow ever tighter. Mr Sincope finds this the height of hilarity and thinks his wife must be joking. As such, he lets rip a huge, mocking laugh.

'Good one, dear.'

He then turns and looks into her eyes and what he sees there is distinctly unpleasant to him. It seems his wife was being entirely straight-faced about him intervening in the Iberians' battle.

'Why would I want to get involved in all of that?' he asks her, appalled at the suggestion.

'Those men may well kill one another otherwise.'

'I don't know either one of them. What happens to them is hardly my concern, particularly on today of all days.'

'Because they're strangers, you don't care if one of them dies out there in the middle of the road while we stand here watching?'

Mr Sincope takes a moment to collect his thoughts regarding his wife's last query. No, he doesn't care if either of the men fighting in the middle of the road killed the other. It was none of his business as far as he saw it. As usual, this wasn't something he was about to convey to his wife. An exit to this spousal argument then suddenly strikes him.

29

'I'm much more concerned about the woman in the passenger seat of the blue car. Her husband seems a lot more wrapped up in kicking lumps out of the other bloke than in helping her. Particularly given they've stopped less than twenty-five feet from a bleeding hospital!'

This works a charm. Mrs Sincope becomes suddenly obsessed with the poor woman with the head injury in the blue Citroën who is still holding a blood-red handkerchief to her head.

'You're right. Let's go over and at least make sure she gets proper medical attention,' Mrs Sincope says. They begin to stroll towards the accident site, Mr Sincope much more tentatively than his wife. But just as they set off, an ambulance and two police cars arrive on the scene. A gaggle of cops set upon the two men fighting and arrest them both. The woman with the head injury is helped out of the Citroën and into the ambulance, which then makes the comedically short, Marx Brothers-esque journey to the front of the A&E entrance, a trip that takes all of two seconds. All this having transpired in front of them, Mr and Mrs Sincope turn to each other, shrug simultaneously, and then walk along the edge of the park to the next fountain without a further word on the subject of the battling foreigners.

The next stone water chute along is, unlike the Parisian knock-off, impressively British in nature. It features a redcoat sitting on a horse, cradling a bulldog in his left arm while holding a sword aloft with his right, from the tip of which dangles a cross of St. George. The flag is done in stone as well, its ripples from the imagined wind of the scene done kinetically. The water spurts from both the end of the flag as well as from the dog's mouth.

'Now that is more like it!' exclaims Mr Sincope. His wife frowns, a sort of pantomime disapproval. She had correctly hypothesised upon first laying eyes on the fountain that her husband would love it given the fact that she had hated it on sight. She dislikes anything particularly jingoistic. If it was ugly as well, which this monstrosity of a fountain certainly, objectively is, her feelings of repulsion could often become uncontrollably strong. Obviously, her husband picks up on none of these feelings.

'Anything happening down there yet?' he asks instead.

'Could you please stop asking every two minutes? I'll let you know when something changes, I promise.'

Mrs Sincope steers them both away from the patriotic bull-dog with man on horse motif, up the triangle's hypotenuse towards the final of the park's three fountains.

'Oh, now this is rubbish,' Mr Sincope says as they approach what is a Roy Lichtenstein rip-off. It features a green cartoon mouse running away from a brown cartoon Dalmatian which has large, shark-like teeth. Water shoots from the dog's mouth, coming close to hitting the mouse but never quite getting there.

'Everyone knows dogs don't chase mice. Is it supposed to be an artistic statement about something?' Mr Sincope asks his wife.

'I rather like it.'

Mrs Sincope isn't saying this simply to be contrarian; she does genuinely appreciate the piece. On a plaque that sits at the dog's feet, the name of the fountain is displayed: *The Missing Cat*.

'I had a feeling you would, dear,' Mr Sincope says snidely to his wife.

'What is that supposed to mean?'

'Feel anything down below yet?'

'Stop asking me that! How many times do I have to tell you I will inform you when I feel differently!'

'And you don't yet, that's what you're saying?'

'No.'

'No, that's not what you're saying or no, you don't feel anything?'

'I'm bored of walking in the park.'

'So am I. What do we do now?'

'I don't know. What did the doctor tell us to do after the walk in the park?' Mrs Sincope asks her husband.

'Beats me. I wasn't the one who was getting induced up there.'

'The doctor seemed much happier talking to you about it and since you didn't seem to challenge that, I assumed you were taking responsibility for everything,' she says with a lot of sass.

'That wasn't my impression of events. As it happens I was rather hoping that I could shove off right about now,' Mr Sincope says. This is the bomb that had been waiting to go off underneath the whole day. Mrs Sincope turns to her husband, incredibly hurt by what he'd suggested.

'Shove off as in leave me here by myself?'

'You're not by yourself though, are you? There are all sorts of doctors around to look after you.'

'Are you saying you're not going to stay for the birth of our child?'

His wife is so obviously of one, deeply held opinion on the subject of him hanging about that Mr Sincope feels the need to back-pedal as quickly as he can manage.

'Of course, I'm going to come back for that. Obviously! I only meant I could push off for now and get myself something to eat. That's all.'

'I don't want to be separated right now,' Mrs Sincope says. 'You can eat later.'

Mr Sincope looks once again at the Lichtenstein copy cartoon fountain, mostly as a place to put his eyes that were away from his wife's. His dislike is now quickly moulding into hatred, particularly towards the fleeing mouse. He begins to imagine the next frame in an imaginary comic strip the fountain is part of, one in which the canine with the jaws devours the snivelling little rodent. He snaps out of this imagining quickly, annoyed with himself for having not paid more attention to the irritating obstetrician while he was there in front of them. But there was nothing to be done about that now.

'What do you want to do then?' he asks his wife despondently.

'What else can we do but go back to his office and see what happens when we get there?' she responds with. They shrug simultaneously – as you may have noticed by now, a Sincope trope – and start back in the direction of the hospital. As they stroll across the road, giving the accident area a wide berth, Mrs Sincope strokes her ponytail with her right hand, an unconscious habit of hers.

Chapter Four

Mammary Monthly Revisited

'Please have a seat,' Jill the receptionist says in that shrill voice of hers, still obviously feeling the effects of being overmedicated on barbiturates. The Sincopes do as they are told and ensconce themselves in the exact spot they had done immediately before the induction. Mr Sincope briefly eyes the golf magazine and decides he can't face it again; neither the magazine itself nor his wife's likely passive aggressive derision. Instead, he thinks he will use the time to gain some of the brownie points he had almost certainly lost in the park with the 'I thought I might shove off right about now' routine by picking up *Mammary Monthly* and pretending to read an article.

'Are you serious?' Mrs Sincope asks, looking at her husband and then the magazine in his hands as if he'd lost his mind.

'You're always going on at me to read this thing, so now I'm doing it.'

'I'm always joking when I ask you to read it. You do realise that, surely?'

Obviously, Mr Sincope hadn't previously comprehended that his wife was always pestering him in jest. He now faces a difficult choice. Should he put the magazine down and laugh along with his wife, placing in her mind the false idea that he knew it was a gag all along? Or should he insist that he was actually interested in the magazine for its own sake the whole time? There is only one road to go down as far as he is concerned.

'I was joking myself when I said I only wanted to read it because of you going on at me to. In actual fact, I've been looking forward to reading this magazine many months now for personal reasons. I just never found the time.'

'Oh really?' Mrs Sincope asks, completely incredulous.

'Really. I am taking my role as a father seriously, not to mention the state of your breasts.'

He garners a few stares from the other people loitering in the waiting room with that last statement. Mr Sincope, not knowing how else to react to this unsolicited attention, proceeds to bury his face in the mammary-related periodical. Now wedded to the thing for at least the next five minutes, he quickly figures out that he will actually have to read one of the articles in earnest in order to stave off crushing boredom, something he hadn't seriously pondered doing up until that moment. Deciding that choosing an article at random is the best way to go, he comes upon a piece that is not about breasts at all. It is instead about what makes for a good marriage. Beginning to tuck into the column, the suggestions for what constitutes marital bliss strike Mr Sincope as hopelessly naïve and old-fashioned, even by his own hopelessly naïve and old-fashioned standards. The first tip on the list is that wives should bake for their husbands more often, preferably cakes or biscuits. The only nod to the twenty-first century given in this proposal is that the baked goods should endeavour at all times to be low fat.

'*Substitute vegetables such as courgettes and aubergines for butter and lard.*'

35

If my wife made me a batch of courgette biscuits, I'd bloody well divorce her, thinks Mr Sincope to himself.

'Cakes with veggies? What next, eh?' comes a cracked and unfamiliar female voice over Mr Sincope's left shoulder. He turns to face the source; it had come from a significantly pregnant woman sat beside him. She introduces herself as Josephine with no prompting.

'You two married? Or are you brewing a bastard in there?' she follows up with before Mr Sincope can formulate a response to her original rhetorical query. Mrs Sincope is about to lean forward and inform Josephine that she and partner's marital status is none of her concern, but Mr Sincope gets in slightly sooner than his wife.

'Oh, we're married all right. It's a good story, my wife and I's wedding day.'

Mrs Sincope feels immediately ill. She hates it when her husband tells the story of their day of matrimony, particularly to complete strangers, which he is commonly favourable to doing.

Mr and Mrs Sincope met while they were simultaneously working for the same large corporation. Mr Sincope was in the finance department while his future wife was a high-powered executive in Human Resources. I use the past tense here by means of capturing the historical element but in fact, by the time of the Big Day both of the Sincopes are still working for the same company, doing the same jobs. There is little interface between their departments and it is unlikely the two would ever have crossed paths had it not been for the fact that one of Mr Sincope's payslips contained an error – according to the slip, he had been double charged for his end of National Insurance. For both selfish financial reasons and the never-ending struggle to maintain numerical accuracy in all walks of life, in his mind this error needed to be corrected as quickly as possible.

As a senior HR executive, Mrs Sincope was never likely to handle a complaint so routine. But Mr Sincope's claim got bumped up the chain when he became infuriated with what he took to be the stupidity of the assistant dealing with his problem ('You, madam, clearly cannot add up,' he had said, in his usual debonair style, causing tears to ensue.)

When Mr and Mrs Sincope met it was not exactly love at first sight. She did, as it happens, immediately spot the taxation error, and understanding what had gone wrong pledged to Mr Sincope that the payslip would be duly reprinted with the correct amounts, the taxation records updated accordingly, and, of course, he to be bank-transferred the shortfall in his pay within twenty-four hours. Their dalliance went no further than this exciting start for some time.

Having met on that occasion gave Mr Sincope the wherewithal to approach the obviously not-as-yet Mrs Sincope at the summer office party, one which occurred a few weeks after they had first met. On this occasion, fuelled mostly by alcohol, the two had a closer encounter involving some tepid conversation followed by a rather desperate heavy petting session in the gents'. He agreed to call her afterwards. From her end, she figured that would be the end of it. Three days later, Mr Sincope delivered the promised telephone call and with it asked if she wanted to go for dinner the following evening. She accepted the offer. The first date went swimmingly, with the future Mrs Sincope being dazzled by her date's seeming indifference to pretty much everything, something she found oddly appealing. The two slept together that night. This was unusual behaviour for her as she was usually reasonably chaste. As often was the case in his dealings with the fairer sex, it was Mr Sincope's utter lack of interest that did it for her; she couldn't bear to think that he didn't care if they had intercourse or not and therefore felt compelled to blow his mind. She did not, on this occasion, succeed in the mind-blowing; he thought her fair to middling in the bedroom department at best (no Aleida, in other words). They began seeing each other anyhow. It was a simple, convenient relationship for them both. They worked in the same building, which made it all the more straightforward.

The not-as-yet Mrs Sincope told Cindy, who was her flatmate at the time, that Mr Sincope was like the corner store: easy to find, takes little effort, and has most of the stuff you need. She was never going to marry a man like that, as she was looking for a Waitrose: a little pricey but delicious, filled with life-changing items, hard to get to sometimes but always worth the effort. Despite this supermarket analogy given to Cindy at the time, when Mr Sincope proposed out of the blue six months later, she found herself saying yes.

A big part of the reason that the soon-to-be Mrs Sincope agreed to marry Mr Sincope despite feeling lukewarm towards her husband-to-be was twofold. One, she was worried about being in her thirties and not finding someone else to have a child with before it became too late to do so. The second reason cut deeper: she fretted about finding anyone else who wanted to marry her at all and ending up alone. Like many career women who were outwardly confident and capable, she had found dating an almost impossible minefield, getting worse with each passing year. Perhaps she had to grow up and accept that she was never going to be able to afford to shop at Waitrose; that she was going to have to settle for the corner store for the rest of her life and there was nothing wrong with that.

Cindy confronted Mrs Sincope on two occasions prior to the wedding on whether or not, given the parameters she'd laid out beforehand, Mr Sincope was indeed the right husband for her friend. During both incidents, the two principals were drunk. Mr Sincope's fiancée gave a slightly different version each time on the same theme: that she'd had an epiphany; that she'd finally seen that Mr Sincope was indeed the Waitrose of her dreams. But she was lying to her living companion, and during the hangovers that accompanied these dual incidents she pondered all day long whether or not she was doing the right thing in ignoring Cindy's advice.

The day before the wedding, a Friday, the finance team put on some drinks for Mr Sincope while the HR team did the same for his fiancée. The groom was restrained with his alcohol consumption that evening, citing his need to get a good night's sleep for the following day's festivities. In the meantime, his soon-to-be wife got plastered beyond belief, the most pissed she'd ever been and indeed would ever be for the rest of her life. One of the girls from payroll dropped Mrs Sincope off at her flat, scared that she would never be able to get home by herself on the tube. Once there, the drunken bride-to-be cried to Cindy about what a terrible mistake she was about to make and asked repeatedly how she thought her friend could help her get out of it. Cindy told her to go to sleep and that they'd discuss it in the morning.

When dawn arrived and with it the most crushing hangover of her life, the quickly scheduled-to-be Mrs Sincope was single-minded in her determination involving two things: one, her insistence on going through with the marriage and two, and related to the first ambition directly, her certitude in avoiding picking up in any way on the drunken conversation of the previous evening with Cindy regarding whether the first determination of the day was justified. The only thing she would readily accept from her friend that morning were a few slugs of Scotch to ease her pain, despite Cindy's repeated and increasingly desperate pleas not to rush into anything.

The service itself was routine, although Mrs Sincope had the urge to run down the aisle and away from the church as quickly as her legs could carry her throughout. On one occasion, just before the portion of the ceremony where the rings come in, she came very close to actually shooting off. But she stayed until the end and married Mr Sincope.

At the reception, Mrs Sincope consumed more alcohol in the conscious hopes of easing her growing fear that she had done the wrong thing, in the subconscious hopes of getting too drunk to have to continue being present at some reasonably early point in the evening. Her deepest urges saw their fulfilment, with her sloping off to the honeymoon suite in the hotel they had booked for the reception around ten p.m., just after the cake had been cut.

When Mr Sincope came upstairs round midnight, at a point when the reception was winding down, he found his wife practically comatose in their love nest. He tried everything he could to wake her: turning some loud music on, making an annoying buzzing noise directly into her ear; he thought about throwing a glass of cold water across her face but then thought better of it when he imagined how angry she'd be with him if it worked. Short of that, nothing would revive her, it seemed. Mr Sincope shrugged and left his wife to lie still while he opened the complimentary bottle of Cava the hotel had given them and drank it while watching a Russ Meyer film that was playing on Channel 5. The newlywed couple waited until the following morning to consummate their marriage. Mr Sincope initiated proceedings by jumping on top of his wife while she was still unconscious and cajoling her into intercourse; not quite forcing himself upon her but getting uncomfortably close to doing so.

Sadly, Mrs Sincope and Cindy's friendship broke down after the wedding day, the marriage acting like a wall between the two former close mates. In fact, Cindy moved out a week later, determined not to stay with the newly married couple a moment longer, while the flat where Mrs Sincope lived with Cindy remains the Sincope abode up to the present day.

'Russ Meyer movie, you say? I do so adore his output. Nothing like a big pair of tits to get your day started right,' Josephine, the intrusive pregnant woman, says in response to the conclusion of Mr Sincope's story about he and his wife's wedding day. Mrs Sincope is now seething with rage. She had been since about midway through the wedding story, prompted by her husband repeating the part about her begging Cindy to help her get out of her engagement. This detail had been revealed to Mr Sincope after one particularly bad fight a few months into their marriage during which his wife had snapped and told him all about the drama involving Cindy and the extreme doubts she herself had experienced in regard to following through with the marriage. He found the whole thing oddly amusing and even more bizarrely, touching; all those doubts about him and she still went through with marrying him. Mr Sincope doesn't notice his wife's anger until he turns away from Josephine, having laughed at the strange woman's line about breasts in the morning.

'What's wrong? Are you in pain? Hoorah!' Mr Sincope exclaims with glorious insensitivity when he sees his wife's face. Mrs Sincope is going to release her wrath upon her spouse after this outburst but is interrupted by Jill telling them that Dr Blots will see Mrs Sincope now. Mr Sincope gets up with enthusiasm and starts to walk towards Dr Blots' office, the one with 'obstetrics' misspelled on the door.

'No, not in there,' Jill shrieks to his surprise. 'He wants you to head up to the antenatal ward.'

Jill, having delivered this piece of information in her weirdly terrifying, squeaky voice, all while standing in front of her desk, turns around and starts trudging back to her seat with notable lethargy, even by her own low standards for the day. Mr and Mrs Sincope turn to one another and then each shrug simultaneously. The couple then walk back out to the hospital corridor towards the lift. When they arrive there, they both realise that they have no idea where exactly they're going.

'Excuse me, where is the antenatal ward?' Mr Sincope asks a woman working behind the nearest reception desk to the lift. She looks at him with a hopelessness that is all encompassing, as if he had asked her to solve a calculus equation involving matrices.

'I have absolutely no idea, sorry,' she says.

Just then, a handsome young male orderly approaches the Sincopes with a smile.

'Did I hear you're looking for the antenatal ward? Follow me, folks,' the orderly says enthusiastically in a soft Antipodean accent. The Sincopes duly follow their newfound saviour without a further word.

Chapter Five

Room 1928

It turns out to be a fortunate thing that the handsome orderly happened to come along when he did; the antenatal ward is extremely cryptically located. After a long trek up and down many floors, and along several corridors, the Sincopes arrive in front of a brown, half-painted, unmarked door, through which they get to the reception desk of the antenatal ward, manned on the Big Day by a spotty-faced boy in his late teens named Gregory.

'Here you are,' the good-looking Antipodean male orderly says as the Sincopes are parked in front of Gregory's desk. Mrs Sincope is so desperate for the orderly to stay she almost makes a move to physically restrain him from going, yet thankfully manages to come to her wits before attempting this.

'Do you people have an appointment?' Gregory asks from behind his overlarge desk in a nasal Lancastrian accent that immediately gets on Mr Sincope's nerves. Fantastic, another northerner to navigate, he thinks to himself.

'Dr Blots sent us himself,' Mr Sincope says in that patronising, Lord-of-the-Manor way he unconsciously always uses to address people he thinks less of.

'When did he tell you to come up?'

'Around ten minutes ago.'

Gregory smiles in a patronising manner.

'Dr Blots has been here on the antenatal ward for the last twenty minutes, so that would be an objective impossibility.'

'Right, as it happens it wasn't he who told us to come up, it was his receptionist,' Mr Sincope confesses, sighing heavily as he does so, in a tone of voice notably less cocksure than his initial statement to Gregory.

'So, when you said that Dr Blots sent you up himself, you were lying. It was Jill who told you to come here.'

'That's a harsh way of putting things, don't you think?' Mr Sincope snaps at the orderly.

'I'll need to see some paperwork before we go any further with this,' Gregory says snidely, looking down at the scattered mess of stationery on his desk and ignoring the substance of Mr Sincope's hurt comeback.

'Well, we weren't provided with any. And I must mention at this point that I'm getting a little sick of your tone, young man,' Mr Sincope says while leaning over the massive worktop in front of Gregory and trying his best to be intimidating. It doesn't work in the slightest as Gregory had grown up in Blackburn, toiling away in his local in order to save the money to go to university. Some of the regulars in the pub had been genuine psychopaths, hell bent on spreading as much human misery as they could. Thus to him, quite understandably, Mr Sincope is nothing more than another middle-class Southern drip, and no leaning over furniture was going to have the slightest effect on his decision-making process.

'If you both could have a seat, please,' the northern lad says blankly to Mr Sincope without even bothering to look back up at him. But the older man isn't ready to back down yet.

'That isn't good enough, I'm afraid. You are going to need to do a great deal better than that, sonny Jim!' Mr Sincope shoots back. Gregory finally looks up at his newfound adversary.

'I think it's going to have to be good enough for now, isn't it?' he says with some steel in his voice. This does the trick. Mr Sincope retreats without a further word thrown Gregory's way.

'Let's have a seat then,' he says to his wife in a voice he attempts to make as decisive sounding as possible; as if he hadn't been bounced into sitting down without further info but rather, had come to the decision it would be a good idea to do so independently. He tries to steer her quickly away from the front desk as part of the whole routine.

'What's happening?' Mrs Sincope asks, now confused. She hadn't been listening to her husband and Gregory's conversation at all, having been distracted by a discussion she'd managed to eavesdrop on taking place between a couple who were sat in the reception area nearby. The man involved had seemingly been apologising for some indiscretion involving the woman's sister.

'I'm sorry again, all right.'

'Do you fancy my sister then?'

'A bit, yeah. I mean have you seen her?'

The man then gave the international symbol for 'large breasts': a cupping of one's hands in front of one's chest. This could be said to have been an ill-advised move at that stage in the conversation.

'She's my bloody sister! So, obviously, yeah, I've seen her once or twice!'

'Exactly. As she is your sister, she resembles you a little bit, right? That's why I fancy her – if I find you fit, I should by rights find your sister shaggable, am I right?'

'No, you shouldn't!'

He was clearly not winning the argument. Yet he continued giving it the old college try, ironic given his clear lack of post-secondary education.

'Right, we're about to have a child together, yeah?'

'Unfortunately.'

'That's because on some level I'm after your genetics, right? Now, your sister, she's got them same genes as you, right? Only makes sense that some part of me is thinking, "Hang about, if Marla isn't up for it again, Trudy can do the business", am I right?'

'I can't be dealing with you right now!'

Marla waved her hands at her boyfriend as she got up and exited the antenatal reception area. The father of her child reluctantly rose as well, waving his hands in the air himself as he followed her out.

'Come on, love, are you going to refuse to deliver our baby because I tried to get off with your sister?' he shouted after his irritated partner.

'Don't fret, dear. Gregory is apparently sorting things out for us,' Mr Sincope says by way of putting his wife into the loop on the less interesting conversation she had missed, drawing her attention away from the conclusion of Marla's boyfriend's exit from the ward. Mr Sincope had gleaned the name of the receptionist from the lad's prominent name tag; it is massive, the size of a small computer screen. Mrs Sincope nods and capitulates, resulting in both husband and wife having a seat in the now otherwise empty waiting room. Mr Sincope, as is his wont, surveys the magazines available. To his chagrin, there is only one magazine on offer: a solitary copy of *Mammary Monthly*. Adding insult to injury, it is an even older edition than the one downstairs in Dr Blots' waiting room. Faced with either flicking through the out-of-date periodical or having a stultifying conversation with his wife about the absurdity of their present situation, which he knows would mostly involve him repeatedly asking whether or not she felt any differently and her becoming more and more agitated about these constant queries, he reluctantly opts for the former. The article he indiscriminately opens the magazine up to is strangely enough about gardening. Its link to breasts is that apparently there are certain fertilizers that can be harmful in the long term to your infant should you be exposed to them either during pregnancy or in the period post-birth while you are nursing.

The dust from these chemicals can easily get into your blood supply via your nose and then into your breast milk. There it can cause irreparable damage to your child, the article reads, in what strikes Mr Sincope as a hysterical tone. *Always remember that your child gets all of its nourishment in the first couple of months from you and you alone. Never in your life will the dictum 'you are what you eat' be more relevant. For your child will also be what you eat during this period – and in the case of FH561 fertilizer agent, what you breathe as well.*

This passage reminds Mr Sincope of a long-standing disagreement between him and his wife, this one thankfully resolved long before the Big Day. It was around whether or not Dorothy/ Faith – he remains miffed about throwing in the towel on the name, particularly as it turns out they'd mostly be waiting around all day together and so would have had plenty of time to argue about the subject were he courageous enough to broach the topic – was to be breastfed exclusively for the first few months or whether there should be some formula involved. Mrs Sincope was dead set on the idea of breastfeeding her baby exclusively. Her own mother had tried for several weeks to feed her via this method but had ended up abandoning the idea.

Apparently, there simply wasn't enough milk being produced to fulfil the infant Mrs Sincope's needs. As a direct result, she felt that she'd missed out on something which she wanted Faith to enjoy. Mr Sincope, on the other hand, was fed formula from the start and felt it hadn't done him any harm. All this adoration of lactation was to him fetishism; some sort of New Age tosh that had pervaded society. Like the name debate, and to be honest, most other fights he ever picked with his wife, this was an argument he was destined to lose.

'They're my breasts,' she ended up saying, a statement which did the job and closed down any further discussion on the matter.

While he is turning this incident over and over again in his mind, an attractive woman in a white lab coat who wanders into the antenatal waiting area diverts Mr Sincope's attention. He watches intensely as she leans over the reception desk and says something quietly to Gregory. The northern lad proceeds to then point at the Sincopes, after which the attractive woman looks over at them, something that makes Mr Sincope's heart jump as if he were a teenaged boy suddenly being checked out by the girl in his school class he'd had a crush on for months.

'Mr and Mrs Sincope?' the attractive woman asks the couple.

'Yes!' Mr Sincope responds, rising to his feet overdramatically. 'That's us!'

'Could you follow me, please?'

The Sincopes trade brief glances and then do as the attractive woman had commanded. She leads them down a short corridor which is adjacent to but not actually on the antenatal ward, taking them eventually to a room which has emblazoned upon the front of it the number '1928' in large stencil. Once all three of them enter the room, the attractive woman in the white lab coat spins round and proceeds to address the Sincopes.

'Hello, I'm Dr Sharp,' she says. 'I'm afraid that Dr Blots is busy with another patient at the moment so you'll be in my care for the time being.'

Both of the Sincopes are happy with this turn of events for different reasons. Mr Sincope is obviously overjoyed to have new medical representation given his antipathy towards Blots, particularly in the form of the goddess in front of him now. From Mrs Sincope's perspective, she had often been annoyed by the fact that all of the gynaecologists and obstetricians she'd ever been to see were men. She had actively hoped for a female obstetrician when she first became pregnant, ultimately to no avail. It had struck her as sexism at its worst. In short, having a woman doctor to look after her is something of which Mrs Sincope heartily approves.

Mr Sincope meanwhile finds his attraction to Dr Sharp deepening by the moment. He had always wanted to date a medical professional but had never managed to pull it off. Something about a woman with that much authority, although in no areas which would threaten his masculinity, appeals to him.

'Could you please get undressed and into this robe for me, Mrs Sincope?' Dr Sharp asks. The pregnant woman nods and then proceeds to undo belts and zippers and the like; she does this under the assumption that the doctor will leave during the process. However, Dr Sharp doesn't depart the room and instead stares at Mrs Sincope's body while the pregnant woman begins to disrobe, ogling her almost. This obviously makes Mrs Sincope feel a bit uncomfortable but she decides she doesn't want to rock the boat with the new doctor just yet.

'Prop yourself up on the table and then lie back, please,' Dr

Sharp says to Mrs Sincope once she is ensconced in the white gown. She does as she is told – being helped up by the doctor as she does so, which is noted by the pregnant woman – and then Dr Sharp, now wearing a pair of surgical gloves, wastes no time in diving in. Mrs Sincope reflects to herself that she thought a fellow woman would be a little more delicate with her feminine parts than all of her male doctors had been. But Dr Sharp is, if anything, even more relentless than Dr Blots when it comes to finger work. Mrs Sincope, who up to this point had been giving Dr Sharp the benefit of the doubt, now takes a slight dislike to the female doctor.

'Jesus Christ, did Blots do this induction? What a shambles!' Dr Sharp says pointedly as she digs around near Mrs Sincope's cervix with little care and attention as to whether or not her patient is entirely comfortable. The doctor then wriggles her fingers in a way which causes Mrs Sincope to feel a sharp, searing throb in her abdomen, causing the patient to instinctively cry out.

'If that's the way you respond to that little niggle, all I can say is I'm glad I'm not going to be around for labour,' Dr Sharp says sardonically as she removes her surgical gloves. 'Right, that should do the trick. Walk around a little more – remaining vertical is key – and in a couple of hours you should be having your first serious contractions. Whatever happens, please return to the antenatal ward at half four.'

The good-looking, female doctor then departs, leaving the Sincopes all alone in room 1928.

'Should we go back to the park?' Mr Sincope asks following an awkward, extended, silent pause. His wife scowls.

'Why don't we get something to eat instead?' she asks. Mr Sincope smiles; this is the obvious thing to do given that the afternoon was wearing on and they hadn't eaten since breakfast. He had not thought about his stomach at all since they'd been in the park, where he had used the prospect of eating as a way of trying to get out of the hole he had dug for himself on the question of his continuing presence at his wife's side. After the suggestion of lunch, Mr Sincope realises all of a sudden that he is ravenous.

'We should go to that nice little place that's opened round the corner, you know the Love Café,' Mrs Sincope says excitedly. Mr Sincope is notably less enthusiastic about the prospect of eating at the Love Café than his wife. They had driven past it several times during their dry runs to the hospital – it had been the desire of both of them to be mentally prepared on that count – and Mrs Sincope had remarked on how happy she was that it had opened and how nice it looked. Mr Sincope thought the café represented something sinister, a completely prejudiced viewpoint given he'd yet to set foot in the establishment. It looked to him like one of those set-ups that did food that wasn't all that different from a local sandwich shop, only served on nicer plates for double the price with a free copy of the *Guardian* available to read.

'I think we should stay in the hospital as we haven't all that much time,' Mr Sincope says. 'I'm sure the cafeteria is perfectly fine.'

'Yes, but I don't want perfectly fine. This is our Big Day. We should enjoy it all as much as we can.'

Given how easily he had caved in on the name their child would have for her entire life, you can imagine the lack of fight Mr Sincope offers on the lunch venue front. He soon finds himself ordering a black coffee and a cheese toastie from the girl with a nose ring and a neck tattoo who stands behind the counter of the Love Café.

'Can I take your coat, sir?' a foreign-sounding man asks Mr Sincope after he had ordered for both himself and his wife – no table service, Mr Sincope notes. How *liberal*.

'I think I'll leave it on, thanks.'

'It gets warm in here, sir. I think you should let me take care of it for you.'

He now recognises the accent: Portuguese, of course. There are a lot of them in the neighbourhood now, something Mr Sincope secretly frowns upon. He imagines the Iberian man taking his coat and then leaving out the back of the café with it on, boarding the first plane to Faro, the most expensive item of clothing he would ever have in his possession wrapped around his shoulders the whole time. Still, it now feels awkward to continue refusing.

'There you are then,' Mr Sincope says through gritted teeth as he hands over his coat.

'Thank you, sir.'

Mrs Sincope points to a table near the window and her husband, now deprived of his coat, nods in agreement.

'Feel anything yet?' Mr Sincope asks as they sit down.

'You couldn't have waited until we'd at least tried to have a decent conversation first before asking that again?' Mrs Sincope says resignedly. 'Same thing applies as it did in the park. I will let you know when I feel something down there, relax.'

'Looks like you sure felt something back there when the doctor adjusted your thingy,' Mr Sincope says in a moment of particular inarticulacy. His wife smiles to herself; his vocabulary always evaporates whenever they have to discuss anything related to her anatomy. Mrs Sincope decides to try and take this offering from her husband and run with it; perhaps even inject some bonhomie round the table.

'It did bloody hurt but it's all part of the process. Don't know what she did up there. Let's hope that it was worth the pain and gets things moving a bit.'

Their food arrives. It is a little prompt for Mr Sincope's liking. Sure, he doesn't like it when it takes ages to get one's meal in a dining establishment, but if the grub shows up quasi-instantaneously then perhaps something suspect is afoot.

'Oh, this is good. Have a bite,' Mrs Sincope says while her first mouthful is still being masticated. She had taken a chance on the 'Love Café Platter', something which seems to consist of artisanal salad and exotic pulses. She is completely happy with the purchase. Mrs Sincope is the type of person who would eat almost anything so long as it had been given some sort of middle-class seal of approval beforehand. Having been raised in a working-class family, she is desperate to disguise her roots and appear as bourgeois as humanly possible. As a result of this, she often ends up trusting the judgement of others over her own on matters of taste.

'No, that's fine, thanks,' Mr Sincope says, laughing. 'It's all a bit green for the likes of me.'

A few tables over, a couple roughly the same age as the Sincopes are eating as well. The man and the woman sit opposite one another and yet they could have been thousands of miles apart from the attention they each give to one another. Parked beside their table is a buggy which contains an infant, the gender of which is hard for either of the Sincopes to ascertain given the unisex clothing. The child is between nine months and a year old. It is strapped into the buggy both by the standard shoulder straps but also by some additional clasps on its wrists and ankles, buckles that look suspiciously as if they had been added to the design of the pushchair by one or both of the parents. As the Sincopes gaze at the child held captive, the infant starts to try and get free of its multiple clamps, mostly by wriggling ineffectively. When it begins to understand that this plan will not result in freedom, the baby begins to shout obstreperously. The mother, almost automatically, reaches her right hand over to the buggy and deftly pulls a plastic, opaque covering over the child, helping to smother the sound of its cries. She then goes back to staring at the table.

'That is absolutely horrible,' Mrs Sincope says to her husband, pointing at the couple. 'We're not going to be like that, are we? Please tell me we won't be.'

'Don't worry, we won't be,' Mr Sincope says sincerely. After all, if he were caught in that same situation he would make an excuse, slip out of the overpriced Love Café, and leave the kid and his wife to sort everything out themselves.

Following the completion of their meal, the Sincopes depart from the café and unconsciously drift back towards Four Fountains Park. They soon end up sitting beneath the Roy Lichtenstein rip-off fountain by unspoken consent, both of them wanting to be as far away from the hospital as possible for the moment. They stare across the park in silence.

'I keep thinking about what you said, about pain being desirable when you're in the position I'm in,' Mrs Sincope finally says to break the calm.

'Desirable is probably pushing it.'

'You kept asking me whether or not I felt anything and every time I got upset with you because I wasn't feeling it yet. I was definitely hoping for pain.'

'I think hoping for something and desiring it are two separate things.'

'That's not true; they are synonymous,' Mrs Sincope says, confused at what her husband has just proposed.

'I disagree. Hoping for something is a complex emotional state. It is about looking forward to the possibility of something occurring without it being life or death. Desire is all encompassing; you can't keep your mind on anything else when you desire a person, a thing, or an outcome,' says the man who had never experienced such a thing first-hand in his whole life. This isn't lost on Mrs Sincope, who finds the idea of her husband giving a lecture on complex emotional states more than a little rich and decides to change the topic.

'That Dr Sharp is pretty,' she says.

'She certainly is,' he responds with, rather more lasciviously than consciously intended.

'You fancy her a little, don't you?' Mrs Sincope asks playfully.

'Maybe just a little. She is pretty as you pointed out yourself.'

'Do you fancy her more than me?' Mrs Sincope says jokily, elbowing her husband lightly in the ribs as she does so.

'My dear, you are my wife and the mother of my child. Stop being silly,' he says sternly and then stands up to indicate he's ready to return to the hospital. As she gets herself up from the rim that edges the Roy Lichtenstein knock-off fountain, as usual with no help from her husband, Mrs Sincope can't help but notice that despite her other half taking her light-hearted comment seriously, he had not in fact answered her question.

Chapter Six

Synergised

Upon their return to the hospital, the Sincopes have what is a predictable degree of difficulty relocating the antenatal ward. They take several wrong turns and end up lost, having multiple tedious arguments with each other as they wander. By the time they have found their way in front of Gregory again, Mrs Sincope is experiencing a great deal of abdominal pain.

'Definitely feeling it now. It has most assuredly started to work. Next time you ask me if the pain has kicked in or not, expect a strong answer in the affirmative,' she says to her husband, over and over again in slightly differing variations during the struggle to find the ward. This is mainly done as conscious retribution for the constant probing over lunch and in the park beforehand.

'We need to assign you to a bed on the ward given you appear to be having contractions,' Gregory says once the Sincopes arrive and explain the situation, a comment from the northern lad that places a smile on both of their faces. They are now getting somewhere at what feels like long last. After a brief wait while Gregory makes a phone call to shore things up, the Sincopes follow a middle-aged female orderly onto the antenatal ward itself. Once there, the couple's bright, optimistic mood dims somewhat as all of the women present there lie in their beds looking bleak, tired, run down. It is as if they'd all been there for weeks – for some of them, it looks like months – without bathing or going outdoors. Several of the women are crying; eerily, all of the teary ladies look like they haven't been on the ward as long as the other women who simply sit staring straight ahead of themselves, completely dead-eyed. Mrs Sincope feels a flush of terror at this realisation before rationalising the situation; pregnancy is difficult and it's logical to expect most of the women to be finding it all a bit tricky, here at the end in particular. She is determined, now that the ball is finally rolling, to be as chipper as she possibly can be about the journey that lies ahead.

'Your doctor will be round shortly to check in on you,' the orderly says as she departs from the space now assigned to the Sincopes. It is a small hospital bed Mrs Sincope has been given, built for a single thin person, with the space on each side being minimal, bordered by a white cloth that goes round two sides of the faux cubicle (the one facing out onto the corridor and the one closing them off from the bed to the left). As luck would have it, they have been given one of the beds at the end of the ward, so they at least have real bricks on one side and even a tiny window.

'Which doctor does he mean, do you think: Dr Blots or Dr Sharp?' Mrs Sincope asks her husband after the orderly has disappeared from sight.

'Who knows any more,' Mr Sincope says. 'Perhaps there will be another doctor thrown our way.'

Mr Sincope draws the white sheet fully round them so that while their neighbours' dolorous moans can still be heard, at least their miserable faces will be hidden from sight. Mr Sincope sits down in the chair that is placed about two feet from the foot of the bed at a slight right angle. Once there, he consults his smartphone. As he does this, he wonders why he hadn't whipped the gadget out sooner. This was his innate Luddite tendency coming to the fore. Times of stress, such as he is currently dealing with on the Big Day, tend to bring out this aversion to technology unconsciously.

'What are you looking at on your phone?' Mrs Sincope asks him in a slightly accusatory tone of voice after he'd been at it for a few minutes. He can't possibly tell her the truth, which is that he's gazing at the website of a lads' magazine where there sit pictures of the 'Ten Best Pairs of Funbags in Britain'. How ironic – he'd been annoyed at himself for having forgotten about his phone's capabilities, a lapse in thought that had resulted in him having to resort to looking at breast-related periodicals, only for him to have remembered that he held the entire collected knowledge of the human race in his hand and then decided to look at a bunch of tits anyhow.

'I'm trying to download an app that helps you time your contractions. It's called Synergised.'

If you're wondering how exactly Mr Sincope had managed to think this fast on his feet, it is because he had searched out an application of this type three days previous. Not, it should be stressed, because he had actually been looking for something to assist in capturing the temporal lapses between his wife's contractions; he had searched out the application so as to be prepared for precisely this occasion, a moment when he might be caught out by his wife while looking at soft porn. Mr Sincope: mentally prepared, as ever.

'That's the sweetest thing I think you've ever done!' Mrs Sincope says, blown away by what she assumes is her husband's out of the blue thoughtfulness. Here she was assuming he was looking up some sporting website and all the while he was valiantly searching for something to help the Big Day along. This earns him some brownie points that he will be sure to throw away at the nearest opportunity.

'You know how I am with these things,' he says to his wife. 'How badly does it all hurt down there now? Oh bother, sorry, I forgot I wasn't supposed to ask.'

She smiles at him; Synergised has bought him this one at least.

'No, it's all right, dear. Now that the contractions have kicked in it's all right for you to ask after my welfare.'

'Contractions? You think?'

Mr Sincope gets a little excited by this news; the moment when he can remove himself from the hospital and his wife's side now seems to creep into sight. He figures he might be able to sneak away once she is heavily medicated and perhaps she wouldn't even notice the difference.

'I think so. All I do know for sure is that I'm in a huge amount of pain right now.'

Mrs Sincope's face then distorts into a look of sheer horror as a new wave of more intense pain kicks in. She shrieks and closes her eyes, clutching her bump as she does so.

'Should I go and find a doctor?' Mr Sincope asks.

'If you would, dear.'

Mr Sincope gets up promptly and leaves the confines of their cubicle in search of medical attention. Seeing no one who obviously fits the bill lurking about the ward, he tries Gregory at the reception desk.

'I think my wife is in labour.'

Gregory nods and then picks up his office phone. Satisfied

59

that the wheels are in motion, Mr Sincope returns to his wife. She now appears to be in even more torment than when he left her.

'Are you all right?' he clumsily asks her. She is literally shaking with pain, it is now so intense.

'I'm having a constant, searing agony. I think something must be wrong.'

Mr Sincope panics. He doesn't deal with this type of situation well; ones where he has little control. He paces for about a minute in the cubicle, doing an unconscious impression of Dr Blots, while his wife clutches her abdomen in torment. Finally, he can stand it no longer. He marches back out to Gregory's desk.

'My wife is in real pain now and she thinks the baby might be in danger,' he says to the spotty adolescent receptionist. Gregory's face doesn't change a single, notable bit.

'I've called upstairs already. Someone should be with you shortly.'

'How shortly is shortly?'

'I myself would normally define shortly as between ten minutes thirty seconds and fifteen minutes, forty-five seconds.'

It then strikes Mr Sincope that Gregory must have been the pedantic bloke on the other end of the telephone line when he had made the appointment with Dr Blots' office the previous day.

'So, *you're* the chap I spoke to yesterday!'

'Excuse me?'

'When I called. To make the appointment with Blots. You were the bloke who took the call!'

Gregory shakes his head defiantly.

'I don't work in Dr Blots' office, so it couldn't have been me.'

'No, no, it was you. "Make sure you arrive early or there may be consequences". That was you surely, come on now.'

'I'm sorry, sir, but you must be mistaking me for someone else.'

Mr Sincope remains certain that Gregory had indeed been the person he'd spoken to over the phone – further, that Gregory's motives for covering this up are possibly sinister. This is despite the fact that the man on the phone the previous day had sounded much older; Mr Sincope had forgotten about that detail already. He wonders how many northern receptionists who are male and anal retentive about time could possibly work in the same hospital (real answer: quite a few; six at the time of the Big Day. As it happens, there is a strong correlation between being born north of the Watford Gap, moving to London in your late teens, being neurotic about timekeeping, and manning the phones at a hospital.)

Mr Sincope stands glowering at Gregory for another fifteen seconds before the receptionist finally looks back up at him.

'What?' Gregory asks Mr Sincope.

'Why won't you admit that it was you on the phone yesterday?'

'Because it wasn't. I think you'll find that's a pretty decent reason not to admit to something.'

Mr Sincope thinks about pushing it further until he remembers that he might need Gregory at some point during the rest of the day, and thus it is probably best to keep the relationship as fresh as is still possible.

'You're right, of course. Sorry, it's been a difficult day.'

'Don't worry about it.'

'I'm sure you must see all kinds of weird behaviour from expectant fathers, eh?'

'Not as weird as you, mate.'

The battle definitively lost at this stage, Mr Sincope retreats back to his cloth-shrouded sanctuary.

'When's the doctor coming?' Mrs Sincope practically shrieks as her husband re-enters. Her condition has not seemed to have improved.

'Gregory and I had a good chat about it. Don't you worry, dear, someone's on their way. Should be here any moment, as a matter of fact.'

'Who the bloody hell is Gregory?'

'The northern lad on reception. Spotty-faced kid out there, you remember him.'

Oddly for her, she doesn't remember Gregory, not even slightly. As a details person, she not only usually remembers pretty much anyone she comes into contact with, but a notable detail about each one. Perhaps it is a side-effect of the induction, she thinks to herself though a fog of pain.

The next hour and a half is hell for both of the Sincopes. Mrs Sincope experiences excruciating physical torture the whole time, her abdomen feeling as if it is being torn asunder, her only outlet being her ability to plead with her husband to liaise with Gregory yet another time to find out when a doctor is due to arrive. For Mr Sincope, it is spent responding to these pleas for information by leaving the cubicle and wandering around for a bit, pretending to be speaking to Gregory only to wander back a few minutes later and fib to his wife by telling her that the receptionist had given him every assurance that medical assistance was on its way. Finally, Dr Blots turns up, putting an end to this ninety-minute float down the River Styx.

'Where the bloody hell have you been?' Mrs Sincope barks at the doctor soon after he melodramatically throws open the white curtains surrounding the Sincopes' little area and bellows an overloud 'Hello, patient!' at the bed.

'Attending to other expectant mothers, of course, but now I

am all yours. How is she?' the doctor asks Mr Sincope. Mrs Sincope is annoyed anew that the doctor is again up to what he had been during the induction, namely directing all conversation about her body through her husband. Only this time round, she is in no mood to quietly grin and bear it.

'I'm over here, Doctor, and I am a bloody wreck!' she shrieks, her northern accent making a rare appearance. As she says this, Mrs Sincope realises herself that she is being slightly hysterical. Her earlier decision to remain in an optimistic frame of mind then re-emerges with this moment of clarity, which she uses to take a deep breath, hoping it will calm her down.

'Shhh, there, there, sweetheart,' Dr Blots says patronisingly as he strokes her hair. 'That's the ticket. Breathe in and out. In and out.'

As he speaks to her this way, the doctor moves his hand up and down in front of Mrs Sincope's torso, keeping it hovered a centimetre above her body. He breathes in and out too, mimicking her respiration.

'Now tell me, Mrs Sincope, where does it ouch?'

She hates the childish tone Blots has suddenly decided to adopt but feels that if the doctor can relieve her pain or better still, get her put onto the labour ward straight away, all of his sexist drivel would become bearable. She rubs her uterus as she tells the doctor about her symptoms.

'It's a constant dull ache with a few stabbing pains here and there. But it's so painful; the most pain I've ever been in my whole life.'

Dr Blots takes the stethoscope he has around his neck and puts it into his ears. He then places the chest piece upon Mrs Sincope's navel and listens intently for several seconds.

'Afraid to say this, but you are not in labour quite yet,' he says, withdrawing the stethoscope from Mrs Sincope's personal space.

'What? I must be!' she says desperately.

'Not until you start having contractions. Moments of intense pain followed by a respite. What you have now are simply the unpleasant side-effects of the induction implant taking effect. Those should go on for another couple of hours before labour kicks in.'

'Another couple of hours! I can't possibly handle that without some pain relief!' Mrs Sincope says, allowing herself to get worked up again.

'You'd be surprised what one can handle when it is required,' the doctor responds with and then immediately turns around to leave. Mr Sincope unconsciously grabs Dr Blots by the arm, forcing him to momentarily halt. He had imagined another few hours in that cotton draped limbo with his wife moaning in agony and decided he'd better do whatever he could to avert such a fate.

'My wife said she needs some pain relief,' he says to the briefly startled obstetrician. Blots betrays panic at having been lightly assaulted without warning but quickly returns to pretending to be cool; badly, of course, as the man is a terrible actor after all. He grabs Mr Sincope's hand and melodramatically removes it from his appendage with disgust, as if it was a small woodland animal that had landed there.

'I will speak to the staff and see what can be conjured up for her,' the doctor says through a badly faked smile, clearly offended beyond words at having been startled into letting his soap opera doctor façade slip, even for a moment. Dr Blots then departs, leaving the Sincopes all by themselves again.

Chapter Seven

The Man who is Not a Doctor

For the three hours following Dr Blots' departure from their cubicle, both of the Sincopes manage to sleep reasonably soundly. In spite of the tremendous amount of pain that Mrs Sincope is experiencing, fatigue simply overwhelms her. Mr Sincope passes out in the chair sat two feet from his wife's hospital bed, finding her unconsciousness contagious.

It is hunger that awakens Mrs Sincope. With cognisance comes the consciousness of the pain once more, washing over her like a wave constructed of tiny, razor-sharp nails.

'Oh, bloody hell!' she splutters, waking up her husband with her exhortation. He looks at his watch immediately, a habit of his when he arises from slumber.

'Swearing, dear. Not good for the foetus and all that,' he mumbles half-heartedly.

'What time is it?' Mrs Sincope asks her husband, ignoring completely his garbled condemnation.

'Almost half seven. Jesus, it's that late?'

'No wonder I'm bloody starving.'

'They must feed you in this place,' he says. 'I mean, if they expect you to stick around.'

'Can you go and find out for me, dear?'

Mr Sincope nods his head. As he does, his less-than-ideal encounters with Gregory at reception pop into his mind, making him feel annoyed. There is little way of avoiding speaking to the lad this time round as he can't bring his wife pretend food. He exits the cubicle and sneaks towards the reception desk with trepidation. However, when he gets there he finds that it is not Gregory manning the post, but rather Jill from Dr Blots' office.

'Oh, it's you,' Mr Sincope says as he recognises her. Jill looks up with bloodshot eyes caused by the barbiturate hangover of surprising intensity she is nursing. She says nothing in reply, so Mr Sincope continues.

'Is Gregory done for the day?'

'He's gone down to Dr Blots' office.'

The high soprano of Jill's voice takes him by surprise again. He quickly recovers his senses enough to decipher the tasty morsel of information Jill has unwittingly delivered unto him.

'Dr Blots' office, you say? Gregory does sometimes work there then?'

'Yeah, he works down there all the time.'

'I knew it!' Mr Sincope shouts loud enough to cause several of the couples sat in the waiting room – and it had got surprisingly full during the Sincopes' kip – to jump slightly as he pumps a victorious fist in the air.

'How can I help you, sir?' Jill asks, now a little concerned as to whom exactly this madman in her presence is, having forgotten most of the day's events and therefore not remembering him in the slightest.

'Yes, sorry. My wife is on the ward and I'm wondering when dinner will be served.'

'Food trays come round at eight sharp.'

'Wonderful, thank you.'

Mr Sincope turns around to spread the good news to his missus. Jill, who reaches out over the reception desk to grab his arm, stops him before he goes.

'There'll be none for you though,' she says in that squeaky intonation of hers.

'I assumed as much, thank you.'

''Cause you know, you aren't the one carrying an infant around in your guts.'

'That is true enough.'

Mr Sincope turns to leave once again and successfully escapes this time round. As he walks away however, Jill has a parting shot, one that she shouts full-throated at him as he walks away.

'You'd be surprised how many blokes think that because they're hanging round waiting for their wife to drop child they deserve a free meal! You can go down the chippie, mate! The hospital isn't a meals-on-wheels service for blokes with swimming sperms, thank you kindly!'

It is clear, even to Mr Sincope, that this rant is about something other than his gastronomy. Whatever it concerns, it is something he wants to know less than nothing about. He beats an even hastier retreat back to his wife's bedside.

'Eight sharp, I've been told.'

'How long is that from now?'

He consults his watch again.

'About another twenty minutes.'

Mrs Sincope makes a sad face.

'Can you go to a vending machine and get me some chocolate? Please?'

He thinks his wife is being childish, not able to wait what is a short period of time before her dinner is due to arrive. Yet he decides to concede. Better than a fight, he thinks, and he works out that he could use the space anyhow.

'Of course, dear.'

Mr Sincope considers further how getting off of the antenatal ward might do him some good as he sails past Jill and walks out of the brown door. Once outside the confines of the ward, however, Mr Sincope almost immediately gets lost. The route back to the hospital entrance is so convoluted and counterintuitive that Mr Sincope soon finds himself completely baffled as to his whereabouts. He keeps trying to follow his nose, going up and down stairwells, until he comes to a large, poorly lit corridor that is without doors, one he doesn't recognise in the slightest. He wonders to himself about what the purpose of such a passageway could possibly be. A flash of panic hits him – what if he has wandered into the incineration department? The horror of this is so acute that he dry heaves slightly. Thankfully, the terror passes once he spies a window at the end of the corridor, one that would have been immediately obvious to someone with greater powers of observation than Mr Sincope, i.e. almost anyone at all. He bursts into a jog towards it and arriving at the end, looks through the transparent barrier, which, to be clear, takes up the whole of the end of the corridor, as in, it is a wall-sized window. There he can see a busy hospital thoroughfare on the other side, doctors and nurses streaming to and fro. He now becomes worried that someone on the other side will see him, possibly standing somewhere he shouldn't. But it seems to be a one-way window, as one male doctor in particular stops in front of it and begins to preen himself, looking at what could only be, from his vantage point, his own reflection. Mr Sincope sees what appears to be the main entrance to the hospital, which is exactly where he is trying to end up. This seems odd to him given he hadn't taken the lift, and though he had climbed down a few sets of stairs, having come all the way down to the ground floor seems logistically impossible. But there it is solid visual evidence to the contrary, so Mr Sincope knows he has to trust what his own eyes are telling him. He then turns around and starts walking back to the corridor's entrance, determined to concentrate on his destination now that he knows he is on the right floor at least. But he soon finds himself falling back into his own thoughts again, this time trying to imagine what life will be like once the baby arrives. It was something he had tried repeatedly to do over the past couple of months, but never once in all that time had he managed to conjure up a definitive image of what he and his wife's existence would be like post-pregnancy. All he could think of when he tried to create a similitude of fatherhood was a dark, empty space, a null void.

This meditation is brought to a sudden end by Mr Sincope's realisation that he had found the main reception of the hospital completely by accident. The vending machine that has been his destination is now directly in front of him, fifteen feet away. He saunters up to it and surveys the chocolate for sale. He tries to recall whether it was the one with biscuits in the middle or the one with peanuts in it that his wife likes best. After considering this for a few seconds, he finds that he can't remember. After another brief period of internal consultation, he goes with the peanuts because he likes them better himself and figures that if she doesn't want the confectionary item at least there will be something he can munch on. She's getting a free meal anyhow, he thinks to himself as he plonks into the machine the change that he has in his pocket, selects the appropriate button, and then watches the bar of chocolate crawl to the edge of its compartment followed by a dive sharply to the bottom of the apparatus. Retrieving his prize, Mr Sincope steels himself for what he imagines will be a difficult journey back to the ante-natal ward, made particularly arduous by the fact that he had not been concentrating even slightly during the forward journey.

As Mr Sincope examines the various exits to the main reception and is disheartened by the fact that he cannot even immediately identify which of them he had entered through mere seconds before, he spots Dr Sharp walking towards him. She is lost in a chart she is staring at intently. Mr Sincope has a sudden urge to speak to the doctor, consciously because he thinks that having spoken to her and gained her insight into his wife's pains would earn him brownie points back at the cotton cubicle, unconsciously because, of course, he fancies Dr Sharp. He strolls towards the doctor, placing the peanut-laden bar of chocolate into his jacket pocket, and halting his progress right in front of where she is heading, makes out as if he hadn't seen her whatsoever and indeed had managed to stop short of running right smack into her accidentally.

'Dr Sharp! Goodness me, I'm sorry. I was completely in my own world there.'

'Mr Sincope! Yes, sorry I was doing the same thing.'

His stomach makes a little leap as she remembers his name.

'Quite all right, quite all right. I suppose we're both dreamers.'

He immediately wishes to slap himself for that line. Thankfully, respite is immediate in coming.

'I'm going to grab some dinner in the cafeteria,' Dr Sharp tells him. 'Would you care to join me?'

Mr Sincope almost chokes on his tongue upon hearing this invitation. He struggles valiantly to remain cool.

'I would be honoured. After you,' he says, the confidence of the old hound dog dining outside of his league coming flooding back suddenly.

'How is your wife doing?' Dr Sharp asks as they stroll the hospital hallways together.

'She's still on the antenatal ward. No dilation as yet.'

Dr Sharp shakes her head, in doing so making her long blond locks float deliciously through the air, much to the delight of her walking companion.

'Inductions,' she says. 'They can take their sweet time.'

As the two of them enter the cafeteria, they each take a tray. Dr Sharp asks for the vegetarian special of the day, which is mushroom risotto; Mr Sincope requests the three-meat lasagne. Both have black coffee to drink. When they get to the till, the doctor pays for both of them. Mr Sincope allows her to do so without so much as a thank you. Dr Sharp isn't offended; she likes to pay for things, particularly for men, as it makes her feel powerful. She had grown up poor, in the lower middle class – her father had been a failed photographer – and so to be a woman with her own money is a key element to her sense of self-worth.

'She'll be on the labour ward before you know it,' Dr Sharp says as they take a seat at a long, otherwise vacant table. She says this to try and move the conversation on; it has the odd effect of killing it completely. A strange tension has now developed between Dr Sharp and Mr Sincope, one he thinks is down to her possibly fancying him. Normally when Mr Sincope gets this feeling he is wrong – his intuition when it comes to whether a woman is attracted to him or not is almost always perfectly inverse. However, on this occasion he is, by pure chance, on the money. Dr Sharp has taken a shine to Mr Sincope due to the reason that

71

he resembles her father, i.e. the failed shutterbug, enough at least; always an essential factor in turning the blonde doctor's head. The echo is entirely physical, mostly down to a likeness between the two men in the lower face region: the jaws, lips, and chin. Dr Sharp also has a tendency to fancy the fathers of the children she helps deliver, an urge she tended to fight off but with Mr Sincope, whether this is due to the vague likeness to her dad or something deeper, she is letting float to the surface.

After the meal has reached its dénouement in silence, they both arise and Mr Sincope follows Dr Sharp towards the lift in a sort of pique of blind instinct. They get in together, with Mr Sincope not sure whether to wander around some more or to check in on his wife, having now forgotten completely his wife's urgency in receiving the bar of chocolate he had put in his pocket upon seeing Dr Sharp. The lift comes to a halt on the third floor. Dr Sharp gets out and motions seductively with her finger for Mr Sincope to follow her. He does as she requests without a word. The two of them walk several feet until Dr Sharp halts before the open doorway to a small room where she turns dramatically to face Mr Sincope.

'This is my office in case your wife's condition doesn't move on quickly and you need an ally or even some advice. If I'm not here, I'm out on calls so park yourself in that chair over there and wait for me.'

The tension she has now created between them is so intense, Mr Sincope thinks for a brief moment about going in for a kiss. He thankfully decides against it, as it would have been too much too soon, even for Dr Sharp.

'I'd best see how the wife is doing,' he says instead. He then jogs off in a sudden hurry without waiting for a reply from his dinner companion. Dr Sharp, her flirtations having had their desired effect, smiles as she watches him scurry away. She knows he'll be back.

In front of Mr Sincope is the mission of getting back to the antenatal ward. He manages most of it correctly through sheer luck before taking one wrong turn near the end that has him on a bit of a wander. He finds himself roaming down another corridor that is completely unfamiliar, this one painted an unpleasant shade of puce. He takes the bar of chocolate out of his pocket to look at it, considers having a bite, and then thinks better of it, allowing it to rest in his palm fully intact.

Thankfully, standing in the middle of the puce corridor, reading some sort of chart is a man who appears by his mode of dress to be a doctor; he is wearing a sharp suit covered by a white medical gown.

'Excuse me, Doctor, terribly sorry to bother you.'

'Oh, I'm not a doctor,' the man who looks a lot like a doctor says drily.

'Right, I see. Sorry. I'm trying to get back to the antenatal ward. You wouldn't happen to know the way there from here would you?'

'I would in fact know the way. And I'm more than happy to take you there myself.'

'Splendid! Thanks.'

'In return for a bite of that bar of chocolate you are holding, that is.'

Mr Sincope looks down at his leading brand chocolate treat which contains peanuts. He is now in a bind. If he gives this bloke who apparently isn't a doctor a piece of the chocolate, he will then have to explain to his wife why he'd opened the chocolate that was meant solely for her. However, if he refused to give the non-doctor any chocolate at all, and the man in a white

73

coat held firm to the terms of his offer, it might take Mr Sincope hours to find his way back to his wife. He comes to the conclusion that his only option is to give the man in the doctor's outfit some of his bar of chocolate; he would tell his wife he got hungry and took a bit of it himself. Having come to this decision, Mr Sincope unwraps the end of the bar and breaks off the now exposed portion between his fingers.

'There you go,' Mr Sincope says as he begrudgingly hands it over.

'That's it? That's all I'm getting?'

Mr Sincope looks down at the bar again and is about to break off another small piece when the man who isn't a doctor slaps him hard on the shoulder and breaks into uproarious laughter as he pops the bit of chocolate he had received into his mouth.

'I'm only taking the mickey. Come on, follow me.'

Mr Sincope does as he is told and within two minutes is back in front of Gregory. It turns out that he was amazingly close to finding the antenatal ward when he had made the chocolate bargain. The ease of getting there makes him instantly regret having surrendered any of his supplies to the bloke who had turned out to not be a doctor.

'Thanks for the chocolate, mate,' the man who had brought him there says before departing. All Mr Sincope can do now is shrug, head back to the cubicle and once there try as best he could to elucidate on why he was returning well over an hour after he'd left, armed with an unwrapped, partially eaten bar of chocolate in hand. Perhaps unsurprisingly, his attempt at an explanation does not go down well.

'Why did you get me that one? You know I don't like peanuts. And why the hell is it open already?'

It doesn't help matters that Mrs Sincope is in a foul mood.

Despite her husband having been gone for an epic length of time, her dinner still hadn't arrived. She had tried to get up a couple of times to ask about what was going on herself but found she was in too much pain to stand.

'I got a little hungry along the way,' is Mr Sincope's lame response. He says it like a scolded schoolboy.

'Why didn't you get one for yourself while you were down there if you were so famished?'

'I wasn't hungry when I bought it. But I got a bit lost on the way back and then the hunger kicked in and I couldn't help myself.'

Mrs Sincope feels instinctively that her husband is lying about something. Her mind goes wild, dreaming up things he had been up to. Common to a lot of women in the last few months of their pregnancies, she'd had a few nightmares about her husband either leaving her or at least cheating on her with another woman. She then suddenly dreams up a scenario in which Mr Sincope had gone off to get her chocolate and then actually spent most of that time getting off with Dr Sharp, perhaps down some darkened corridor. The more she thinks about this, the more convinced she starts to become that this was precisely what had actually occurred. It was one of those strange accidents that can take place in which someone dreams up something wild, borne purely out of their own paranoia, which in fact turns out to be at least partially true.

Mrs Sincope swipes the partially eaten bar of chocolate out of her husband's hand and with no further ado proceeds to inelegantly wolf it down. Meanwhile, her husband settles himself into his little chair, whips out his phone, and begins surfing for pictures of ladies' bosoms once again, as if he'd never left the cubicle.

Chapter Eight

Leka the Albanian

Mrs Sincope's dinner finally arrives at quarter past ten that evening. She pointedly asks the woman dispensing the meals out of a tray holder why it had come so late, but the woman appears to speak little to no English. Probably Turkish, Mr Sincope incorrectly concludes – she's from Poland. The supper brought to Mrs Sincope consists of a shepherd's pie composed mostly of peas, the one vegetable in the whole world Mrs Sincope detests. Yet she is so in need of nutrition by this point, she scoffs down the vegetable heavy dish regardless. The one plus of the whole situation from Mrs Sincope's perspective is that her pain has subsided to a semi-tolerable level now.

Following the departure of the Polish dinner lady, no one visits the Sincopes in their little fabric-shrouded den again until four a.m. the following morning when they are both awoken from their restless slumbers by the visit of Dr Sharp.

'How are you, Mrs Sincope?' the pretty blonde doctor asks after she enters the cubicle. The pregnant woman almost weeps at seeing the doctor, both in relief and anger, but successfully keeps her emotions in check. Several hours previous she had imagined this woman having designs on her husband; at this stage she is willing to put those thoughts aside. Mrs Sincope is focused on one thing only now: getting admitted to the labour ward.

'I'm still in pain, Doctor. I must be close to labour by now.'

'Why don't we find out? I'm going to examine you – is that all right?'

Mrs Sincope nods in affirmation as she realises that for all the poking and prodding she had received over the past day no one had actually asked permission to invade her personal space until that moment. This makes her even more confident that things are about to start going her way at long last. Dr Sharp dons a pair of surgical gloves that she removes from her lab coat pocket. She then slips her fingers inside of Mrs Sincope and prods around. The experience of this is incredibly painful for the pregnant woman, but she grits her teeth and makes not a sound. She has to remain tough for another minute or so and then she will be home free. Or so she thinks.

'Sorry, nothing happening down there as yet. Your cervix hasn't dilated a single centimetre since I examined you yesterday.'

This news hits Mrs Sincope hard. She is now unable to hold back the emotions that have been building up. Tears flow down her cheeks within moments of Dr Sharp's analysis. It is the first time she has cried in years.

'If that's the case why am I in so much pain?' she asks the doctor pleadingly, through sobs that almost choke her. The doctor laughs softly, trying to lighten the mood.

'It's the induction doing its job. We should get the breakthrough in the next couple of hours. I'll come see you before say, ten this morning, promise. Hopefully by then we'll see enough movement to admit you upstairs.'

Mrs Sincope wants to say more but given she has now had assurances from the doctor that she would be back in less than six hours, she decides to simply thank Dr Sharp and leave it there. The doctor departs with a final, fleeting look towards Mr Sincope that makes his mind wander in all sorts of interesting directions. Well, interesting by his standards at least.

The Sincopes then mercifully fall right back to sleep after that, Mr Sincope taking slightly more time than his wife to nod off due to his increasing discomfort in the tiny chair.

They are next awoken by the breakfast trolley at half nine that same morning. Mrs Sincope turns up her nose as a plate full of buttered kippers is placed in front of her by a woman from the Czech Republic.

'Can I have something less fishy, please?' she asks the trolley girl with little hope of a coherent response.

'I see what they have,' the Czech girl says in heavily accented English with a friendly smile. 'But they give me what they give me.'

Mr Sincope, who until then had still been half asleep, arises fully, standing up out of his chair. He finds himself in a foul mood that isn't bound to be accommodating towards the foreign breakfast girl who is only trying to be helpful.

'I suppose that's the way things are done in Turkey, but not here in England, young lady! My wife wants something without fish and that is what she shall have!'

The Czech girl, who had only come to London the previous month and was still getting her head around English attitudes and customs, takes this rant from Mr Sincope as a sign that she must have done something notably wrong.

'I'm so, so sorry,' she says as she slinks away with her trolley, managing to hold back from crying.

'Why did you speak to the poor girl that way?' Mrs Sincope asks her husband as soon as the Czech girl has vanished.

'I was trying to stick up for you, dear.'

'Don't harass any women on my account, please.'

Mrs Sincope is hungry enough to literally eat a horse and so she decides to tuck into the fishy breakfast anyhow, containing a gag reflex as she does so.

'I thought you hated fish,' Mr Sincope helpfully adds.

'I'm hungry enough to eat anything.'

She is in no frame of mind to have one those typical conversations with her husband. She knows exactly what he is after: a row followed by her handing her breakfast over to him in a way that would in no way implicate him for having started the whole mess. He mercifully gets the hint in this instance that his indirect claim on her meal would not end in success and leaves the cubicle to forage for his own breakfast without a further word. As he departs, Mrs Sincope steps up her paranoid speculations of the previous evening, imagining that her husband is off to shag the desirable Dr Sharp. The root of this fear, it should be added here, is not simply down to her late pregnancy hormonally addled blues, but in part informed by something that had happened to Sarah, her neighbour, when she had been eight months pregnant. Her husband, Dave, had decided to have an affair with their next-door neighbour – the one in the next flat over – who was named Vanessa. The worst thing from Sarah's perspective was that she'd invented the idea of this affair months previous to it becoming a reality and had only found out it was concrete fact via following Dave around during his early evening jogging routine. He would leave the flat in his running gear and have a jog round the block clockwise only to run right up to Vanessa's place and into her bed. The second worst aspect of the whole affair for her was that Vanessa is older and quantifiably less attractive than Sarah.

'All I can say is thank God I saw it coming,' Sarah said to Mrs Sincope when they first discussed it all. Mrs Sincope wondered at the time why she and Vanessa had never become friends in the same way that Vanessa and Sarah had – at least, before Vanessa started sleeping with Sarah's husband. It always seemed that way, in all avenues of her life. She was unpopular at school, didn't make any permanent friends in university. She always felt like the odd girl out.

In the end, Sarah stayed with Dave after he promised to break it off with Vanessa starting immediately.

'I suppose I have to give the bloke a break – I was pretty intolerable at the time,' Sarah told Mrs Sincope. 'And at least I know if Dave wanders away from the nest ever again he'll be so uncreative about it all that I'll be sure to find out in no time.'

Mrs Sincope openly expressed doubt at the time that Sarah and Dave's relationship could remain the same after the Vanessa-related blow.

'When you marry a guy that you know is not your absolute dream bloke, but a good man who happened to come along at the right time, you let a lot of things slide, don't you?' was Sarah's response. Then came the killer blow.

'You of all people should know all about that one, love.'

Mrs Sincope thinks again and again about Vanessa and Dave and the quote above while she waits for her husband to return from wherever he had gone to feed himself on that morning following what should have been the Big Day. At least this is what consumes her thoughts until a pain like nothing she had ever experienced before in her life kicks in; the horrors of the previous day are not even on the same scale. It feels like a knife has been stuck into each of her ovaries and then savagely twisted.

She shouts at the top of her lungs for a full minute, pleading for someone to come and help her as she spits tiny shards of kipper all over the front of her white hospital gown. No one comes.

Mr Sincope meanwhile has decided he can't eat in the cafeteria again for reasons he can't quite articulate and so he leaves the hospital – after another protracted search for the main entrance – to find sustenance. Once outside, he takes note of how chilly it is and regrets having not brought his coat along from upstairs. It is then that he flies into a miniature panic; his coat wasn't up on the ward, of that he suddenly felt certain, so now he isn't exactly sure of its whereabouts. He thinks the best place to look first is the car. But the coat turns out not to be inside the Skoda either, as he discovers when he goes to check for it in the car park. As he locks the vehicle back up, he then suddenly remembers where he left it: that Portuguese git had taken it off him when they ate at the Love Café the previous day and as it had warmed up during their meal, he'd forgotten to grab it back before they departed. Annoyed with himself for not having been sufficiently 'mentally prepared' at a moment when it was required, he huffs and puffs under his breath to himself as he walks towards the exit to the car park. He then trots along the pavement beyond the hospital, rubbing his arms to warm them up as he does so. Spotting the Love Café fills him with dread. He thinks about bottling it, but then realises this would be idiotic; he needs his coat back, so he will attempt to be in and out of the place as quickly as humanly possible.

'Excuse me, my wife and I were in here yesterday and a man took my coat off me, a Portuguese chap it was, and I'm afraid I forgot all about it and left it here.'

'That was kind of stupid,' comes the bloke behind the counter in a thick East London accent.

'Yes, I suppose it was. You wouldn't happen to still have it by any chance, would you?'

'I'll have a look. Describe it for me.'

'It's light bluish-grey, an overcoat.'

'Right.'

The Londoner leaves the counter and goes into the back of the café. He returns a few seconds later, shaking his head.

'No luck, I'm afraid.'

'Are you sure? Are there no coats you have from yesterday that were left here?'

'There are, but none fitting your description.'

Mr Sincope is starting get annoyed at the cockney café worker, who seems to be playing some sort of a game with him.

'Can I see the ones that you do have back there then?'

'What, all of them?'

'How many can there be?'

'So, I bring them all out and you point to the one that's yours? That seems dodgy.'

'Come on, give us a break here.'

'Fine then. Hang about.'

The cockney again disappears into the back of the café. While Mr Sincope stands waiting for him to return, he surveys the patrons. They are mostly mothers accompanied only by their young children. It reminds him of the fact that London seems to be going through a sort of baby boom at present. This leads him to further ponder school spaces and how there might not be one for his daughter when she reaches the appropriate age. He paints a scenario in which his daughter is home-schooled by his wife and ends up socially ill-equipped for adult life. This would mean she'll never find a husband and would have to live the rest of her life in the basement of whatever house they had moved into by then, playing video games, drinking beer, rarely communicating with the outside world. The Londoner who had gone into the back to fetch the coats thankfully returns quickly, breaking up Mr Sincope's morbid train of thought.

'Right, here they are.'

Despite having used the plural, the cockney holds in his arms a single, solitary coat. It also happens to be Mr Sincope's.

'That's it, that's mine,' Mr Sincope says, going to grab it back, but the cockney from the café moves backwards to prevent Mr Sincope from doing so.

'I thought you said it was a bluish-grey overcoat.'

'That's because it is a bluish-grey overcoat, as anyone can clearly see.'

The café worker examines the coat in a semi-forensic fashion.

'This one is grey, plain grey. Also, it's too short to technically be considered an overcoat. I would describe it as more of a kind of normal coat.'

'Are you a tailor in your spare time or something?'

'I know an overcoat when I see one, mate. And this isn't one.'

'May I have my coat back, please?'

Mr Sincope is now livid. He had made the major error of letting his guard down yesterday and now he was being made to pay the price. After a moment of further tension, the café cockney reluctantly hands Mr Sincope his coat back.

'Thank you. And now I shall wish you adieu, good sir,' Mr Sincope says indignantly while putting on his newly reacquired coat, regretting all the while having used a French word. As he begins to leave the café, the cockney has one last jab at him.

'What, no tip?'

Mr Sincope leaves without a further word, swearing internally to never find himself a customer of that establishment, even at his wife's insistence, ever again, all while the cockney chap laughs mockingly at him.

Mr Sincope is reminded of his hunger as he walks out of the Love Café. He goes to the nearest off-licence and buys a chicken tikka sandwich, eating it as he trudges back to the hospital. The sandwich is truly horrible, almost inedible, but he forces it down. By the time he gets back to the hospital entrance he is in a deeply foul mood.

Mr Sincope's bad humour is deepened by the state of his wife upon his return to the cubicle, which follows another torturous journey back to the antenatal ward.

'Get me pain . . .' Mrs Sincope breathlessly shrieks as he enters, confusing him to no end before, after a few breaths, she manages to finish her sentence.

'Relief.'

He sighs gently. It feels to him as if he is having to carry an enormous burden here. His mind focuses again, for the first time since he and his wife had discussed the subject in Dr Blots' office the previous day, on the question of exactly how long he would be required to stay at the hospital. Given they had spent a night there and still had yet to reach the labour ward, perhaps it was time he shoved off. But he'd have to ease his wife's pain first, if only to have an intelligible conversation about his departure with her.

'I'll sort this out, dear. Back in a moment.'

He marches towards Gregory with newfound determination. He will end his wife's pain and then this will allow him to stage an exit.

'My wife's in labour.'

'That's news to me.'

'She needs to get onto the labour ward immediately.'

'I haven't been told anything. Which doctor confirmed this diagnosis?' Gregory says, as drily as humanly possible. Mr Sincope decides he has to be authoritative if the desired results are to be achieved; the gloves now had to come off with this acne-pocked, teenaged, northern git.

'The diagnosis was given by Dr Screw You, mate.'

'Clever, sir. I'll send someone round to check it out, all right?'

Mr Sincope mistakenly takes this offhand remark to get rid of him as a victory.

'Wonderful. In the meantime, my wife needs something for her pain.'

'All I can give her is paracetamol.'

'Now listen here, this is proper pain she's in, Gregory my lad. I'm going to need something stronger than that.'

'That's all I've got.'

'What about that then?'

Mr Sincope points at a gas canister that is parked behind Gregory. The receptionist turns around to observe what is being gestured at.

'What about it?'

'I'll have that then.'

'You can't.'

'Why not?'

'Because it doesn't belong on this ward.'

'Yet it appears to be on the ward at present.'

'It's not on the ward; it's in the ward's reception.'

'Why is it in the ward's reception then if doesn't belong on the ward?' Mr Sincope asks.

'It shouldn't be here. Someone's coming to take it away.'

'Too right: me.'

Mr Sincope marches behind Gregory, picks up the gas canister's handle, and wheels it out onto the ward floor.

'Hold on there, you can't do that,' the receptionist says to him in an uncharacteristic fluster as Mr Sincope makes to depart with the canister.

'Watch me.'

Mr Sincope's heart is racing a mile a minute as he walks away from Gregory. That was the biggest direct confrontation he'd had for years with anybody. I must get up in people's faces more often, he thinks to himself as he re-enters the cubicle like a returning hero. When Mrs Sincope sees the gas canister she treats him like one too.

'Gas and air! Well bloody done!'

Mrs Sincope jumps up off the bed and uneasiness on her feet be damned, stands up, turns some dials on the front of the canister like an old pro, grabs the mouthpiece, and inhales with all her might. As she exhales, the mood in the cubicle changes completely. It is as if Mrs Sincope had suddenly been immersed in Valium and instantaneously absorbed every molecule.

'Man, I feel real chilled,' she says in a three-martini voice. The calm that comes over his wife is infectious and Mr Sincope finds himself unwinding swiftly as well. Mrs Sincope offers him a suck on the gas and air; he doesn't refuse and in fact jumps up and grabs the inhaler and goes to town.

'That's some good shit,' he says as the euphoria sets in instantly for him as well. His wife nods at him while smiling; a lovely, stoned grin.

For a period, perhaps of an hour, maybe two, the Sincopes are both silent. Mr Sincope spends the time gazing at the various stains on the ceiling. After a while, he falls asleep and has a dream that he is driving a car through some unknown continental country. Probably the south of France but could be Spain. His wife is asleep beside him. In the back, sat in a child's car seat, is Faith. In his nocturnal vision of her, Faith is as beautiful to Mr Sincope's eyes as any human being could possibly be. He turns around to look at her smiling face and finds himself completely enchanted, needing to gaze at the child again and again. On the seventh or eighth time of rotating to stare at his daughter briefly before facing the road again, Mr Sincope finds he cannot turn his face away from his daughter. Faith finds this incredibly amusing and laughs the kind of laugh only very small children seem able to muster, a complete body, infectious type of all-encompassing joy release. Mr Sincope then realises he hadn't looked at the road in some time and whips his head round to face frontwards. It is too late, however; the car is mere nanoseconds from hitting another vehicle, an articulated lorry. A head-on collision jolts the car the Sincope family are travelling in swiftly backwards, sending it hurling into a roadside tree. Miraculously, no one is hurt. But as Mr Sincope is counting his blessings, the driver of the lorry emerges. What emanates from the vehicle isn't entirely human, something that becomes clear as it gets closer to the Sincope's vehicle. It is some kind of black, mist-like phantom that is semi-person-shaped. The bizarre apparition floats towards the car and then hangs outside. Mr Sincope understands somehow that the ghost is calling for him and him alone; that it will spare his family if he offers himself up as a sacrifice. In the dream, Mr Sincope doesn't know what to do when offered this choice. Thus, he sits in the vehicle, trying desperately to decide which judgement to make.

While her husband is out of it, Mrs Sincope simply lets her mind wander randomly, effortlessly. For the first time in a long time she feels at peace. Prior to becoming pregnant, alcohol was her escape valve. Having to quit drinking was perhaps the hardest thing about the whole pregnancy for her to bear. Getting outside chemical stimulation once again is heaven. A few minutes on from her last puff, Mrs Sincope begins to hallucinate mildly. First it involves the colours of the objects surrounding her becoming more vivid, but soon she is having all sorts of time/space distortions. She looks over at her slumbering husband and he appears to be some sort of goofy looking puppet. She goes to laugh but no sound will emerge from her mouth. Then a little bluebird flies over from the window and lands right beside Mrs Sincope's head. This startles her not in the least, a realisation that ironically slightly unsettles Mrs Sincope. She wonders how the bird could have got into the room as the tiny window to her right definitely appears to be closed.

'Expecting any moment, are we?' says the bluebird in Mrs Sincope's ear in a London accent. The fact that the bluebird is speaking to her in clear, intelligible English doesn't seem at all incongruous to her.

'It seems to be taking for ever,' Mrs Sincope says in response to the bluebird.

'For me as well, love,' the bluebird says and then pats its own oddly engorged belly. 'As a matter of fact . . .'

The bluebird then throws her head back and wails with pain. Mrs Sincope oddly finds this incredibly funny and is about to say something to Mr Sincope about the bird, yet when she looks at her husband she is then reminded of the fact that he has become a silly puppet and besides that, is still asleep.

'Oh my, the labour pains,' the bluebird says through gritted teeth, its face becoming more anthropomorphised by the moment. Mrs Sincope looks at the bottom of the bird so as to catch the moment when the egg emerges. Yet what comes out of the pregnant bluebird is not an egg but a little baby chick, as if the bluebird was not actually a bird at all but simply a birdlike mammal. Once the newborn bluebird emerges from its mother, the class confusion continues with the mother bluebird bringing the winged infant up to her teat – located where the nipples would be if the bird were a primate – whereupon the baby chick sucks in milk through its tiny beak. Mrs Sincope blacks out at this stage and wakes up some indeterminate time later, desperate for another puff of the gas and air as the pain has kicked in again. But as she sits up to satiate her urge, the valve on the gas pump starts to malfunction and the gas is impeded from reaching her lungs.

'I need you to look at the gas and air for me, dear. It's not working all of a sudden,' she says to her husband as psychological withdrawal kicks in almost immediately. Mr Sincope, awake again having had a few more puffs from the gas himself, shakes his head to clear it, gets up from his seat, and walks over to the gas and air canister to investigate what had gone awry. Not knowing what he is doing in the slightest, Mr Sincope pushes a few buttons and pulls at a few bits, hoping to make a difference. It works, but not as intended; a pipe becomes dislodged, sending gas wheezing into the air.

'What have you done?' his wife asks him, horrified her new toy appears to have been broken.

'I was trying to fix the stupid thing, like you asked me to.'

'Perhaps you could try and put it all back together again with Sellotape!'

This is an extremely pointed comment that relates to an incident which had occurred six months previous, right around the same time they had bought the Skoda. Mr Sincope had decided at the time that if they wanted to sell the flat for the best possible price, the bathroom needed to be upgraded. Mrs Sincope, who was averse to the idea of moving anyhow, hated the thought of having her bathroom torn to pieces. At three months pregnant, she was not particularly keen on the thought of having the loo closest to their bedroom disabled for several weeks when she was having to get up to pee three times a night. Despite these protestations, her husband pressed ahead with the work anyhow. Worst of all, he hired a group of Albanians whom he had met outside of the local hardware store. Mrs Sincope couldn't understand why her husband, who was normally so wary of foreigners and often liked to talk about 'British jobs for British workers', would hire a group of them that weren't even in the country legally. She knew the answer, of course: because they were extremely cheap. Economics always trumped everything for her husband. Even worse, the leader of the Albanian crew, Leka, would often make lewd comments to Mrs Sincope when it was only she and him in the flat together. A few choice favourites that got a lot of airtime were:

'A pregnant woman very sexy.'

'Pregnancy make boobs much, much bigger.'

'Woman with child much more wonderful than virgin girl. She is real woman.'

Mrs Sincope dealt with this by one day telling Leka, after he'd uttered one of these quasi-come-ons, that she would in no uncertain terms remove his testicles if he ever said anything of a non-professional nature to her ever again.

After that, she made every effort to not be around when the Albanians were there as the tension was too much. But given her husband worked long hours while hers had been cut more and more the deeper into her pregnancy she had got ('You must take time to be with your bump,' she had been told repeatedly by her supervisor when Mrs Sincope had enquired as to why her contracted hours were being reduced), she had become the unofficial mission leader on a project she hadn't wanted to embark on in the first place. All of this created huge resentment between the Sincopes.

'This isn't my bathroom, it's yours,' she would often say around this time to her husband. 'You're going to need to sign off on it when they're finished because I'm not going to.'

Truth was Mr Sincope quickly became fairly terrified of the Albanians and of Leka in particular shortly after hiring them. Partly it was his general fear of foreigners, but a large slice of his wariness was down to his terror of workmen, builders, or indeed any working-class male who did a job that involved his hands, whatever his country of origin. Mr Sincope was completely non-functional when it came to anything that incorporated mechanical reasoning. Being around macho blokes who knew which end of a wrench was which intimidated him; made him feel like less of a man. Leka was particularly testosterone-charged, and unintendedly compelled Mr Sincope to feel effeminate when the Albanian foreman was around.

'We fix this bathroom up for you good, Mr Sincope. You no worry.'

Mr Sincope tried his best to take Leka's advice. Yet he was constantly terrified that his decision to go with such a cheap option would come back to haunt him – and so it did. The day came when the Albanians were done with their work and Mr Sincope walked around to inspect the new bathroom. He checked the taps to see that everything worked and flushed the loo. It all seemed all right to him. He paid Leka in cash and with a smile on all of their faces, the Albanians departed.

When Mrs Sincope got home that evening, she did an inspection of the new bathroom herself. This was a more thorough job and she quickly came upon something big that her husband had missed: the pipe adjoining the sink to the wall had only been Sellotaped there. The stationery item was all that was holding the main pipe to the rest of the house.

'That's never going to last!' she shrieked. 'And when it goes it will flood the whole bloody flat!'

Mr Sincope tried to get Leka on the phone, but the Albanian dodged his calls. Mr Sincope had been had. He'd trusted a foreigner, something he himself thought was a bad idea, and had his fingers burned.

'I'll call a plumber tomorrow and have it fixed, dear,' Mr Sincope said to his wife after formally giving up on Leka, feeling utterly emasculated along the way.

'This time British jobs for British workers, if you please,' she said. Being chided by his wife on something that was for him a guiding principle made Mr Sincope feel even worse about the whole situation.

Over the week following the Albanian-Sellotaped pipe incident, Mr Sincope fell into a deep depression. He found himself completely obsessed with the poorly affixed duct, even going so far as to stare at it for several minutes each evening when he arrived home. His wife would nag him instantly upon his entrance about whether or not he'd rung a plumber yet to come around and fix the problem. Due to this obsessive staring, he was avoiding doing so for the time being.

At night, he would lie staring at the ceiling and think about the Sellotape and how it seemed like the perfect metaphor for his entire existence. Although he felt like he was on top of things most of the time, when he looked under the surface of his life he found that it was mostly being held together by the flimsiest of materials and that not much was keeping it all together before the inevitable metaphorical flood appeared. Now that he was going to be a father, this idea scared him even more than it normally would have.

An orderly neither of the Sincopes has previously seen bursts into the cubicle and stares at the hissing gas canister in absolute horror.

'What the bloody hell is going on in here?' he says as he marches over and stops the leaking gas by pressing a button on the face of the canister. 'How did you get a hold of this? There aren't supposed to be any of these on this floor!'

Mr Sincope thinks on his feet and decides to take an opportunity to do over Gregory.

'The northern kid at the reception gave it to us.'

'Gregory?'

'That's the chap. I asked for it and he wheeled it in.'

'However you got it, I'm taking it away. They're strictly not allowed on this ward.'

'Why not?' shrieks Mrs Sincope as the orderly starts wrapping up the canister and all of its accoutrements. She is ready to get up and pounce on the man, immobility be damned.

'Because they're not. It's the rules,' the man lamely offers.

'That's not good enough. I want to see a doctor.'

'They're all busy at the moment. I'll put your request through.'

The orderly then begins to leave, with the gas and air canister in hand. Mrs Sincope makes a face to her husband that implores him to rescue her euphoria machine from the retreating orderly. Mr Sincope simply shrugs at her in resignation as the no longer leaking canister leaves the cubicle for good, running through in his mind once again all of the abuse regarding the Sellotaped pipe he'd had to weather months back and feeling that he was perhaps now exacting a small portion of revenge.

Chapter Nine

'I'd Put That In The Pro Column'

No doctor, nurse, midwife nor any other healthcare professional bothers to visit the Sincopes' cubicle for the remainder of Friday following the Thursday that was to have been the Big Day. Not even Dr Sharp, whose promise of a pre-ten a.m. visit becomes a blanket no-show.

Finally, at two in the morning on the Saturday, near the start of their third calendar day since arriving at the hospital for the induction, Dr Blots appears in the cloth-draped domicile that has become the Sincopes' temporary residence. He subjects Mrs Sincope to another test of her cervix; once again, she is told there is no movement, but that labour will hopefully be coming soon.

In the meantime, Mr Sincope has become increasingly aghast at his wife's behaviour; what he sees as all that moaning in pain and agony. He had expected a little more mental toughness from his wife and is surprised to see her so caught off guard by the whole experience. The not inconsiderable amount of time they expended on those execrable NCT classes is now looking more and more wasteful. Mr Sincope had initially tried to steer his wife around the idea of NCT altogether. She would have none of this ('If we don't go to NCT classes, how will I know what to do on the Big Day?') and two months before what was initially scheduled to be Faith's birth date, Mr Sincope found himself sitting around a circle in the lotus position with five other couples at the first class dedicated to helping them understand better the tsunami that was about to envelop them all.

'Thank you for coming today, I'm Pauline,' said the notably attractive (to Mr Sincope at least) brunette woman who was to be their NCT instructor. 'I'd like to start by finding out where everyone is from. So, as you can see, I've put a map of the UK up there on the wall along with little tags with each of your names on. If you could all stick your tag on the spot where you were born, that would be grand.'

Of course, this being London, most of the tags went unplaced due to the fact that almost no one in the room was born anywhere whatsoever within the confines of the United Kingdom. Apart from the Sincopes, there was only one other fully home-grown couple – a working-class pairing from Penge – in addition to an English bloke who was married to an Italian woman. The Italian lady was notably attractive as well, a fact also not lost on Mr Sincope.

The embarrassment of the map incident delicately and deftly handled by Pauline, the rest of the day was a supposedly subtle attempt to brainwash everyone into having a home birth. The very notion of this was anathema to Mr Sincope. Having birthing fluids spread all over their Ealing flat was never going to be a priority of his. The Brit who'd married the Italian was of the precise opposite bent; he was clearly some sort of home birth Nazi, something he made abundantly clear on several occasions.

'Let's now talk about the pros and cons of having a home birth,' Pauline said after she'd been through the step-by-step procedure regarding the DIY nascence of a human being. The

Englishman who was extremely taken with the idea of his gorgeous Italian wife having their child on the linoleum added, as you'd expect, a great deal to the pro argument.

'Your kid knows where he lives, straight off,' struck Mr Sincope as amongst the more dubious items to be added to the list by this man who'd married off the farm. After the pro tally had been made into almost novella length, mostly by the Home Birth Nazi, the cons were briefly touched upon.

'The big minus we have to consider about a home birth is the fact that at home there won't be the opportunity to have any sort of serious pain relief,' Pauline announced solemnly to the group. There were lots of nods and grunts under their breath from the ladies sat round the circle.

'I'd put that in the pro column,' the home birth aficionado said with a sleazy grin. This earned him the evil eye from all of the women in the room bar his own wife. Home Birth Nazi either didn't seem to notice or didn't mind the attention as he continued wearing a pleasant grin on his face for the remainder of the session.

The rest of the NCT instruction, both that class and the one on the following Saturday, went by in a blur for Mr Sincope. He mostly tuned out completely, pondering things like how they could cut their gas bill further. It wasn't until the third and final session, the one marked out for breastfeeding, that things got hellish enough for him to tune back in. The other chaps had obviously fought their corners more successfully to stay away. Mr Sincope's wife aggravated him further by inviting the home delivery fascist and his lovely Italian wife out for a drink following the udder-related session. The two couples took separate cars to the pub, which allowed Mr Sincope the chance to raise his anger passive-aggressively with his wife.

'Unusual this – we don't normally go the pub after an NCT class,' was his lame, limp-wristed opening statement.

'There have only been two previous classes, dear, so precedence is a hard thing to cite,' was Mrs Sincope's response.

'Thing is, I didn't think you liked that bloke and his, as you put it last week, misogynistic world view.'

'Actually, that's exactly why I asked them to come for a drink, now that you mention it. I want to get him alone, question him further on all of that sexist rubbish he came out with during the classes.'

When they got to the pub, in spite of trying to be located anywhere but, Mr Sincope found himself parked next to the pain in the pro column bloke in a way that isolated him a great deal from the two women. Mrs Sincope and the Italian wife meanwhile seemed from Mr Sincope's vantage point to get on like a house on fire almost immediately, which made the whole situation even more pressure-packed for him. The two men started off by reminding one another of their first names – the home birth obsessive turned out to be called Gerald. He was also, as luck would have it, a fellow accountant.

'How long ago did you qualify?' Mr Sincope asked after discovering the Home Birth Nazi's occupation.

'Ten years now. You?'

'Eleven this May.'

Having this slight superiority in terms of experience gave Mr Sincope a testosterone hit. He cheered up considerably and decided to give Gerald half a chance.

'When's your year end?'

'Two months from now. Yours?'

'We run co-terminus with the calendar year.'

The conversation only got even more crushingly dull to any

objective observer from there, to the mutual glee of Gerald and Mr Sincope. There was even an aged creditors joke at one point, for good measure.

Mrs Sincope meanwhile was actually in a sort of personal hell, deeply regretting initiating the pub trip. She was almost overwhelmingly intimidated by Isabella, the sexy and glamorous Italian wife of Gerald. Isabella talked about her journey from the back streets of Milan to the house in West London that she lived in with her husband. It appeared to Mrs Sincope to have been seamless and her current life a vision of cosmopolitan wonder.

'The only thing about England that drives me crazy is the weather. I miss the sunshine sometimes. Do you and your husband travel often?' Isabella asked Mrs Sincope. When the Sincopes had gone on holidays together, it tended to be an unmitigated disaster. The pattern had started early on – the Sincopes took a city break to Nice as their first trip abroad together, one which was a comedy of errors from start to finish. Mr Sincope put his wife's bag down for a moment on the Promenade des Anglais and it was almost immediately nicked. The couple spent the rest of the trip in the police station filling out a series of forms, in triplicate, in French.

'We don't travel often,' was another lie from the mouth of Mrs Sincope to Isabella. 'What about you? Do you miss Italy?'

'Oh my word, I am so glad to leave Italia far behind me,' she said with a sardonic chuckle that unnerved Mrs Sincope further, as she had no idea what it was meant to signify. 'The corruption, the rampant racism that is everywhere – and that is before you get to the way politics is in Italia. Everything is corrupt. This is one of the many reasons that I left for good.'

Mrs Sincope found her drinking companion's dismissal of her own country discomforting for reasons she couldn't understand.

'Surely you must miss something about where you grew up?' she asked in semi-desperation. Isabella flicked her hair in a way that made her seem incredibly inviting, even to the flustered Mrs Sincope, as if she were a character from a Fellini movie who had walked off the silver screen and into real life. Isabella wore her pregnancy in a way Mrs Sincope felt she could never pull off; as if being pregnant brought out her womanliness, her sexual desirability.

'The food is the only thing I miss a little about Italia. That and the *calcio*; English football is so boring.'

On the way back home from the pub, there was a stark contrast between the moods of the two Sincopes.

'That turned out to be rather lovely, dear,' Mr Sincope said with a smile about halfway through the journey (they had both been completely silent up to that point). 'Thank you for putting that together.'

Mrs Sincope's stomach turned. She had hated the whole experience but since it was her idea in the first place she couldn't rubbish it. It also occurred to her just then for the first time that she hadn't been able to say one word to the Home Birth Nazi, her ostensible reason for having put the whole occasion together. She thought for a moment and, in an effort to pick a fight with her husband about something, anything other than the pub meal they had experienced being dreadful for her, she found herself greatly overreaching.

'I saw the way you were looking at Isabella. I know you found her attractive.'

'No, not really,' he fibbed. 'Not my type.'

'I wish you didn't feel the need to lie to me, particularly about petty things that don't matter.'

'If they don't matter, why bring them up?'

She felt he had her there and so she dropped the line of enquiry.

That evening, Mrs Sincope had dream after dream about Isabella. Most of them involved the two of them being friends, going on strange adventures together. A few of them were sexual in nature, which shocked Mrs Sincope as she had never had those sorts of feelings towards another woman in the whole of her life up until that point.

Over the coming months, Mrs Sincope thought about Isabella often, usually with some hint of sexual yearning involved. This was accompanied by occasional feelings of intense dislike for the Italian woman, sometimes coupled with an urge to find her and confront her about something; what that challenge would or even could be about never being clear to Mrs Sincope, despite the feelings being very real in the moment. Her intense emotions towards Isabella disturbed her greatly. Sometimes she wouldn't think about her for weeks and then suddenly she'd be there, her Milanese accent and wonderful hair floating back into her mind, stirring up all the same, awful feelings once again inside of Mrs Sincope.

Chapter Ten

The Old Grist Mill

Following Dr Blots' two a.m. Saturday morning visit, the one which yielded the fact that Mrs Sincope's cervix had not yet dilated a single millimetre, another fourteen hours pass without a further call from a health care professional to the Sincopes' cubicle. Mr Sincope sleeps through a lot of this downtime; Mrs Sincope meanwhile has become so wracked with pain that sleeping more than ten minutes at any given time has become impossible. On a few occasions during the morning of the third day in hospital, she gazes over at her husband snoozing, a contented grin on his face, and finds that she has the sudden urge to throw something at his head. She miraculously manages to resist this temptation each time.

The Polish dinner lady brings lunch at one p.m., a stew-like substance that is once again laden with peas. Mrs Sincope is now past caring about food saturated with generous portions of her most hated vegetable and so she eats her lunch, slowly, methodically, but also completely. Like when one does exercise, she counts each spoonful, stopping when she gets to twenty and then having a minute-long breather.

When the Sincopes finally do get a medical professional in to see them late afternoon on Saturday, it is a new male nurse.

'A doctor, at long last,' Mrs Sincope says to her husband mistakenly as the young man in a white coat wanders in.

'I'm not a doctor. Only a nurse, I'm afraid. Everything all right, Mrs Sincope?'

This question permits Mrs Sincope to unload on the poor man.

'No, it's not bloody all right! I've been here for three days now and I want to go up to the labour ward!'

'But you're not in labour. At least not according to the charts.'

'If I'm not in labour yet then why am I in so much pain? It's getting worse by the hour!'

'I don't know, I'm afraid. Probably best to ask a doctor.'

Mrs Sincope breaks into tears, frustrated almost to the early stages of insanity by her position.

'I feel like I'm trapped in a Kafka novel!' she shrieks. The literary reference is completely lost on the male nurse, unfortunately, who simply shrugs out of anything better to do in response.

'I suppose I could examine you, if that would make you feel better,' he says.

'If you aren't a doctor what good will that do?'

'Like I say, I thought I'd offer to make you feel better.'

'Please leave.'

'I'll make sure and send a doctor round to see you,' the male nurse says as he departs.

'I've bloody heard that one before!' Mrs Sincope shouts after him, loudly – or at least her husband thinks so. He is becoming increasingly dismayed with his wife's behaviour and is even close to attempting a passive-aggressive conversation with her about it. He decides against it after the male nurse departs, opting instead for another nap. He has decided for now that he can't leave the hospital until his wife is in labour and safely ensconced in the ward upstairs.

Mr Sincope is awoken several hours later by the sound of his wife sobbing. He looks at his watch: it is ten p.m. Even he can tell that this time his wife's tears are not entirely petulant; she seems to be in the midst of a sort of breakdown.

'Are you all right, dear?' he says, trying his best to convey warmth, even going as far as getting out of his seat and touching his wife's hand.

'That nurse said a doctor was coming. It's been hours and hours now. Please, I need you to find me a doctor. I'm in so much pain.'

'All right, I'm on it,' he says resignedly as he dashes out of the cubicle, at least somewhat happy to have a mission and be away from his manic wife for at least a few minutes. He decides what he should do is go past Dr Sharp's office and see if she can be of assistance. She did say that he could call on her any time. Given the hour, she would most likely not be there but it remained his best lead. The only problem would be finding her office again. He takes the lift to the third floor and then makes a left and a right and then a left again, not knowing if he is getting warm, all the time simply following his nose. Recalling how close the office seemed to the lifts on his maiden visit, Mr Sincope is now baffled at how it does not seem to be anywhere near them. And then, seemingly out of nowhere, he finds himself standing in front of a door that reads: DR SHARP – OBSTETRICS. Adding further luck to the pile, the good doctor herself is actually in, sat behind her desk. Mr Sincope is instantly reminded of how attractive she is as he looks at her. Her long legs, her wavy blond hair, her impressively pneumatic figure. As she looks up to acknowledge him, Mr Sincope's heart does a little flutter.

'Why hello, handsome,' she says with a huge grin. 'What can I do for you?'

'It's about my wife. She's in terrible pain and rather losing her wits about it all and I was wondering if you could possibly examine her. We've been waiting for hours for someone to come round to no avail.'

Dr Sharp takes the dull end of the pencil she had in her hand and begins to seductively chew on it.

'I can do you one better,' she says, taking the pencil out her mouth and pointing it at Mr Sincope. 'I can have her moved up to the labour ward as soon as possible.'

'Really? Well, that would be marvellous!'

To immediately prove that she meant what she had just said, Dr Sharp picks up the phone and dials a number.

'Have one for the ward . . . yes, a Mrs Sincope . . . in the ante-natal ward, yes . . . next hour? . . . thanks, Jay.'

She hangs up the phone.

'All sorted,' she says to Mr Sincope.

'Wonderful. I don't know how to thank you, Doctor.'

'Don't worry, I can think of something. Follow me.'

Dr Sharp gets up from her desk and whisks past Mr Sincope, grabbing his hand as she does so, compelling him to follow her as she races down the hallway outside of her office towards God knows what. He finds it a little exciting as he jogs in her wake, feeling his palm getting sweaty next to hers. After numerous twists and turns and dashes up stairwells, Dr Sharp comes to an abrupt halt. Mr Sincope immediately recognises where he is: at the mouth of the long corridor that has the one-way window at the end of it, looking out on to the hospital's main entrance. Mr Sincope feels disorientated by the fact that this means they are on the ground floor. Like the first time he'd happened upon this location, the number of stairs they had walked down seemed incongruous with that fact. Dr Sharp walks them both to the end of the corridor, almost until she is right up against the one-way mirror looking out onto the hospital entrance at the end.

'I'm sorry for dragging you all the way here,' she says to Mr Sincope a little breathlessly as she flicks a patch of her blond locks seductively away from her eyes. 'I wanted to get you somewhere where we would be able to speak undisturbed.'

Mr Sincope tries to think of something to say but finds himself strangely mute. He has no idea what the situation expects of him, and this leaves him feeling uncomfortable. He gets a sudden urge to make a run for it, but consciously knows this would be idiotic for many reasons, not least of which is the fact that Dr Sharp had arranged to have his wife put on the labour ward, solving most of his immediate problems. He then suddenly finds himself thinking about his Argentinean ex-girlfriend, Aleida – he has an incredible desire to be with her again in that moment and even has a fleeting feeling that breaking up with that feisty, sexy Latin woman was a huge error, perhaps the greatest mistake of his entire life.

'My husband died eighteen months ago,' is what Dr Sharp breaks the awkward silence with.

'I'm sorry to hear that.'

'We were close. I loved him more than anything in the whole world. When he died, I felt I couldn't go on living myself. In order to be able to keep going, I buried myself in my work. I didn't allow anything of a personal nature into my world.'

She walks towards Mr Sincope, ever so slightly. He notices the doctor is trembling a little.

'He unfortunately left me with a reasonable amount of economic concerns of which I was previously unaware. I was wondering if, perhaps in light of the favour I've just done for you, you could have a look at my personal accounts for me – at a discounted rate?'

After Dr Sharp says this, Mr Sincope feels a let-down so crushing he thinks for a moment he may be having a heart attack. He wasn't sure what to expect from this rendezvous, but he'd somehow hoped for something more than a request for his financial expertise. His sudden breathlessness is not lost on Dr Sharp.

'Jesus, are you OK?' she asks. Mr Sincope touches his chest and then gives her a nonchalant smile. She must not think for a moment that I thought she was taking me somewhere for sex, he thinks clearly to himself for the first time.

'I'm fine. All this sleeping in a chair isn't so good for me, I think.'

'I can probably get you some light barbiturates if you're not sleeping well.'

'No, no, no, I'll be fine.'

'What do you say? About my proposition, I mean?'

'I'd be happy to look into your financial affairs at a suitably modest price, Doctor.'

'Thank you.'

She kisses him on the cheek and then dashes past him, down the corridor and out of sight. Mr Sincope looks to the floor for a moment and then raises his head to gaze out at the bustling hospital staff in the corridor beyond the one-way window. A deep shame around his desire to engage in adulterous behaviour with the doctor sets in. He would have to do something – going to a pub and having a pint seems the immediately attractive option – before seeing his wife again.

After getting lost several times while trying to locate the exit, Mr Sincope walks out of the hospital and through Four Fountains Park. He stops briefly to gaze at the jingoistic fountain with the bulldog on it, which has the odd effect of deepening his shame about what he had wanted to happen with Dr Sharp in the corridor. He almost wants to apologise directly and out loud to the lifeless redcoat on the stone horse; instead, he carries on out of the park and ambles aimlessly for a while, lost in his thoughts, which mostly consist of him thinking about Dr Sharp and what he would have done had she tried to seduce him. The rumination that he had never cheated on his wife – at least, he'd never had full-blown sexual relations with anyone since they had been married – and yet less than an hour ago found himself actively prepared to do so breaks through to the core of his conscience, no matter how hard he tries to keep it out. Even Mr Sincope realises that the incident represented a major crossing of the Rubicon for the way he would see his marriage from now on.

Mr Sincope breaks out of his cogitation to find himself exactly where he'd hoped to end up when he set out from the hospital – in front of a dingy-looking old man pub that he'd never previously been to in his life and would almost certainly never visit again, which is exactly what he's after right now. Even its name is perfect: The Old Grist Mill.

As Mr Sincope walks inside, he finds the place as predictably quiet as you'd expect an old man pub on a side road in West London at that time of the evening to be. Looking at his watch and discovering the time, he is surprised the pub is still serving. Mr Sincope is one of only four customers and the sole patron under the age of sixty. He goes to the bar and orders a pint of real ale, one from the West Country with a typically funny name. Holding it in his right hand, he surveys the room briefly and then takes a seat at the table most strategically removed from everyone else in the pub. This doesn't prevent one of his fellow punters, an elderly gentleman in a flat cap and floods, from wandering over and helping himself to a seat at Mr Sincope's table.

'I see you're a Smelly Fungus Toe man,' he says by way of an opener. Mr Sincope is utterly baffled until he realises that the old man is referring to the ale in his hand.

'Yes. I suppose I am,' Mr Sincope says in a snarky voice designed to get rid of the pensioner as quickly as possible.

'It's funny though – you don't look gay.'

This seeming non sequitur has Mr Sincope understandably baffled.

'Excuse me?' he asks the old man, who laughs in return.

'You wandered past and thought you fancied a tipple, I suspect. This, young man, is a pub for active homosexuals.'

This seems utterly impossible to Mr Sincope, but he also can't see why the old bloke would make up that piece of information either. Perhaps he's joking? Mr Sincope doesn't want to offend anyone's sexuality. That's like being racist these days; simply not the done thing.

'Yes, I stumbled upon the place. My wife's having a baby at the hospital,' is what Mr Sincope thinks is the perfect rejoinder given it also happens to be the truth. It gives his visit context while clearly spelling out his heterosexuality for the old bloke.

'Well, young man! You should have said so off the bat! Jimmy!' the old man shouts, addressing the portly, middle-aged landlord who is behind the bar with a pint of what appeared to be Smelly Fungus Toe himself in his right hand. 'This chap is having a kid today!'

'You don't say!' Jimmy answers back in a thick Dublin accent. 'Is it your kid or your partner that's the father?'

The old man at Mr Sincope's table laughs and then shakes his head at Jimmy.

'He's not gay. He wandered in by mistake.'

'Oh, right. Either way, congratulations are in order,' the landlord says. The other customers all wander up to the table to offer their congratulations as well, one by one. Then another punter gets up and approaches the bar.

'Jimmy, whatever the lad is drinking, his next one's on me.'

Now extremely uncomfortable with the whole situation – he had only chosen to come into the pub in the first place because it seemed an easy place to sit and have his thoughts to himself – Mr Sincope wants to try and finish his pint and leave as quickly as possible. He now formulates a plan to gulp down the pint of ale he currently has as quickly as possible in the hope of escaping before the next pint that was being purchased for him began to be poured. However, the old man at his table, the one who initially approached him, catches Mr Sincope off guard with a question.

'I know you're not gay, right, but if you were, let's just say that you were gay, just for a second here, who would you rather sleep with, George Best or Denis Law?'

'They're both dead,' Mr Sincope points out to his invasive drinking companion, thinking on his feet for once in his life.

'I know, but I don't mean them as they are now, obviously. I mean in their prime, like.'

'As I mentioned before, I'm not a homosexual, so it is not a question I can answer.'

Mr Sincope starts to sweat profusely. He is way outside his comfort zone and begins to panic a little.

'But you must have a feel for which bloke you'd rather sleep with,' the punter at the bar buying him his next drink comes in with. 'I mean, if you had to shag one of them, which would it be?'

Mr Sincope had, quite honestly, never thought about having sexual relations with any footballers, living or dead, and certainly never pondered which former Manchester United legend he'd rather go to bed with. But he senses that this topic isn't about to be dropped in a hurry and he can see then that he is definitely trapped in the pub for the second pint anyhow as Jimmy the landlord had already begun to pour it. He has to cough up an answer.

'Denis Law, I suppose,' he says, having picked one of them completely randomly via his normal method on such an occasion: reverse alphabetical order. The old man sat at the table across from him makes a face of real disgust.

'The Lawman? Really? But Georgie was such a good-looking chap. How could you go for that filthy Scot over him?'

'You see? Told you so! I've been telling you for years that being a Denis Law man was perfectly acceptable, haven't I?' the punter at the bar who was buying a drink for Mr Sincope shouts triumphantly as he hands Jimmy some change in return for said beverage. It is apparent that the man whose generosity Mr Sincope is about to enjoy had been waiting for years to hear someone come down on the Denis Law side of the Georgie-Lawman debate.

'I can't believe you're a Denis Law man,' the old man across from Mr Sincope says to him in utter disbelief, as if Mr Sincope had admitted to sometimes fancying small ponies as sexual partners. His pint then put before him by the pensioner who fancied Denis Law himself, Mr Sincope's newfound aim is to finish it as quickly as possible without seeming to guzzle it and to then extricate himself from the premises with as little excitement as would be realistically possible.

'To my daughter, Faith,' Mr Sincope says, raising his glass to the other drinkers. This is the right tactic and gets the old gay men back on side, including the appalled Georgie Best fan across from him. They all raise their pints to Faith. Mr Sincope takes a huge slug of his drink, finishing half of it one go. This

110

turns out to be overreaching and has potentially immediate damaging effects on his plan to scupper.

'Looks like the lad is thirsty – Jimmy, pour him another one. This one's on me,' the man across from him shouts towards the bar. Time is now of the essence. Mr Sincope instantaneously formulates a plan. He looks at his watch and then pretends to be alarmed.

'Actually, chaps, I've realised the bleeding time. I need to get back to the hospital as soon as possible,' he says and he finishes the pint in front of him in one go, gets up and walks swiftly to the door.

'Thanks for the drink!' he shouts as he makes his exit. He wasn't entirely lying when he said time had become a factor; looking at his watch, Mr Sincope actually did realise that with the Dr Sharp/corridor incident and then the gay pub shenanigans, he had been away from his wife for almost two hours. He quickens his pace in the direction of the hospital. When he gets back to the cubicle, he is surprised to see his wife in the type of mood he hadn't seen in her in for some time without the aid of chemical refreshment.

'My dear, have you heard? I'm being moved to the labour ward!' she squeals with joy.

'Great! When?' he says, playing ignorant.

'Right now! Another few moments and you might have missed me. Dr Blots says I'll be on the ward in less than twenty minutes. Can you believe it?'

Mr Sincope smiles and kisses his wife. Whatever way they had got there – and it appeared he would have to do some cut-rate work in his own free time for a woman he had been prepared to sleep with in a hospital corridor as compensation – it looks like they were about to finally arrive on the labour ward.

Chapter Eleven

Double-Barrelled First Names

The labour ward, sitting high atop the rest of the hospital on the twelfth floor, is everything that Mrs Sincope had hoped it would be. The colours there are warm and inviting, vermilions and deep purples. The doctors smile at you as you pass them in the pristine corridors. It feels cleaner than any other part of the hospital.

'We've made it,' Mrs Sincope says to her husband as though they were pilgrims who, having completed a three-week trek on foot to the Cathedral of Santiago de Compostela, now stumble warily to the narthex. Mr Sincope thinks his wife's comment is melodramatic and wants to nip any latent triumphalism in the bud.

'Long way to go yet, dear. We must remain mentally prepared.'

As Mrs Sincope is being transferred from the passenger bed she has resided in for more than three days to the plush cot in her new room on the labour ward at the stroke of midnight leading into Sunday, the woman who is to be their new midwife enters the Sincopes' new domicile.

'Hello, I'm Marie-Marcia.'

'Hi, Marie,' Mrs Sincope says, trying to convey as much warmth as she can to the woman who would now be helping her baby to be born.

'Sorry, Marie-Marcia is my first name.'

A double-barrelled Christian name: is that posh, working class, or neither? This is the question Mr Sincope puts to himself as he watches Marie-Marcia scurry about turning various machines on. Meanwhile, Mrs Sincope feels stupid for having got the name of the midwife wrong on the first go and is fretful that her relationship with this woman, which is going to be so critical to the birth of her child, has got off to such a bad start. Marie-Marcia silently examines charts and continues springing machinery to life while Mr Sincope reads a paper – the first one he'd seen lying around the hospital. A day-old copy of the *Sun*, but hey, beggars, choosers and all that.

Mrs Sincope can't help but stare at Marie-Marcia the whole time, focusing the entirety of her attention on every little thing the midwife does, as if by studying her she will be able to glean enough information to know what to say and do in order to make this latest health care worker like her.

'How far away do you think we are from the birth itself?' Mrs Sincope tries to ask calmly. Marie-Marcia laughs. She'd seen all this before, many times.

'From what I can tell from the charts there hasn't been any dilation as yet. But the doctor brought you up here so she must think there will be movement soon.'

Mrs Sincope picks up on the reference to the doctor in question as 'she'. Her mind wanders back to all sorts of conspiracy theories involving her husband and Dr Sharp; the secret affair they've been having over the last couple of days that she has invented.

Marie-Marcia continues, 'What is likely to happen is that your contractions will kick in over the next hour or so and after that we will probably have to manually break your water.

Once that happens, things will move pretty quickly. Eight, maybe nine hours from now, you'll be holding your baby in your arms.'

Mrs Sincope smiles at this news and allows a few tears of joy to trickle from her eyes. Eight or nine hours constitutes a long interval, certainly, but at least it is a definitive space of time. It is the first such estimate she has received since she set foot in the hospital three and a half days ago.

'I'm in a lot of pain at the moment,' Mrs Sincope says to the midwife with the double-barrelled first name. 'They wouldn't give me anything on the antenatal ward – now that I'm here could you get me something?'

'I can do that right now, Mrs Sincope,' the midwife says. True to her word, she hands her new patient a pill; a tiny oval-shaped green one that looks a bit like a miniature rugby ball. Marie-Marcia then turns to the sink in the far corner of the room to pour some water into a plastic cup.

'There you go,' the midwife says as she gives Mrs Sincope the liquid. The pregnant woman takes the pill diligently and smiles up at the midwife. As she does so, she thinks about asking Marie-Marcia what exactly it was that she had now ingested, but then becomes shy about the idea and doesn't bother.

'I need to check something,' Marie-Marcia says. 'I'll be right back.'

As the midwife departs, Mrs Sincope becomes even more emotional. She thinks about how holding Faith in her arms might feel; the sensation of it all is so vividly imagined, it is practically lucid. Mrs Sincope can almost feel the softness of her newborn baby's skin; can almost smell that newborn baby smell; can almost feel Faith's thin, wispy hair through her fingers. His wife's almost religious emotional moment is entirely lost on Mr Sincope, who at that moment is completely enraptured by an article in the out-dated copy of the *Sun* he'd snagged in which a man who had been on benefits his whole life said he was going to vote for the Conservative Party at the next election because he didn't like the shape of the Labour leader's lips. It looks like he's had collagen implants, says Sammy the Scrounger, the man on benefits' nom de tabloid. Mr Sincope looks up from the newspaper with a desire to engage his wife about one of the more humorous passages from the article and it is only then that he notices her hyper-emotional state for the first time.

'What's wrong?' he asks over-paternally, almost sternly.

'Nothing. I'm thinking about Faith. Come here and hold my hand, dear.'

Mr Sincope acquiesces to this request immediately. He had long since learned that it was much better to swim with the tide than fight against it when it came to moments like these. He still gets up slowly and then sort of limps over to his wife, making hay about how arduous the whole thing is by way of sighing heavily. Mrs Sincope notices the obvious signals but chooses to ignore them. What she's after is some matrimonial bonding time and she is prepared to put up with a reasonable amount of her husband's immature crap to get it.

'Think about this,' she says, holding her husband's hand a bit too tightly for comfort, her only way of extracting any sort of revenge for his adolescent behaviour. 'In a few hours' time, Faith will be here with us.'

'I don't know if I'd summarise nine hours as "a few", dear.'

This flippant comment almost causes Mrs Sincope to lose her temper. But she holds it in check. She simply squeezes her husband's hand even tighter, cutting off most of the circulation to his fingers, causing them to go mostly numb at the tips.

115

'However long it turns out to be, the end is in our sights now.'

'I suppose that's one way of looking at things.'

Realising that another snarky reply from her husband could see her jumping out of bed, pushing him to the ground, and then proceeding to smother his face with her distended belly, Mrs Sincope instead decides to keep silent at this stage and simply try and enjoy the moment, such as it is, as best she can as she drains the life from her husband's palm and digits. This lasts for about five seconds until Marie-Marcia makes her return.

'You feeling any relief from the pain yet?' she asks Mrs Sincope. The pregnant woman is all ready to pooh-pooh the idea from the midwife. She had only swallowed the pill a few minutes previously; surely it couldn't be that fast-acting. But thinking this causes her to re-examine how much discomfort she is actually in at the moment. She finds to her pleasant surprise that the pill had indeed worked its magic. She is now experiencing nary a spasm.

'Actually, yes, now that you mention it. The pain is almost completely gone.'

Marie-Marcia allows herself a tiny, self-satisfied grin. She loves her work and especially enjoys moments like these, when a woman who has been in such agony can receive solace from the folds of her garments.

'Lie back and relax, Mrs Sincope. What we need you to do right now is to sleep.'

Doing as her midwife had instructed, she lays back and rubs her belly contentedly. Within three minutes, Mrs Sincope is out cold.

'I didn't tell her this, but the pill I gave her has a mild sedative effect to it,' Marie-Marcia explains softly to Mr Sincope, who has his nose in the newspaper again and hadn't actually noticed his wife drifting off at all.

'She'll be fine, I suppose?' Mr Sincope asks once he'd looked up and twigged what was going on.

'If she starts having contractions, we'll all know it pretty quickly, don't worry about that.'

The midwife then departs again, leaving the Sincopes alone in their pristine room. Mr Sincope decides all at once that an opportunity had now been handed to him – he has to act fast and leave the room himself before his wife wakes up. Not to leave and not come back, not yet; even Mr Sincope knows a move like that needed to be discussed with his wife first. He just wants to depart briefly in order to take a break, lest he be subjected to more tortured platitudes, all while having the life squeezed out of his fingers once again.

He makes the decision to leave the hospital and go to the greasy spoon a few doors down from the Love Café. He recalls it has a sign out front that reads 'Breakfast Served 24 Hours', so it's somewhere he can get fed that isn't far from the hospital at such an ungodly hour.

It is cold outside. As he walks along the perimeter of Four Fountains Park, he thinks deeply about how exactly he might extract himself from the hospital permanently now that his wife had managed to get on the labour ward – with his help, no less, which he congratulates himself for, conveniently forgetting for the moment that his part in the whole scheme had involved him seriously considering committing adultery.

He decides that after he had eaten his dinner, he would go back to the new room on the labour ward and tell his wife that while she was asleep he'd received a call from work and that he was required to be in the office the following morning. Terry, that boss of his, what a ballbreaker! Mr Sincope then thinks about his job for the first time in a while and how nice it will feel to be back in the office after the nightmare of the last few days. He knows he'll probably come in for some gentle ribbing around the Thursday and Friday he'd taken off at the end of the week in order to be at the hospital ('A day, fine, but two whole days with the missus, hanging about waiting for her to drop? Excuse for slacking, mate!' He imagined something along those lines from Terry). However, it would be great to be back in an environment he knew and had some control over again.

'Full English,' he says to the woman behind the counter of the greasy spoon. She simply nods and then scratches at the almost fully formed moustache growing under her nose. He takes a seat and does some people-watching. Everyone in the café seems to Mr Sincope to be working or non-working class. Being surrounded by people not of his socio-economic group makes Mr Sincope distinctly uncomfortable, so he reaches for the copy of that day's *Sun* that had been left on his table by the previous occupier. 'Croatian Scroungers Already Planning to Besiege Dover', reads the headline. Even Mr Sincope, a true xenophobe if ever one walked, laughs at the hysterical tone of the headline. He has to concede that when they'd gone all mental about the Bulgarians and Romanians arriving in droves a few years back, few in the way of actual Balkan natives turned up in the end. Mr Sincope's thoughts are broken when a fat Turkish man puts his breakfast down in front of him.

'Thank you,' Mr Sincope says as the Anatolian immigrant retreats. Bloody Turks: come to this country and they can't even be polite, he thinks as he surveys his meal. He suddenly doesn't feel all that inclined towards a plate full of grease, which is a rarity for Mr Sincope, who is generally grease-inclined at all times. Still, he'd ordered it so he'd have to eat it. As he tucks into his baked beans, his thoughts go towards a place they had often been

118

early in his wife's pregnancy but had not travelled to recently. How he had always dreamed of escaping Britain and living abroad, perhaps for a little while, perhaps for the remainder of his life. He desires, like many xenophobes often strangely enough do, to be a foreigner himself. Perhaps that is even the root of Mr Sincope's dislike of immigrants: he is envious.

This leads him to think about Aleida again, the Argentinean who had been his final woman but one, the gal who had unsettlingly popped into his mind the other day for the first time in a long while. As he imagines her face, Aleida's beautiful, perfectly formed visage, he wonders what was he thinking letting a woman like that go? He turns this question over and over in his mind as he pops a piece of bacon into his mouth, the bean-munching having now got him prepared for the grease at last. The idea of getting up and walking out of that West London greasy spoon, leaving behind his plate full of carcinogens, hailing the first cab to roll past and then heading to Heathrow so that he could buy a ticket on the first plane leaving for Buenos Aires, seems almost irresistible to Mr Sincope for the briefest of moments. But then he flips the *Sun* over, starts reading the sports section while tucking into his egg, and such a temptation then becomes the furthest thing from his mind.

Returning to the labour ward after his meal, he finds his wife not only awake but with Marie-Marcia present as well. The midwife is setting up what looks to Mr Sincope to be an ECG machine.

'Hi, dear, where have you been?' Mrs Sincope asks her husband innocently enough. She appears to be in a better mood for the rest, much to her husband's relief.

'Grabbed some food down the road.'

'That's sensible. Marie-Marcia is setting up the Electronic Foetal Monitor. It can measure the size of my contractions.'

'You're having contractions at long last then, eh?'

Marie-Marcia turns to Mr Sincope and gives him a grave-faced shaking of the head to indicate that this was not the case, the sort of thing a medical professional might do to signal to a relative that their seemingly recovering family member was not going to make it in the end.

'Not yet,' Mrs Sincope says in an optimistic tone of voice. 'But they are round the corner, I can feel it.'

Marie-Marcia goes to leave the room but as she does she subtly calls Mr Sincope out into the corridor with her eyes. He manages to get the hint and leaves the room behind the midwife.

'Dear, I'll be back in one second. Need the loo,' he says as he departs.

'But the room has an en suite,' she says back as he races off. Once outside the door, he sees Marie-Marcia standing twenty feet away, waiting for him.

'I have to let you know that your wife still hasn't had a single contraction. We are starting to get into a region of concern here, Mr Sincope.'

This sounds serious, he thinks. Her tone of voice is the kind of thing health care professionals use when discussing someone in mortal peril.

'Is my wife or the baby in trouble?' he cuts to the chase.

'Not for the moment. But I don't know where we take it from here. I'm going to keep doing everything I can to induce labour but nothing has worked so far.'

'So, what next?'

'I'll get a doctor to come in for an update in the next couple of hours. In the meantime, please stick around and try and get her spirits up. It is hard for expectant mothers in her position and a loving, supportive partner can go a long way.'

The last bit is clearly a criticism of him personally and what Marie-Marcia had obviously perceived as a bad attitude on his part. Perhaps he had been a little brusque with his wife, he thinks to himself. *Apply a little TLC now and I can probably get the hell out of here and back to civilisation a great deal quicker.* This might put a delay on his departure but make it easier to move when they get over this little hump.

'I'll do better,' he says with a smile, which is precisely what Marie-Marcia wanted to hear. She smiles back.

'Tell her I'll return shortly,' the midwife says. 'I need to check in on another patient. In the meantime, please do what you can in there.'

As Marie-Marcia trots off, Mr Sincope re-enters the room where his wife is stationed, walks right up to her, and kisses her on the lips. This completely befuddles Mrs Sincope as her husband had never before so spontaneously kissed her in that manner during the entire course of their relationship.

'What was that for?' she asks.

'For everything you're going through and for how brave you're being.'

As he says this, his voice cracks. Although he had steeled himself to 'do better' simply on the advice of Marie-Marcia and is following this guidance simply as a way of bringing his escape from the hospital closer to hand, as the words come out he finds that he actually deeply means every one. He even has to think about the rugby match he'd read about in the *Sun* during his visit to the greasy spoon to halt an emotional outburst that could have got messy for everyone involved. Mrs Sincope says nothing but grins at her husband, happy to have found this oasis of connectivity in the desert of disengagement that was their marriage.

121

Five mostly silent hours then pass, during which Marie-Marcia occasionally comes in to read something on the various whirring machines in the room, write something down on Mrs Sincope's chart, and then depart once again. Sometimes one or both of the Sincopes sleep, but mostly they are awake. The good mood that had been established between the Sincopes as a result of Mr Sincope's rare emotional semi-release dissipates slowly over this time frame, like air escaping from a punctured tyre. There emerges in its place a hard to define dread. Neither of them feels like the birth of their daughter is particularly imminent now. The morning of their fourth day in the hospital is upon them and with it, no ending in sight. Mr Sincope keeps building himself up to tell his wife that he has to leave; to throw the work routine at her, but every time he is about to open his mouth and do so, he ends up losing his nerve.

The whole of Sunday turns out to be incredibly tense, with Marie-Marcia's appearances becoming less and less frequent along the way. Mrs Sincope assails the midwife with questions on the rarer and rarer occasions when she shows up. What she gives back sounds a lot like platitudinous nonsense to both of the Sincopes, obviously uttered to keep their fears at bay for as long as possible. This pattern goes on all day and into the evening and then into the early hours of day five. Then, at around three a.m. on the Monday, a midwife they hadn't seen previously enters their room.

'Hello, are you Mr and Mrs Sincope?'

They both answer 'yes' simultaneously, something, anything breaking the tedium being immediately stimulating to them both given how dull a day they had both endured.

'I know this is probably not what you're going to want to hear right now ...'

This is all it takes. Mrs Sincope begins to silently weep, the sobs sticking in her throat. She knows what the unknown mid-wife is going to say next.

'But since you haven't progressed to labour yet and we've got a real rush on tonight and the beds are at a premium ...'

'Can I at least go home until labour starts?' Mrs Sincope asks desperately, knowing full well what the answer to this query will be.

'I'm afraid not, Mrs Sincope. You're going to have to return to the antenatal ward. But hopefully, you'll be back up here in no time,' she says. Two male orderlies enter the room at this point. They pick up Mrs Sincope and plonk her in a wheelchair that a third male orderly who entered behind them has wheeled in. They do this in a forceful manner, and notably without ask-ing Mrs Sincope about it first.

The journey out of the labour ward feels like the walk of shame to Mrs Sincope, even though she is not actually ambula-tory herself. She weeps the whole way back down to the antenatal ward. She is angry at her own failings, her own body. There is no one else to be choleric towards; it is *her* inability that is letting everyone down, at least in her mind. What makes the whole return even worse is the fact that she is deposited in pre-cisely the same cubicle as she was in previously. She had been hoping against hope that she would at least get a new bed, but she was in for no such luck. Mrs Sincope is right back where she had started almost five days previously.

Chapter Twelve

All This Young Flesh

The further it sets in, the more the move back to antenatal from the labour ward feels like the most crushing defeat of her entire life to Mrs Sincope, regardless of what her husband or the doctors might be telling her in an effort to keep her spirits level.

'It is only temporary, Mrs Sincope. Down to a shortage of bed space – you will be back on the labour ward within hours,' Dr Blots tells her as he visits the cubicle shortly after she had been moved back downstairs.

'We have a real rush on at the moment, so we need to make room for the women who are due to give birth at any moment. Please bear in mind that you'll probably be one of them in a day or two if everything goes well, which of course it will,' Dr Blots continues. The fact that being given a forty-eight-hour window for birth is now being put in the optimistic category is deeply unsettling to Mrs Sincope.

'Everything will be fine. Let nature run its course. We both need to remain mentally prepared,' Mr Sincope says to his wife at nine a.m. on the morning of their sixth day in the hospital, the Tuesday after they had been put back on the antenatal ward and seen neither hide nor hair of a doctor since Dr Blots' truncated visit early the previous morning.

Mrs Sincope feels an overwhelming sense of depression and helplessness of a kind she had never experienced previously in her adult life. As a strong woman who had built up an executive career from nothing, she considers herself to have a tough hide. Yet somehow this move back to the antenatal ward feels existential in a way she cannot rationalise. It feels almost like the consequences of it are consuming her. She realises she has to get a hold of her feelings and yet finds this impossible.

Mr Sincope does not appear on the surface to be in any way put out or disappointed by them being relegated from the labour ward. His wife thinks he almost seems happy about the whole thing, although this is in fact a form of paranoia on her part. Mr Sincope is actually deeply upset about the whole affair. He missed work on Monday when he was supposed to have been in, and he is now in the process of missing a whole other day's work as well. But his wife's recent relegation made bailing out on her ever more precarious. His exit routes are narrowing by the hour and he feels more claustrophobic than ever in that tiny seat at the foot of his wife's hospital bed. As a means of coping with the stress he is under, Mr Sincope revives his reveries of Aleida, the ones that he had left off with in the greasy spoon the other night. His thoughts turn, oddly enough, to having children with the Argentinean beauty. In the vision that haunts him as he sits back in that incredibly uncomfortable chair within touching distance of the sheet that defined the cubicle, this half-Argentine child creation is effortless, wonderful, a joy. Not like the current limbo he is being forced to reside in, more and more against his will.

'What are you thinking about over there?' Mrs Sincope enquires of her husband at a point when she can stand his silent thousand-yard stare into the tiny window to her right no longer.

'Nothing much.'

He thinks this is better than telling her the truth – which it is, obviously. However, Mrs Sincope is not in the mood for any vagueness from her husband.

'Don't you care about what's happening here? To me? To Faith?' she asks, exploding into tears. As soon as she has done this, she internally castigates herself for her emotional outburst. She feels increasingly detached from herself somehow, unable to fully control her own mind.

'Of course I do. Why do you think I'm still hanging around?'

Mr Sincope thinks this expression of his martyrdom will lay the fight to rest. Of course, it only ramps it up another gear as it lays bare, for the first time since his fumble on the subject in Four Fountains Park a few days' previous that he'd only just managed to successfully navigate, the fact that Mr Sincope is seriously debating how long he is required to stay. It also confirms all of Mrs Sincope's fears that her husband had been lying when he had assured her that being by her side during the birth of their daughter was a priority for him and he wasn't coming along for the sake of avoiding a row.

'If you don't want to be here, you can leave any time,' she says, still sobbing furiously. This is obviously a huge bluff on Mrs Sincope's part. The thought of her husband leaving her there alone, all by herself in the cloth cubicle for the rest of the time it takes to get back on to the labour ward, existentially terrifies her, particularly given that everything seemed to be moving in the wrong direction. If he decides to call her on it and leave, things look almost unbearable for Mrs Sincope. Thankfully, he does not.

'I'm staying. I said I would. I'm still here, aren't I?'

Mr Sincope is being a sadist about the whole matter but Mrs

Sincope isn't about to push her luck any further. She lets the whole thing go.

'Thank you,' Mrs Sincope says to her husband. They are the hardest two words to say in her entire life up until that point.

An almost completely silent hour later, Dr Sharp enters the cubicle.

'How are we feeling today, Mrs Sincope?'

'Bloody miserable,' the pregnant woman answers and immediately feels embarrassed for being so stroppy. As she is admonishing herself for being uncivilised, she notices a glance passed back and forth between the doctor and her husband. It's brief but loaded. She finds her imagination running wild again as the doctor dons a pair of gloves and begins to examine her, this time without having asked first at all. But Mrs Sincope is too caught up in thoughts of what the hell is going on between Sharp and her husband to notice the doctor's lapse in bedside manners.

'No movement at all still, I'm afraid,' Dr Sharp says. 'Someone will be round in another few hours to check you out again, give you another update on the situation.'

And with that, Dr Sharp leaves the Sincopes alone in their fabric cubicle once more.

'What was that all about?' Mrs Sincope asks her husband. He looks up at her, genuinely baffled as to what she is asking.

'What was what about?'

'That look you and the doctor gave each other.'

'What look?'

'I saw a look, no question. You two traded loaded glances at each other.'

'They were not loaded.'

'You're not denying there were glances exchanged then?'

'*A* glance perhaps. I looked at her in admiration of her medicinal abilities and she thanked me with her eyes. That's all it was.'

'Bollocks – you tried to get off with her, didn't you?'

Mr Sincope laughs in fake incredulity that manages to come across as convincing, as he is genuinely shocked by his wife's ability to have worked out that he had spent more time with Dr Sharp than he had told her about with only a momentary meeting of eyes to go on as evidence.

'When? How? Are you suggesting that she and I disappeared at one point and that I then made love to her in a hospital corridor?'

Mrs Sincope begins to realise that she is being hysterical – having no idea, of course, how close to the truth she has stumbled by accident.

'I'm sorry. I don't know what came over me,' Mrs Sincope says, shaking her head.

'Exhaustion, dear. That's why you need to get some rest. I bet that's the problem. It's like your body knows you're too tired to go into labour.'

'Stop it, that's rubbish.'

'I'm serious. I will bet you any money you care to wager that if you were to lay your head on that pillow and get forty winks, when you wake up it will be because you've gone into labour.'

While she grapples with this idea emotionally, Mrs Sincope's subconscious agrees with her husband's assessment of the situation as she turns her head to the right and is almost immediately asleep.

While his wife is slumbering, Mr Sincope wanders the hallways of the hospital trying to work up the courage to make a return trip to Dr Sharp's office. Despite this being his mission, he has mixed feelings about seeing the doctor alone again. During this period of meandering he recalls at length an incident a year or so previous when he first met Bill, an accountant from his firm's Birmingham branch, someone who was in London at the time for the company's Annual General Meeting. They were sat next to each other in a pre-AGM get-together and immediately hit it off. Bill asked Mr Sincope if he wanted to grab a pint after the AGM and the offer was accepted. Mr Sincope said he knew a place down the road that was his work local; Bill insisted they go to a place a little further on that he had in mind instead.

'I go there every time I come down to the Big Smoke for these things. It's worth the extra walk to this place, trust me here.'

When they arrived at the pub that Bill had picked, Mr Sincope was horrified. It was wall to wall with young men and women in their early twenties and late teens, all of them stood about listening to alienating, loud rock music. Mr Sincope's image of Bill, who had seemed such a solid, respectable, conservative sort of a chap back at the office, had now taken a knock.

'Great place,' Mr Sincope said with as much sarcasm as he could muster. However, the combination of Mr Sincope's inability to convey irony and Bill's delight at having arrived at his favourite haunt conspired to obscure this statement's true meaning.

'It is, isn't it? All this young flesh. Let's get stuck in!'

Bill did precisely that. After getting a round in, the accountant from Birmingham started chatting with an attractive blonde girl who looked to be about nineteen years of age. After a conversation that lasted around eleven seconds, she slapped him hard across the face and stormed off.

'What did you say to her?' Mr Sincope asked as he re-approached Bill, who was notably cheerful despite the physical assault.

'I said what I always say to the young birds whenever I'm in here: I'm in town for one night only, how would you like to go back to my hotel room with me and have a private drink?'

'No wonder she slapped you. That girl was a bleeding teenager.'

'I happen to like bleeding teenagers.'

Although wild horses could not have dragged it out of him, Mr Sincope liked teenaged girls a wee bit himself. Being with an eighteen- or nineteen-year-old lass had a certain amount of appeal to his imagination. They are so innocent at that age, so lacking in the cynicism that invades all women's hearts some-time around the age of twenty-five, he would reflect to himself sometimes while daydreaming at work. Having said all of that, the idea of actually sleeping with a girl of that tender an age slightly repulsed Mr Sincope at the same time as exciting his urges. It was somehow completely, inexorably *wrong* in his worldview. As a result, he kept his appetite firmly in check and would never have dreamed of going into a young person's pub if he had not been taken to such an establishment blindly, and certainly not with a view to hitting on teenagers.

Bill continued speaking to young women and either getting slapped, having drinks poured in his face or, in the lightest of cases, being laughed at and walked away from. After a long dry run, he finally found a girl that seemed to at least tolerate his affections. Unfortunately for Mr Sincope, she had with her a friend who was around the same age, which from the looks of things was about eighteen. Mr Sincope soon found himself act-ing wingman and chatting to – and indeed without intending to, chatting up – a teenager named Clarissa who had come into town to stay with her friend Sharon (the one Bill had his sights on), her friend from school who had moved to London about a year back. Clarissa did most of the talking; she found Mr Sincope immediately attractive, in that inexplicable way that a scary percentage of the insecure girls he had ever come across in his life had found him alluring. She decided talking for England was a way to solve her jitteriness problem in front of this man of the world who almost certainly owned property and had a real job. Within a couple of hours, all four involved in this intrepid group were drunk. Mr Sincope looked over his shoulder at one point to see Bill and Sharon snogging furiously. Before he had time to think about what to do next, Clarissa had chosen her spot and attacked Mr Sincope, burying her tongue as deep as it would go in his mouth. He did nothing to stop her.

They all stumbled out of the pub at closing time, around midnight. It was clear to Mr Sincope as they did so that Bill had already arranged with Sharon for her to accompany him to his hotel room.

'See you round the next time I'm down here, mate,' Bill said to Mr Sincope casually as he and his young date wandered off into the night, making it abundantly clear to his original drinking companion that he had only been used as fodder for Bill getting into someone's pants. Now alone with Clarissa, it being just the two of them for the first time despite the snog in the pub, Mr Sincope turned to the young woman, unsure of what to do next.

'Now that Sharon is going back to your friend's place, I have Sharon's flat all to myself,' Clarissa said. Mr Sincope froze. He had no idea what to do next. On one hand, he found her unbelievably attractive and hey, when would he find himself in this circumstance again any time soon, standing on the pavement debating whether or not to go to bed with a stunning eighteen-year-old girl who was clearly quite up for it. Clarissa took Mr Sincope's silence to mean that he hadn't grasped fully what she was offering, so she spelled it out even further for him.

'Come back there with me and spend the night, yeah?'

He kissed her again – that he couldn't resist – but as he pulled away from her lips he gave her the brush-off.

'I have to be up early. Thanks, but no thanks.'

Not trusting himself any further than that, Mr Sincope turned his back on her and began to walk towards the tube station. Thankfully that did the trick; Clarissa didn't run after him to make another overture. He couldn't have possibly resisted again had she done so and as a result, Mr Sincope would have cheated on his wife that evening.

When he returns to the cubicle, Mr Sincope finds his better half still asleep. Watching her at peace, he gets a sudden rush of love for her. Despite their problems, their differences, here they both were, together and waiting for their first child to arrive in the world. He decides he will stay and wait for Faith to be born. Well, he'd stick around for another couple days at least. He'd have to call work and tell them what was happening at some point, he realises, before deciding to put that off as long as possible.

Mrs Sincope blearily opens her eyes and smiles at her husband when she sees him standing over her.

'How long have I been asleep?'

'About four hours.'

'Any doctors come by in that time?'

Mr Sincope shakes his head.

'Predictable.'

'How is the pain?'

'Same as it was when I passed out: persistent, dull but so fierce as to be practically unbearable. My womb feels like my head at month end when Chuck has been doing payroll.'

This was a reference to Charles 'Chuck' Innes, a low-paid, long-standing employee of the firm where both the Sincopes worked who was known for his general incompetence.

'I guess you'll be glad never to have to deal with Chuck ever again,' Mr Sincope says. His wife's face instantly melts into a position of anger and hurt. He has no idea what he has said to provoke this reaction, but Mr Sincope at least realises he's said something wrong.

'What do you mean, "never have to deal with Chuck again"? I'm only taking six months off and then I'll be back in the same office with the same job. I don't think Chuck is going anywhere in a big hurry, unfortunately.'

Mr Sincope laughs.

'Dear, you're going to be a mother now. Sure, maybe you'll go back to help the firm out for a few months, but after that everyone will understand completely when you leave.'

'Are you suggesting that I quit my job?'

They had never discussed this sensitive issue even once during Mrs Sincope's pregnancy. Mr Sincope had simply assumed his wife would quit her job when the time came; she took for granted the fact that after an appropriate period of time she'd go back to work and they'd hire a nanny.

'Is there another option?' Mr Sincope asks.

'We hire someone to look after Faith while I'm at work.'

'You can't be serious.'

Mr Sincope is completely aghast at this idea being put forward for the first time by his wife. He can't believe that she would even consider the idea that she shouldn't be at home with their daughter as much as possible. What is particularly strange about his assumption is the fact that his mother continued working after he was born and a nanny looked after him. This is what had led Mrs Sincope to assume that her husband would be fine with such an arrangement, without it having to be discussed.

'Why is it assumed that *I* quit *my* job?' Mrs Sincope asks her husband, looking to deepen the fight. 'For instance, if you're so opposed to the idea of someone other than the two of us looking after Faith, why don't I take the first six months off to look after her and then you take the next six months off to stay at home?'

This suggestion makes Mr Sincope burst out laughing again; he assumes his wife must be joking. When he looks at her face and realises that she is completely serious, he is horrified.

'That's completely absurd,' he says.

'What's so absurd about it?'

He has to think for a moment.

'My job has more potential for advancement.'

'That's debatable. You only picked that because I make more money than you do, so you couldn't use that as the reason.'

Mrs Sincope is an executive at the company, while her husband is merely a member of the finance team. She actually makes a lot more money than he does.

'It's still an absurd idea,' Mr Sincope spits, whipping his head away from his wife.

'Why? Because you've got a penis and I don't?'

Mr Sincope's gut reaction is to reply, 'Yes, as a matter of fact' – thankfully he realises in time that saying this would be moronic. He thinks on his feet instead, at least as much quick thinking as he is capable of doing.

'Like I said, my career has more ability to grow than yours. Let's face it, HR is a place where women work until they get knocked up.'

This is Mr Sincope's out of the frying pan and into the fire moment. Mrs Sincope is finding her husband's sexism bad enough, but at least that had been directed at women in general; now he had made a personal attack on her profession.

'That's what you think of what I do?' she says through a wavering larynx and huge tears forming in her eyes. Even an emotional midget like Mr Sincope understands at once how deeply he'd hurt his wife with that last insult. His brain reels about how to repair the situation. What he comes up with is rather special, even by his remarkable standards.

'I always thought you were simply biding your time until you could go into something better. Now you're getting the best job in the world – being a mum.'

At this point, Mr Sincope is lucky that his wife is pretty much stationary, otherwise he'd have been in real trouble.

'I need you to go somewhere else for a little while,' she says. 'Right now.'

This comes out of her with such exhaustion and fury that even Mr Sincope takes the hint. He creeps out of the cubicle without a further word.

Chapter Thirteen

Mammary Monthly Re-revisited

Following this big fight with his wife, Mr Sincope wanders around the hospital corridors for a few hours on his own. He often gets lost but always manages somehow to instinctively find his way back to the hospital's main reception, as he had done on his first trek there from the antenatal ward, when he did so in search of chocolate. At the end of this particular long and pointless journey, Mr Sincope decides that the only way to solve all of the problems facing him is for Faith to be born as soon as possible. He then figures that his best chance for helping to make this happen is to put aside his pronounced dislike for the man and lobby Dr Blots directly on the subject. Having reached this conclusion, Mr Sincope goes in search of the doctor-cum-thespian in order to achieve this new aim. He wishes to accomplish this goal before returning to the cubicle to avoid an empty-handed re-entry. He heads first to Blots' office.

'Have a seat, he'll be with you in a moment,' says Jill in a solemn and less high-pitched way than usual to the less expectant by the moment father after Mr Sincope had explained at length why seeing Dr Blots was of the utmost importance.

The receptionist is still taking barbiturates to try and ease the pain of her recent break-up. Doreen had called and left a message on Saturday night – Jill was out getting pissed by herself at her local at the time, eventually ranting at other punters before being unceremoniously ejected by the landlady. This telephonic communiqué from her ex-lover had caused hope to spring anew in the receptionist's heart. However, subsequent attempts by Jill to contact her ex had proved fruitless, which caused the tension that had led to the daily dose of downers continuing.

Mr Sincope does as Jill asks and finds himself in the exact same chair he had sat in six days previous, when the Sincopes had arrived for the induction. What is also reprised, obviously but much to his chagrin, is the same choice of magazines as the last time he sat there (he had once again forgotten all about his phone and its ability to entertain). He picks up *Mammary Monthly* and flips through the pages, not focusing on any of them particularly, until something leaps out at him on one of the sides. It is an article entitled, 'Your Job and Your Child: Which Comes First?' He is surprised that he hadn't noticed this piece the last time he leafed through the magazine. He supposes that perhaps such a question wasn't particularly relevant to him at the time and only his wife's sudden career woman turn had him thinking about the rights and wrongs of the situation. The final two paragraphs of the article read:

Looking at the pros and cons of each possibility, what does come first? Your career or your child? When all is said and done, it is family that lasts. Jobs come and go but when you are in your old age it is your children who will take care of you. They will be the true source of joy in your life. My conclusion is that it is your child that must take precedence. I'll admit that as a committed feminist such a conclusion does not come without difficulty. In my youth, I would have balked at the idea of relying on a man for my sustenance. But when that man in question is also the father of your child, the equation changes significantly. Suddenly, two incomes are not as important as one of you being there to look after your baby. And in the end, I can only conclude that it should be the mother who fulfils this role. Fathers are wonderful, but only a mum can be a mum.

Come on, girls, take the plunge! Quit your job and become a domestic goddess! You know you want to!

Mr Sincope is overjoyed to have randomly come across a magazine article that puts his own view on the matter of women and their careers forward from within a quasi-leftist, intellectual, feminist framework. He then decides he will rip the article out of the magazine and take it upstairs to show to his wife. However, in actioning this desire, he incurs the instant wrath of the semi-dazed Jill.

'Are you destroying the magazines over there, sir?' she shouts at Mr Sincope from across the reception desk, the squeaky quality of her voice returning with a vengeance. The three couples waiting alongside him in the reception area turn to look at Mr Sincope with a mixture of contempt and pity.

'Sorry about that. I saw something . . . my wife is upstairs in the antenatal ward, bored out of her tiny mind and I thought she might like—'

Jill cuts him off, the receptionist now thoroughly worked up about the vandalism to what she considers her own property. She takes great pride in all aspects of the reception area – but oddly in that respect, has never noticed the spelling error on the door to Dr Blots' office – and will not stand idly by as one of her periodicals is torn to bits, particularly by a man.

'If your wife is in antenatal what are you doing in my waiting room, ruining my magazines?' she asks, having completely forgotten the lengthy explanation Mr Sincope had given her before having a seat. Mr Sincope for his part decides at this stage that

138

the best thing to do would be to simply get up and leave Blots' reception area, which he proceeds to do without another peep.

While her husband is getting into trouble by being deleterious to the complementary reading material in Dr Blots' waiting room, Mrs Sincope sits in her cubicle stewing about the argument she and her husband had taken part in which had resulted in his hasty departure. She deeply regrets the whole thing and is eager to apologise. Under the influence of what she thinks is a cool head – yet is really her being atypically emotional due to the trauma of being kicked off of the labour ward – she figures she needs to cut her husband some slack. Yes, she is in a great deal of pain, but he is now missing work, days he had told his supervisor he would be in for, all in order to hang around and comfort her. And how did she repay him but by picking a fight. Now was no time to discuss what the future of her career held; she should have understood this and cut the conversation dead.

The whole episode takes her back to when she had first found out she was pregnant with Faith. It had been revealed by the use of an over-the-counter pregnancy test. She hadn't thought she was pregnant at the time, but due to an impending holiday she figured it might be prudent to find out for sure, mostly to know if she should drink or not during their time abroad. They were going to Marbella for a week the day after Mrs Sincope had taken the test. She had to push pretty heavily for this to be their summer holiday destination that year; Mr Sincope usually got his way on where they went and where they tended to go was somewhere that Mrs Sincope, more times than not, regarded as pretentious. The year before, for instance, the couple had ended up in Ashgabat, Turkmenistan after Mr Sincope had read an article in the insert magazine of a major right-wing newspaper about how the former Soviet republic was becoming an up-and-coming locale for hip young things looking for sun and adventure, as well as those looking to ideally avoid running into anyone working or even lower middle class from the United Kingdom (it was this latter detail that had sold it to Mr Sincope). Everything about the holiday turned out to be, as she had predicted beforehand, hell for Mrs Sincope: the flight was awful, a cheap and nasty near-death experience; the hotel they stayed at was sub-*Fawlty Towers* with notably wretched catering; and the city itself was how she thought Stalingrad must have felt like at the height of the Soviet purges, only Ashgabat was surely a great deal smellier.

Mr Sincope, of course, gave off the air the whole time they were in Central Asia that he was having the time of his life. For his part, he felt that he had to do so because he'd lobbied so hard for the destination. Secretly, however, he hated the whole thing, even more so than his wife did. Everything about Ashgabat offended his sensibilities; the food was greasy and inedible, being some sort of unholy mix of low-end Turkish and normal Russian; he found the people weird and unappetising in the extreme, even on the limited encounters he had managed. The air itself in Turkmenistan seemed stale and fetid to him. They suffered in silence throughout the week, both of them trying to act as if they were having fun, each of them desperate to share with the other how horrid a time they were actually having. They could have shared their horror over a glass of oversweet, overpriced Georgian wine, had a cathartic laugh, perhaps even bonded a bit as a couple. Alas, they both decided to suffer in saturninity throughout the entire trip.

The year following the Turkmenistan disaster, it was unspoken but fully accepted between the Sincopes that it was the turn of the missus to pick the getaway. When Mr Sincope was told by his wife that she had chosen the Costa del Sol as their destination he almost shat his pants – literally. He had eaten a dodgy curry for lunch, and this combined with the thought of going to one of his most hated places on Planet Earth to spend the one escape from London he had during the whole year almost overwhelmed his colon. He was no fan of Spain: paella, tapas, and killing male cows for sport were all low on his list of likes. For him, one of the greatest arguments against Britain remaining in the European Union had been the fact that it meant being saddled with that bunch of cultural heathens that had been run as a military dictatorship well into the 1970s. But Madrid, Barcelona, the Basque country; these were options he could have almost coped with. Marbella was a place where, he felt, English people of a lower class than he inhabited went on holiday. But after the Ashgabat disaster, he had no choice but to quietly give in.

It was two days before the Sincopes were due to fly to Malaga from Luton airport, and from there to board a coach down the Mediterranean coastline, that Mrs Sincope ducked into the Ealing flat's sole bathroom with the pregnancy test she'd bought from a leading food seller. It was the cheapest one going, so she was slightly scared that its accuracy might have been questionable when the result came in. The instructions read that it might take up to a minute before the red line that indicated you were pregnant would appear. However, after Mrs Sincope peed on the stick, the line in question went red almost instantly. Mrs Sincope didn't know whether to think this was proof of the test's fallibility or evidence that she was uber-pregnant. Given this ambiguity in her mind, she didn't know whether to inform her husband about the results of the test or not to bother. She decided she'd better tell him.

'I'm pregnant,' she said as nonchalantly as she could muster as she emerged from the bathroom. Mr Sincope simply looked baffled at first.

'You managed to get pregnant between when I last saw you and when you came out of the toilet?'

He said this, of course, completely deadpan.

'I took a test while I was in there, you bell end,' she said to clear the confusion.

'Oh, I see,' Mr Sincope said in a way that even the most talented psychologist of all time could not have interpreted.

'Glad to see you're so over the moon about it,' Mrs Sincope said, hurt by her husband's impossible to read response. She had figured at worst that he would act happy in a phony way when she broke the news. But no, he wasn't even willing to try that hard. Worse yet, having been admonished, he then clumsily rushed in to try and save the day.

'Listen, I do want a child, I do. More than words can express. I suppose I didn't expect to hear about it right after you'd been to the toilet, that's all.'

Mrs Sincope accepted this typically clumsy explanation and they moved forward with their day, preparing for their holiday. The subsequent trip to Marbella was a complete disaster as it turned out; amazingly enough, perhaps even worse than the Turkmenistan fiasco of the previous year. Mr Sincope came down with a particularly nasty cold on the flight there, one that persisted throughout their time abroad. Mrs Sincope, arriving at Malaga airport determined to enjoy herself in southern Spain, got food poisoning from bad paella on the first evening and spent a great deal of the rest of her stay on the Costa del Sol on the loo. Between her mad dashes to the water closet and her husband's sneezing and sniffling, they cut a pretty miserable image to their fellow Brits on the beach. Worse still, Mrs Sincope spent most of the time she wasn't crapping herself fretting deeply about whether the food poisoning she had come down with had killed the embryo growing inside of her. Like all of their holidays together, what had made it so bad an experience for each of the Sincopes is that they could not share in their grief and bond over it. The horrid experiences they collectively encountered only ever seemed to create even more emotional distance between the couple. Both of them got back from Spain almost desperate to return to work.

With his route to Dr Blots now effectively blocked as a result of his stunt with the breast mag, Mr Sincope surveys his options as he wanders semi-aimlessly through the hospital's corridors once again. Dr Sharp is not in her office – he goes by several times to check – and he can't think of any other viable option that would help bring to a satisfactory close his wife's interminable pregnancy. He supposes he could ask Gregory for some advice, a poor alternative. However, as it appeared to be the only one available to Mr Sincope, he goes for it anyhow.

'Please, Gregory, whatever can be done, whomever you can send round to examine my wife, would be spectacular. I'm sure she must be in labour by now,' Mr Sincope says to the antenatal ward receptionist from Blackburn. Gregory looks at him with steely eyes, trying to place the man in front of him.

'Are you the bloke that stole the gas and air canister from behind my desk the other day?'

'I didn't steal it. My wife needed some pain relief so I borrowed it for her.'

'I thought it was you. I got in a lot of trouble for that, I hope you know. So yeah, not much in the mood to help you out of this one, mate.'

Gregory puts his head down and begins reading anew the

academic book he had been perusing prior to Mr Sincope's arrival at his desk. With even Gregory refusing to be of help, that is that, Mr Sincope thinks to himself. No more cards left to play. As he stands in the antenatal ward reception area and wonders what to do next, he receives a phone call on his mobile from a blocked number. When he answers it, he finds that it is his boss, Terry, barking down the line at him.

'Where the hell are you, Sincope? Forget that Monday and Tuesday are days you are contractually obligated to come in for?'

Mr Sincope knew this call was coming but it still feels brutal in the moment.

'Terry! Look I'm sorry, I'm still at the ...'

He is about to tell his boss the truth when he thinks better of it – he'd sworn to Terry that the only days he needed off around his wife's birth were the Thursday and Friday of the previous week, so Mr Sincope does not feel he can get any mileage from Terry out of the situation around the pregnancy going on and on. Mr Sincope makes something up off the top of his head, never one of his strong suits as we've come to discover already.

'Still at the pub! That's it, yes, still at the pub. From Wednesday when the guys saw me off. Those crazy kooks.'

'Sincope, do you mean to tell me you've been at the Coach and Horses for the past six days?'

It was a completely ridiculous assertion to have made but there was no way out of the lie now.

'That's right, mate. Six days, five nights straight.'

'What about the wife?'

'What about her? No, I'm kidding. She's in the hospital, I think. I don't get too involved in all that. It's woman's stuff, right?'

'Wherever the hell you've been, I need to know you're going to be around tomorrow for sure. I'm moving management accounts up by a day this month to accommodate the Cardiff office.'

'No problem, Terry. I'll be there, don't you worry, mate.'

'Fine then, I won't. See you tomorrow morning, bright and breezy.'

As he puts his phone back into his pocket, Mr Sincope makes the decision to tell his wife that he is going to have to leave as soon as possible. He will spend that night back at the flat and then go from there to work the next day. She'll understand when he tells her that Terry had rung.

'Hey, dear,' Mr Sincope says as he enters the cubicle, hoping a lightness of tone will set the appropriate mood. As it happens, Mrs Sincope had long since forgiven her husband and was eager to make amends.

'Oh, my dear, I'm so glad to see you. I want to say straight off that I'm so sorry about that silly argument we had about my job.'

This is a real gift to Mr Sincope, who not only had been the real villain of the spat in question but knew it too. He decides to bank the advantage.

'Thank you for the apology, dear. I accept. I don't know, I suppose one way of looking at it is that there were things that needed to be said. Having said that, you did say some things that are going to be hard to completely forget.'

He takes this bizarre route simply because he has decided on the spur of the moment to intentionally start another row; if he can initiate another fight, he reasons quickly, he can then use it as an excuse to leave and go home without a heavy discussion being necessary. One fight isn't enough but two fights in a row seems to be the perfect escape plan to him all of a sudden. It's all simple in Mr Sincope's mind, as these sorts of things usually are for him.

'Well, sorry again, dear,' Mrs Sincope says, in actual fact hurt by her husband's words but desperate for there to be no animosity hanging between them.

'Like I say, some things were said that stung, you know.'

'I can only apologise again.'

His plan isn't working. Here we have the male Sincope desperate to start a fight to achieve his ends while at the same time his wife is desperate to avoid one. He switches tack.

'You know, there's something I need to tell you – Terry called, just now, and I'm going to have to go into work.'

'Right this second?'

'Yes. Well, no, I mean I'll have to be there tomorrow morning. Bright and breezy as Terry always says.'

'I thought you told me that Terry was fine with you taking as much time as you needed with the birth.'

He had told his wife this fib a week before the Big Day. This was mostly because he liked to exaggerate to her his status within his department, which given her senior position within the same organisation, she knew was complete bullshit most of the time anyhow. It was also said to put her mind at ease. He'd secured the two days with Terry and at the time he couldn't see how any more were going to be required.

'Something's come up. Emergency, something to do with the Cardiff office,' he says. 'They need me back right away.'

'All right. I guess we'll have tonight and the nights going forward with each other then. Until Faith is born, obviously.'

'You mean here?'

'I'm not going anywhere else in a hurry, dear.'

Mrs Sincope nervously laughs after saying this, a horrible feeling in the pit of her stomach intensifying.

'Right, see, what I was thinking is that I could go home, back to the flat, oh sometime around, say ... now. Then I sleep there, in our bed, and then I get up, go to work, come home and sleep in the flat again. You carry on doing the good work you're doing here in the meantime.'

Mrs Sincope is more upset than angry with her husband's insensitivity. She is terrified of coping with the new reality that her husband had just proposed, which essentially would entail her being abandoned to weather the antenatal ward by herself from here on out most of the time.

'Please don't do that,' she asks pleadingly, tears forming in her eyes involuntarily while she curses herself for not being able to hold it all back, knowing that the cooler she plays things, the better her chances of keeping her husband there are.

'All right, how about this? I go back to the flat tonight, rest up, and then after work tomorrow I come back to visit.'

'Will you stay the night tomorrow night then?'

He desperately wants to say no but finds he can't manage it.

'Sure, why not.'

'All right then. You go home, dear.'

These are perhaps the hardest words Mrs Sincope has ever had to say to anyone in her whole life; even more so than the undeserved 'thank you' she muttered to her husband earlier. She does it because she feels it's the only option. Better to have him tomorrow night than to have to suffer two nights in a row without him.

'Great!' Mr Sincope shouts like a teenage boy being given the keys to his father's Porsche for the weekend. He then kisses his wife's head emphatically, as if they had just won the Wimbledon mixed doubles.

'I'll see you tomorrow then!' Mr Sincope says to her, and then he turns round and dashes out of the cloth cubicle without a further word.

Chapter Fourteen

Old Batty

The day after Mr Sincope leaves the hospital is the worst in all of Mrs Sincope's life up until that point. She is terrified that her husband might not do as he said he would and come by the ward that evening to be with her. The logical part of her says that there is no way he wouldn't do as he had promised; while he had been a scoundrel at times during their marriage, never had he let her down that badly. Yet Mrs Sincope still fears the worst this time round. She feels like this situation is somehow different; that something in the triumphalism of her husband's escape the previous night presaged a new and altogether worse chapter in their relationship.

What punctuates how terrible that wretched seventh day since her induction turns out to be is the fact that not one single health care professional even bothers to stick his or her head into the cubicle to see if she is all right. Even the catering woman seems to have forgotten about her, as Mrs Sincope misses out first on lunch and then supper. Not particularly regretfully, as she isn't in the least bit hungry anyhow. As she sits and gazes at the ceiling blankly, Mrs Sincope imagines a situation in which she has a haemorrhage and bleeds out over the hospital tiling; no one even bothers to notice until it has spread far enough to cause general alarm to the other inhabitants of the ward. Even then, nothing occurs. It is only the antenatal ward after all.

The day had got off to a terrible start when she used her mobile to call Sarah at around nine a.m. She told her neighbour what had happened and asked if perhaps Sarah would come down to the hospital and spend however much time she could with her.

'Would love to help you out, sweetheart, but the kids have swimming today, so there's no way.'

'Even if you only came for half an hour it would mean the world to me.'

'I know it would but I can't. I guess you should have married another bloke, right?'

Sarah using this moment to spring a 'told you so' moment on Mrs Sincope is pretty low behaviour. The conversation stutters to a close and Mrs Sincope spends the rest of the morning crying her eyes out. She had cried more in the last few days than she had collectively throughout her adult life up until that point. The travails of her week in the hospital and the strange turns it had taken had weakened Mrs Sincope emotionally; much more so than of which she is conscious. What makes it worse is that she uses a lot of the afternoon trying to think of people she feels close enough to so that she can then ring them and ask if they will visit her in the hospital. The few she can come up with – mostly work colleagues, women she'd had the occasional drink with over the years – do not even answer the phone when she calls.

Every so often Mrs Sincope turns her gaze towards the chair where she had temporarily forgotten her husband is no longer sat, always with the intention to plead with him to go and find her a doctor as she is in a lot of pain, the rediscovery of the fact that he is absent always stabbing her in the heart and seemingly doubling the amount of discomfort she is experiencing. Each time this occurs, she tides herself over with the idea that Mr Sincope would be returning that evening and this thought gets her through the hurt of it all.

At eight p.m., she begins to get restless, wondering where her husband is. At nine, she starts to panic. Ten minutes before ten, she passes out, too exhausted to stay conscious.

As midnight approaches, bringing with it Mrs Sincope's eighth day in the hospital, she awakens from her slumber via being physically examined by Dr Blots.

'What are you doing down there?' she asks blearily, trying to wake herself up and struggling.

'Relax, Mrs Sincope. Performing a quick spot check.'

She thinks this an odd turn of phrase. A few seconds later Blots pulls his fingers out of her quick and roughly, causing her to shout out in considerable pain. Blots does not apologise for this.

'Still nothing moving down there, nothing at all,' he says instead in a disappointed and even disapproving voice as he removes the gloves from his hands.

'What happens now?' she asks, fully conscious after the pain of the withdrawal of Dr Blots' fingers had forced her fully awake. She looks at the clock on the bedside table to discover the time. It then sets in for the first time that her husband had definitively broken his promise to her. He hadn't come to visit her that evening at all, as he had sworn to her that he would.

'We wait. What else is there to do?' Blots rhetorically asks.

'I've been here over a week already. How much more waiting is involved?'

'It takes as long as it takes.'

Blots then turns to depart.

'Doctor, before you go: do you know if my husband dropped by this evening at any point?'

'I can find out for you.'

Dr Blots jogs off to speak to someone or other outside of the confines of the cubicle. Mrs Sincope already feels sure of the answer she is going to get back – that her husband hadn't come. She begins to prepare herself emotionally for such a reply. Sure enough, Blots re-enters the cubicle about a minute later.

'Sorry, your husband has definitely not been up to the ward tonight,' he says. Mrs Sincope starts to weep softly. She expects Dr Blots to simply turn tail and flee but she is pleasantly surprised when he sticks around to comfort her instead.

'For what it is worth, I think you are better off without him,' he says bluntly after a few seconds of awkward silence. 'Apologies for being so frank.'

'No, it's all right. It's partly my fault. I may have asked too much of him.'

'It is not too much to ask the father to loiter long enough to see his child being born. The man is a brute; I could tell that from the first moment I laid eyes him. I tried discussing my acting sideline with him, after which he attempted to humiliate me.'

Blots' eyes harden into resolve before he continues speaking.

'Mrs Sincope, I have decided I am going to give you something to aid your pain that will also help you sleep.'

Dr Blots removes from his coat pocket a large pink pill. And by large, I do mean enormous; its circumference is that of a bottle cap. Mrs Sincope is the most grateful she has ever been to any other human being in the entirety of her existence in that moment.

'Oh, thank you, Doctor! Thank you so much! I've been suffering with it all for so long now and I'm so, so desperate for some relief.'

'Don't worry about it, sweetie. Rest up, let that body of yours recover its strength. And though I know it must be difficult, please try and forget about your husband.'

Dr Blots leaves and as he does, Mrs Sincope finds herself landed with a newfound dilemma. She has no water with which to take the pill the doctor had given her. Under normal circumstances, she would simply try and get the pill down her throat dry but here one needs to appreciate the hugeness of the object in question. She thinks for a moment of biting it off in chunks, but she is scared of what this might do to the pill's medicinal qualities given she wants the maximum possible effect. Mrs Sincope considers ringing for help briefly, but that hadn't worked once yet all day and so she puts the idea out of her mind hastily. What she does do is slowly, methodically sit up; then, just as haltingly, she swings her feet round so that they are planted on the ground. Using all of her remaining upper body strength, she proceeds to hoist herself upright. She is a little unsteady but feels she can make it to the antenatal ward reception without falling over. When she gets there, which takes around five minutes to accomplish, Gregory is manning the desk.

'Hello, I was wondering if I could get a glass of water from you?'

Gregory looks up from his book, thinks for one moment, and then does as Mrs Sincope asked with a remarkable scowl on his face. Water received, she then pops the gigantic pill into her mouth right there and then, while still standing in front of Gregory. She follows this up with a chug of the water and then tries to swallow the whole thing down. It doesn't work; she unfortunately coughs it all up again, right onto the reception desk itself.

'What the hell are you doing to my work zone? Can you at least barf in your own space?' Gregory says to her, rudely. He then gets up and walks towards the gents', acting like he's been doused with acid the whole way.

Right, this is it, Mrs Sincope tells herself, psyching up for another go at downing the pill. She picks the now damp pill off of the reception desk and steels herself for the task ahead by means of a few deep breaths. The second time round she takes a lot more water in and that seems to *just* push the odds in her favour. Managing to swallow that pill feels like a massive achievement to Mrs Sincope. Knowing that she'd soon be asleep and mostly pain-free, so long as Dr Blots was reasonably honest in his assessment of what he had given to her, makes Mrs Sincope perceive an ease she had not felt since her husband had departed the ward. She turns round and begins to stumble back to her cubicle.

During a period of time lasting a fortnight, starting from when Mr Sincope abandoned his wife to her own devices on the antenatal ward – two weeks that Mrs Sincope spends lying in the hospital, taking enormous pink pills to help her cope, getting progressively emotionally and intellectually weaker – he is back at work and completely out of contact with his wife. At first this reversion to his old life following the week spent on an obscure wing of the local hospital comes as an overwhelming relief to him. He feels the need to fib about his current situation to keep the cover of normalcy; Mr Sincope tells all of his workmates that Faith had been born on Big Day Thursday, healthy and happy, six pounds four, and was now at home with mum. This dishonesty eventually has a ruinous effect on the joy that he feels at returning to the familiar. To take an example, it is now hard for Mr Sincope to navigate an entire morning without having to give an update to at least one female member of staff about how things were supposedly progressing with the wee one. He has to improvise in these moments, something he finds horrendously exhausting given his obvious imagination deficiency, made so much worse by the fact that he has no idea what living with a small baby is like. He falls back on stereotypes for lack of anything better.

'My wife is so tired. All that child does is throw up and poop!'

Mr Sincope is also constantly being asked for pictures of Faith, a tricky situation to avoid forever. Eventually he downloads some snaps a former work colleague of his who now lives in America has on his Facebook page, ones depicting his son when he was first born. This is precarious stuff for Mr Sincope, particularly given his naturally diminished powers of observation. One day he almost puts a picture with a tiny willy visible into the mix, a mistake that would have been surely irreparable.

There is a new chap in the finance department who started working there the same week that Mr Sincope returned to the fold, a bloke from Sunderland named Gary. Mr Sincope and Gary become fast friends, despite the former's general distaste for those born in what he considers England's northern hinterlands. Most of the other people who work in the office seem rather wary of Gary, going so far as to blank the guy when he says hello in the morning, something Mr Sincope can't fathom as Gary seems so personable to him and he had never known the office to be so xenophobic towards newcomers before. Also,

154

if a dyed in the wool basher of northerners such as himself can like Gary, surely anyone could.

Gary's seeming inability to make any other friends in London, combined with Mr Sincope's desire for company that will not ask too many questions about his current domestic situation, see the two men bond at a level that is unusual for either of them. It starts heavy as well – lunch together every day plus drinks in the pub each evening, just the two of them. However, the whole situation is not built to last.

The event that brings this brief phase of Mr Sincope's life to a shuddering halt occurs on one such pub outing, two weeks to the day after he had last seen his wife. A few beers into the night, he finally decides to open up to Gary about his current situation, something that despite all of their time together, Mr Sincope had not yet done with his newfound friend. He tells Gary everything about the ultimately inutile week he had spent in the hospital, from the outrage at the car park prices – which had cost him over one hundred and fifty pounds in the end – until the final departure and unforgivable lack of return since.

'You haven't spoken to your wife in the last fortnight at all?' Gary asks in a neutral tone, neither accusatory nor supportive.

'I've almost dialled her number a couple of times. But something always causes me not to call. And of course, she's called loads of time and I've dodged every one of them.'

'I think you need to see your wife, matey. I mean, whatever happens going forward, you can't leave things as they are.'

'You're right, I know.'

'Call her, right now.'

'No, I think it would be better to see her rather than talk to her on the phone,' Mr Sincope insists.

'Do you know where she is?'

'No. I could call the hospital and find out.'

Mr Sincope takes out his phone and dials the hospital. He asks reception to put him through to the antenatal ward. A few moments later, Gregory answers the phone.

'Gregory! Is that you?'

'How can I help you, sir?' the boy from Blackburn says, annoyed.

'I'm wondering when my wife was discharged from the ward. Her surname is Sincope.'

'Hold on.'

Gregory puts him on hold for a moment before coming back with the news.

'We have a Mrs Sincope still on the ward, sir.'

'Really? Still on the antenatal ward? That's not possible.'

'Well, she's here. Anything else?'

'No, thank you, that's all.'

Mr Sincope hangs up the phone dazed. How could his wife still be on the antenatal ward a fortnight on since he was last there?

'What did the hospital say?' Gary asks.

'My wife is still on the antenatal ward.'

'Come on – finish your drink and I'll put you in a cab. You need to be there as soon as possible.'

'What if she's so angry she won't even see me?'

'She might well be that cross. But she also needs your support and so you two will make it through, at least until you get home and are both in the right space to work it all through properly.'

'You know something? You're a great mate, Gary.'

'Thanks.'

Mr Sincope follows Gary's advice, getting into a cab and

asking to be taken to the hospital. He wonders again how she can possibly still be on the antenatal ward. Logic dictated that she must have given birth to Faith by now. He had assumed before this evening that she had gone to a friend's house with the baby, or failing that, possibly up north to be with her father.

Gary goes home that evening feeling disgusted with Mr Sincope's behaviour towards his wife the more he considers it. By the time he gets off the bus and is back in his flat share, he resolves to avoid Mr Sincope as much as possible from there on. He'll be polite to the man in the office, maintain professional decorum and all that, but he'll always find himself conveniently busy any time Mr Sincope wants to grab a pint ever again. He doesn't need friends in London that badly, Gary decides.

As the cab wanders its way through West London, Mr Sincope begins to have second thoughts about whether this venture to the hospital is actually a good idea or not. He is about to ask the cabbie to simply go on to the flat, not to worry about the hospital, when the cab arrives in front of the pre-arranged destination; he'd been so lost in his thoughts, he hadn't been paying attention to how close they were.

Mr Sincope pays for the cab and then stands staring at the building for several minutes in the rain that had commenced since he had left Gary and the pub behind. Deciding that he doesn't want to stay where he is any longer but having not made up his mind definitively either to enter the hospital or simply walk home, Mr Sincope chooses to wander across the road to Four Fountains Park. He goes to sit under the jingoistic fountain, but finds the idea off-putting before he gets there. He sits instead by the Lichtenstein knock-off, the one his wife had so admired. He looks up at the fountain again, trying to capture some essence of what his wife liked about it. He can find nothing. It still looks like typical post-modern rubbish to him. He suddenly feels a pressing urge to flee; to leave London, indeed England, for good. Hop on a plane to somewhere, any-where, and never return. He begins to think about this idea seriously. Why not? He could give it a go at least. With the thought of doing this alive in his mind, he figures that before he does anything else he should cross the road and see his wife. Yet something he can't define is now stopping him, something far beyond his comprehension. It is certainly way, way beyond what his limited emotional intelligence is capable of overcom-ing. He gets up from the ledge surrounding the *Missing Cat* fountain and attempts to take a step towards the hospital. But it is as if he were trying to lift his legs out of dried cement. His breathing becomes heavy, as if he had completed a jog of ten miles at a rigorous pace. Mr Sincope turns to face home instead. His breathing stabilises as he does this, his legs becoming free again. His body has told him what to do and that is to head back to the flat he had shared for the past several years with his wife. From there, he would have to ponder what his next move should be.

As soon as he arrives back at home, it immediately occurs to Mr Sincope what he has to do next: phone his mother. She was always the person that he turned to when he was in a real bind. He finds her number in his phone and presses call. It rings for some time. He looks at his watch and only then realises the time; it's late to be ringing even his parents, particularly as they tend to go to bed early. Finally, as he is about to give in, Mr Sincope's father picks up the line.

'Sincope residence.'

'Hello, Father.'

'Son. What can I do for you at this full an hour?'

'I need to speak to Mum. If she's around.'

'Where else would she be at this time of night?' his father asks, his nose slightly bent out of shape by even the slightest notion that his wife could be anywhere other than safely ensconced inside of his house. He hadn't, incidentally, thought for one moment of asking what was happening with his grand-daughter. This is a prime example of the apple not falling all that far from the tree.

'Could I please speak with her, Father?'

Mr Sincope is upset but he knows better than to expect any sympathy from his dad. The older Sincope male calls for his wife.

'Dorothy, get down here. It's your son on the phone,' he shouts without even bothering to cover the receiver. Mr Sincope's mother is on the line three seconds later.

'Hello, darling.'

'Hi, Mum. Look, I have something I need to discuss with you, something very important. I apologise for calling so late but this couldn't wait.'

'Of course, of course. I'm here for you, my boy. What's on your mind?'

He fills his mother in on what had transpired two weeks prior between him and his wife and how he has not been back to the hospital since or indeed even spoken with his other half on the phone.

'What should I do now?' he asks his mother with particular urgency once he'd concluded the whole of the tale. Much of what he would end up doing hinged on his mother's advice.

'Son, I want to say straight off the bat that I think you've done the exact right thing. And about time too.'

'Excuse me?'

This was not the answer he had been expecting right off the bat and Mr Sincope is slightly taken aback by his mother's strident tone of voice.

'I always thought it was a mistake, you marrying that woman. You have finally come to the realisation of what an error you made. Good on you. Now you can rebuild your life.'

'What about the baby?'

'You'll have to fulfil your legal obligations, obviously. But I wouldn't go back to the hospital again. Or indeed see that woman other than to sign the divorce papers, if needs must.'

'I'll have to see her if I want to see my daughter, Mum.'

'I would advise against that as well. Think about it: the poor little girl will only form an attachment to you that cannot be fulfilled. Surely it's better if she never knows you at all. Think of the child; life will be easier for her if she's none the wiser about you.'

'She'll obviously figure out at some point in her life that she had to have had a father. What are you suggesting, Mother?'

Mr Sincope's mocking question is merely surface; he's hearing his mother say exactly what he wants to hear her say. What he craves more than anything is to turn his back on everything and never think about any of it ever again and his mother is providing him with moral cover for such an action.

'What she is told and not told is none of your concern. What is your concern is how you rebuild your life now that you've admitted a mistake has been made.'

'But we're married. I can't simply walk away from that. Can I?'

'Her family have never liked you anyhow,' his mother says; a non sequitur that is nonetheless extremely effective. Right before they were wed, Mr Sincope had driven up north to ask permission for his wife-to-be's hand in marriage from her father in person. The soon-to-be Mrs Sincope had warned her fiancé beforehand about her father's temper, his drinking, his overall surliness. This was an attempt on her part to avoid the meeting taking place. Something about the idea of the whole exchange – and exchange was the right word, as it made her feel like a piece of property – discomfited Mrs Sincope. She eventually attempted to make her annoyance felt directly to her husband, to no avail. She even tried instead to prey upon his fear of northerners.

'I must warn you that he's quite mad, my father. Typical aggressive northern bloke, and you know how much you hate that type.'

'I know what to expect in Manchester, relax.'

She tried peddling more along the same lines but nothing would work. Her fiancé was seemingly determined to go along with his plan of asking her father for her hand in marriage.

Mr Sincope decided the best thing to do would be to simply drop by and ring his prospective father-in-law's front door one evening without calling ahead – surprise the old bugger, in other words. The drive north was not going to be pleasant for him; however, Mr Sincope was nothing if not a man of tradition. He felt he needed the father of his bride's blessing on the whole matter before going through with it. Although he was not to know this, the tactic Mr Sincope had chosen was the absolute worst one possible. Gerry, as Mrs Sincope's father was called, hated anyone ringing his front doorbell or dropping in unannounced. It was one of his real pet peeves.

It was a sodden Thursday evening when Mr Sincope left work early to make the long trip up the M40 and then the M6. He had hoped to leave early enough to escape fully from rush hour traffic and had not managed it. It ended up taking him almost six hours to get to Manchester, by which time it was well past ten in the evening. Most nights, Gerry would still have been down at his local, filling his boots, but he'd been feeling particularly depressed that evening and had decided he couldn't face the pub. Instead he got incredibly crapulous on his own, notably so even by his standards, within the comfort of his own four walls. Thus, when Mr Sincope, who this man had never met and, contrary to what Mr Sincope himself believed, had never even heard of – Mrs Sincope weighed up calling her father and telling him she had got engaged and about her fiancé's intended house call but figured in the end that would make things even worse – showed up at his door at ten to ten that night, Gerry was extremely drunk.

'Who the fuck are you?' was his welcome to Mr Sincope, who proceeded to introduce himself and, Gerry not having produced his hand to shake of his own accord, grabbed at his prospective father-in-law's right paw to make the meeting a proper one.

'What are you after, eh?' Gerry shouted, drawing his hand away almost instantly. After Mr Sincope set out to explain again to Gerry that he was his daughter's boyfriend and that he had something serious he needed to discuss with him, Gerry reluctantly let the strange, middle-class southerner into his terraced house.

Mr Sincope's first impression of Gerry's place was of total disarray; the swirling chaotic surroundings of the confirmed, solitary drunk. There was an odd smell that hung in the atmosphere, somewhat like rotting pig flesh, that Mr Sincope wished to know nothing further about.

'Since you're obviously sticking around for a bit, get a drink down your throat,' Gerry instructed his sudden companion. Mr Sincope agreed before he realised what he was in for, which was unbelievably cheap brandy that had a large number of unidentifiable bits floating in it. He took the glass off Gerry with a smile and the intention of letting it get nowhere near his mouth. He planned to drive all the way back to London that evening anyhow and even one drink may have made him too drowsy.

'I'm here because I wish to marry your daughter,' Mr Sincope blurted out the moment Gerry had taken his seat. Gerry laughed, a strong, hearty chuckle that resulted in a great deal of coughing due to his dodgy lungs. When he could finally get his breath back, Gerry looked into Mr Sincope's eyes.

'No,' he said simply.

'Excuse me?'

Mr Sincope had not been prepared for such a reaction. He had somehow thought the father of his fiancée would simply acquiesce to his demand without anything much further being said.

'You heard me. No, you can't have my daughter.'

'Any particular reason for that?'

'You show up here out of the blue at ten o'clock at night and ask for my daughter's hand in marriage. I don't know you from Adam. And you strike me as a bit of a wanker. So, piss off back to London and ask some other bird to marry you.'

Mr Sincope was furious but tried to keep calm.

'I could marry her anyhow, you realise of course.'

'Then why did you bother to drive two hundred miles up the bleeding country to ask for my favour?'

Gerry had a point there. For whatever reason, getting his blessing was transparently of importance to Mr Sincope. The fiancé of Mrs Sincope rethought his tactics. Thinking of Gerry's habits, he came up with a plan on the spot.

163

'Why don't we at least go out for a drink and discuss this further.'

'It'll be getting on to eleven soon. The pubs will be about to shut by the time we get to one.'

'Something tells me you must know of a shut-in somewhere within the walkable vicinity.'

Gerry smiled broadly at this at least.

'Are you paying then?'

'The whole tab.'

'Right then: follow me.'

They left Gerry's house in the following few seconds. Mr Sincope was then led on a rather nightmarish journey through that particular part of Manchester's underbelly. They ended up in the worst pub he had ever been to in his entire life, one that was very possibly the worst pub in all of England. Most of the patrons had shaven heads, with several of them sporting 'MCFC' carved into the top of their skulls, seemingly done with a dull razor. There was a dog fight going on in the back room. It was a small mercy for Mr Sincope that Gerry didn't seem keen on blood sports himself.

'Best give me the cash and I'll order,' Gerry said as they took a seat. 'Your accent could get us some unwanted attention.'

Mr Sincope agreed with Gerry wholeheartedly and handed the man he hoped he could convince over the next hour or so to become his father-in-law a fiver. Faster than Mr Sincope would have possibly expected, Gerry returned with a pint of mild for his guest and three double Scotches neat for himself.

'A fiver got you all that?' Mr Sincope asked incredulously.

'Welcome to the north, son,' Gerry said with a laugh, which brought with it the first signs of conviviality between the two men, much to Mr Sincope's relief.

The odd couple had another round of drinks, then another, then another. Despite Gerry becoming ever more intoxicated, Mr Sincope could not extract a blessing from the man come hell or high water.

'Having drunk with you now, you seem a decent enough chap,' Gerry said. 'But I don't feel like giving my daughter away to anyone right now.'

This comment was overheard by an elderly gentleman at an adjoining table. He came over and put in his own two pence, completely uninvited.

'You should marry the girl regardless,' he said, pointing his index finger almost menacingly at Mr Sincope. 'The whole idea of a man having to ask the father of the girl he wants to wed is all poppycock anyhow. It's treating the girl as if she were her father's possession and the whole idea of marriage as some sort of business transaction. As if you were asking Gerry's permission to buy some carrots from his garden or something.'

Gerry laughed.

'Don't listen to old Batty here. He's a Trot,' Gerry said. Yet Old Batty continued.

'Whatever I am, I know that in this day and age it's for a woman to decide whom she wants to marry. The outdated tradition the two of yous are wrapped up with right now is all about controlling a woman and in particular controlling access to a woman's ability to reproduce.'

Gerry laughed again.

'Go home, Batty. Get yourself scarce and read the *Communist Manifesto* elsewhere, yeah?'

Old Batty simply waved his hand in disgust, got up and walked off. After another round of drinks, Mr Sincope and Gerry left the worst pub in England. Mr Sincope consulted his watch; it was almost one in the morning. He had now drunk too much to drive, particularly all the way to London from Manchester in the middle of the night. He was pondering what to do next when Gerry asked him to stay the night. He graciously accepted, despite the awfulness of Gerry's house, for lack of any other real alternative.

In the morning, Mr Sincope awoke with a splitting headache. Gerry was already up, cooking rashers of bacon.

'I've decided you can have her,' Gerry said, straight off, before even a 'good morning'.

'Excuse me?'

'She's yours. You can marry my daughter. If you still want to, obviously.'

What had caused his change of heart regarding the blessing of his daughter's marriage, Mr Sincope never asked of his father-in-law. It seemed it was all down to the drinks at the pub that Mr Sincope had bought; he had got his wife for a few slugs of Scotch, all purchased at conveniently low, northern prices.

Mr Sincope never saw Gerry ever again. He failed to turn up at the wedding and died a month after his daughter got married, having drunk himself into a coma he never arose from.

'What should I do with my life now, Mum?' Mr Sincope asks his mother over the phone as he tries to leave behind the memories of that evening in Manchester that had flooded back into his head from seemingly nowhere.

'That's for you to decide, son,' his mother replies.

'You're right. I will have to make a decision. In due course.'

'Take your time; you're a young man. You have your whole life ahead of you.'

'I should go now. I've kept you on the phone too long and it's late.'

'Go get some rest, son.'

'Goodnight, Mum. And thanks again.'

'You sleep well tonight. And remember, you're doing the right thing.'

With that, Mr Sincope hangs up the phone. He walks over to the liquor cabinet and pours himself a brandy. One without any floaty bits in it, he thinks to himself, unable to stop going over Gerry, Old Batty, and the worst pub in England. Then, his wife and unborn daughter take over in his headspace. For a moment, he thinks he is going to weep but just manages to hold the emotional tide back. As he gulps back his booze, he pulls himself together again. His mother was right – marrying the HR executive from the north had been a mistake, he thinks to himself. Following that logic to its conclusion, that meant the child would have to be a mistake as well. The double entry of it all demanded that if one was a credit in the balance sheet, there had to be a debit somewhere else of equal value. What exactly all of this means in Mr Sincope's crude accounting analogy isn't clear, especially to him.

He thinks about everything once again and although much remains foggy it becomes clear to Mr Sincope that he can't do as his mother had suggested and never see his wife again, and indeed his daughter even once. He makes a resolution, as he swigs the last of his brandy before heading to bed, to go to the hospital the next day after work and resolve things with his wife.

Yet when the time arrives to do this the following evening, he does not. He wanders past the hospital on his way home, lingers in Four Fountains Park for a little while, staring at the hospital, but then simply returns to the flat for an early night. Too tired, he thinks to himself as he does so, desperate for an excuse. Tomorrow, I'll see her for sure.

He doesn't on that occasion either. He makes internal pacts to go and see his wife in the hospital every day for that entire week but never manages to follow through. After that, the idea of going to the hospital doesn't disappear completely, but it does become more and more remote from his thinking as the memories of his wife become more and more distant.

Chapter Fifteen

Snuffles

It has now been a month since Mrs Sincope was induced. She remains on the antenatal ward, in the same cubicle she has spent all that time except for her ever so brief sojourn onto the labour ward. She is visited every two or three days by Dr Blots.

'Who is the most beautiful woman in the world?' he will ask her every time he sees her during this period. Mrs Sincope usually smiles and then childishly gurgles at the doctor before being quickly examined, Blots then retreating without a further word.

She is receiving a steady dose of the large pink pills, three a day, and these manage to make life almost tolerable for her. They have also considerably worn down her mental faculties. Once a strong-minded, opinionated woman, Mrs Sincope now has trouble focusing on anything for more than a few minutes at a time. At least when she is under the influence of the pink pills, which is most of the time. In the rare moments when their effect has worn off, she has moments of lucidity, but these are inevitably drowned out by the horrific withdrawal symptoms, the pink pills being incredibly addictive.

Mrs Sincope is now almost forty-five weeks pregnant.

There is an incident that happens very early during the fifth week of her time in the hospital, a moment when the effects of the pink pills wearing off coincides for the first time with an appearance by Dr Blots.

'Who is the most beautiful woman ...'

'I need to understand what's happening here,' she interrupts Blots with. 'Why am I still pregnant? I've been here for weeks now.'

Mrs Sincope has lost track of how long she had actually been in the hospital. Amongst its other effects, one thing the pink pills do is make tracking the passage of time extremely difficult.

'Don't take that tone with me, Mrs Sincope!' Blots says to her, exploding suddenly into an angry voice. He had never used this tone with her before.

'Excuse me?'

She is completely dazed by this response from the doctor and asks the question with genuine confusion. Blots then leans in close to Mrs Sincope, until his face is millimetres from hers.

'You will do well to remember who is in charge here. Things could get a whole lot worse for you very quickly. I could take away the pink pills, for a start.'

The very suggestion of this fills Mrs Sincope with deep horror.

'No, please don't. I'm sorry. I will address you in the politest manner possible from now on, Doctor.'

'Promise?'

'I swear on my life. Please don't take the pills away!'

Having got what he was after, Blots backs away from Mrs Sincope and begins to pace, silently for a few moments before speaking again, continuing to walk back and forth in front of his patient.

'Beyond whatever else I can do for you, Mrs Sincope, it must be clear by now that with your husband gone forever, I'm the only one you can trust. I may well be the only person in this world who cares about you at all.'

'My husband isn't gone forever,' she says angrily at first, calming down when she remembers her pledge to speak to the doctor only with reverence. 'What I mean, Doctor, is I think you misunderstand the situation. My husband will return at some point soon.'

Blots laughs derisively at this idea.

'Wake up! It's been over three weeks since he was last here. And you haven't been able to speak to him on the phone over that time either, have you?'

'How do you know that? I mean, sorry, I'm curious to know how you know that, Doctor.'

'I have been monitoring your phone conversations, Mrs Sincope, as few and far between as they have been. That's how I know that not only have you not been able to reach your husband, but seemingly no one else outside the walls of this hospital will speak to you either.'

This was true. Mrs Sincope had tried again and again to reach out to work colleagues, friends, Sarah, basically everyone she knew. No one would even pick up the phone for her now. In her lowest moments over the preceding three weeks, she had paranoid thoughts about her husband having told them all something ghastly about her; something he'd invented out of spite that kept them from even speaking to her.

'Only I care about you,' Blots continues. 'Just bear that in mind, please.'

As Blots departs the cubicle, Mrs Sincope finally accepts that the doctor is correct; her husband has seemingly vanished from her life forever. He is not coming back, for whatever reason.

She absorbs this idea slowly but surely over the next three

days. Doing so crushes something deep inside of her, forever. They had never had the best marriage, of that she had never fooled herself otherwise, and yet she thought he at the very least cared for her enough to make what he had done, abandoning her in the hospital while she was still pregnant, unthinkable. In order to process this and somehow come to terms with the actions of her husband, Mrs Sincope's personality, already dimmed by her time spent in hospital combined with Blots' mind games and the addictive drugs she was ingesting, comes close to imploding altogether.

Four days after the incident in which Dr Blots told Mrs Sincope her husband wouldn't be returning, the doctor makes his next appearance in her cubicle.

'I am going to have to take my leave of you for a little while,' he says first thing upon his arrival. 'So you will not be seeing me after this visit for some time. But don't fret; I am putting you in the able hands of my colleague, Dr Abelman.'

Mrs Sincope is barely moved by this news. Somewhere deep inside there is a sense of betrayal, yet it is dampened beyond recognition by the wounds previously inflicted upon her emotions and the fog of the drugs.

'Will you ever come back?' she just manages to ask.

'Most likely. Although it is difficult to say how long it will take until I can return once more to your bedside, Mrs Sincope. I have been called into head office for something I'm afraid I can't discuss with you. Dr Abelman will take good care of you in my absence though, I promise you. He's a specialist in cases such as yours. He has been handpicked by head office to look over your case, in fact. We are all ensuring you get the best treatment. Until next time, take care, Mrs Sincope.'

'One thing, Doctor, before you leave.'

'Yes?'

'One more time. For old time's sake?'

'All right,' he says rolling his eyes. 'Who is the most beautiful woman in the world?'

'Is it me?'

'Of course it is.'

He shrugs and leaves without a further word. As soon as he's gone, Mrs Sincope briefly feels embarrassed for the behaviour she just displayed – but that's gone in a moment, as her personality sinks back into the quicksand of post-traumatic stress and narcotics.

An hour later, an elderly man with crazy white hair peeps in from behind the cloth barrier and into the cubicle.

'Hello, Mrs Sincope. I am Dr Abelman,' he says with a German accent.

'Hello, Doctor.'

She finds the presence of the new doctor oddly stimulating, emerging from her stupor enough to engage with him a little bit.

'Dr Blots told me that you are an expert on pregnancies of this kind,' she says.

'Pregnancies of what kind do you mean exactly?' Dr Abelman says, genuinely confused by her question.

'Pregnancies that have gone on longer than originally scheduled, I believe.'

'Expert? No, I would not use this word.'

Mrs Sincope doesn't understand from the response whether Dr Abelman is simply being understated or if he is saying that he really isn't in fact a specialist as Dr Blots had told her. Either way, she feels her moment of intellectual perkiness start to quickly fade.

'Are you going to examine me?' Mrs Sincope asks, although she is already beginning to lose the ability to care either way.

'No, not at this time. I would prefer to simply have a discussion with you about your symptoms.'

'My symptoms?'

This perks her up again a little as she finds the notion mildly amusing. It is the first time she has found anything even slightly funny for a very long time, although she doesn't consciously register this fact in the moment.

'This will be a short chat, then, I'm afraid,' she continues. 'I'd be in pain all of the time if it weren't for those big pink pills I keep taking and yet my cervix doesn't seem to dilate. Not one inch.'

'I see. And have you had this problem before?'

'This is my first pregnancy.'

She is confused as to how something that simple about her case could still be unknown to Dr Abelman. It appears that Dr Blots hadn't adequately briefed him on her situation in the slightest.

'I can hear from your accent, Mrs Sincope, that you are not from London. Am I correct?'

The doctor has hit on a sore spot there and this awakens a level of indignity inside that she had not felt in at least a fortnight. Mrs Sincope takes great pains to hide her northern roots; to sound as southern middle-class as possible. She realises she can't be doing such a great job of obfuscation if a foreigner can hear what she is up to.

'No offence meant, Dr Abelman, but you don't sound like you're from round here either.'

He laughs good-naturedly at this counter-offensive.

'This is too true, yes. Many years I have lived in England though you would not know this from my voice. Dresden, I am from originally.'

Since they have now stumbled onto the terrain of the

personal, there is something in particular Mrs Sincope is suddenly dying to ask about.

'Abelman. Isn't that a Jewish name?'

'It is true. My father was a rabbi in fact.'

'The Jewish community in Dresden couldn't have been terribly large while you were growing up there.'

She only realises after it had escaped from her mouth how insensitive a comment this was to have made. Thankfully, the doctor laughs this one off as well.

'No, this is true. My father was one of only four rabbis in the whole of Eastern Germany during the time I was growing up. Can you believe this?'

The conversation has acquired a distinctly 'don't mention the war' flavour somewhere along the way, one that Mrs Sincope is now desperate to leave behind as she finds her spirits flagging again.

'Given my symptoms, Doctor, how do we get this baby out of me?'

The doctor laughs at Mrs Sincope's direct question.

'All in good time, all in good time. That is what I have learned over the years. The baby will come out and face the world when it wants to come out and face the world.'

'Faith is a she, not an it.'

The doctor laughs again – the precise same laugh he seems to have for every occasion, every remark, every awkward situation.

'This is true. Faith – such a beautiful name.'

'Thank you.'

'I will leave you be for the moment. I will be back tomorrow morning to discuss your case further. Good day, Mrs Sincope.'

Dr Abelman then departs.

Mrs Sincope proceeds to spend the rest of the day thinking

over and over again about memories from her early childhood spent in the Yorkshire Dales. The visit of Dr Abelman had stimulated her mind, at least a little bit, and she found that remembering in detail when she was a small child is where her brain had wandered with all of this sudden – relative, at least – energy.

She was from a poor rural family, the kind of people who had been there since feudalism, living as vassals, who had then become the peasantry of the Victorian age, unwilling to travel to the large cities for work like the rest of the rural poor. Her parents were the ones who broke this unfettered line; the family moved from their rundown farm when she was eight years of age after her father could simply not afford to feed them any longer. This was how they ended up in Manchester, which Mrs Sincope quickly grew to detest.

This dislike of her urban surroundings resulted in an overly romantic view of her pre-Mancunian childhood. She had somehow convinced herself that her father's excess drinking and violent temper had only surfaced after they moved to an oppidan environment; in truth, she simply saw a bit more of it in Manchester as they were by then living in much more cramped quarters. Mrs Sincope was particularly fixated the day she had met Dr Abelman on an incident that had occurred on her eighth birthday, the last one she would spend in the countryside, pre-Manchester. It involved the only act of kindness she could ever recall being perpetrated by her mother towards her. On the day in question, eight-year-old Mrs Sincope woke up to discover that no one was in the house. It was a Saturday, and finding herself all alone was nothing new as her mother often went shopping on the weekend while her father was off 'working', which was code for drinking himself senseless down the pub.

It should be mentioned that Mrs Sincope was an only child,

a fact that she lied about to her husband, a fib which required her to invent a wayward older sister named Lucille who had supposedly moved to South America when Mrs Sincope was a teenager. The fact that Mr Sincope had never once thought to question why his wife and this phantom sister had never once conversed on the phone during the course of their entire relationship, or indeed why Mrs Sincope had not a single picture of Lucille, said a lot about why she felt relatively comfortable being untruthful with him about it in the first place.

As to why she had lied about having a sister named Lucille, that was harder to explain. Mrs Sincope had always felt both uninteresting and scared of revealing too much about her childhood to new people. She thought of Lucille on her third date with her eventual husband, making the whole story up off the top of her head as a way of creating conversation about herself which revealed nothing that was true.

Despite not unduly panicking when she found herself alone in the house on her birthday, the eight-year-old version of Mrs Sincope had been expecting some demonstration from her parents that they were aware of what day it was; a card and a small present on the table would have sufficed. Even her parents could be relied upon not to forget about the day she came into the world entirely; apparently, no longer. She had a seat in front of the television set, as she often did when she was temporarily orphaned, picking up the remote with the intention of turning it on to watch cartoons. But before she had a chance to do this, her attention was attracted by a ribbon fluttering near the bay window at the back of the house, which the young Mrs Sincope could just spot from where she sat. She got up from her seat and went to examine this phenomenon. She gave the ribbon a tug and received the surprise of a lifetime – it was tied around the neck of an adorable Border Collie puppy. The eight-year-old Mrs Sincope squealed unconsciously with delight at seeing the animal and went to wrap her arms around its neck in a flood of emotion. As she did so, her mother jumped out from around the corner of the house, right in front of the bay window.

'Surprise! Happy birthday!'

Mrs Sincope was lost in an unconditional love for the dog of a kind that she had never experienced before – and sadly, would never experience again. She decided to name the animal Snuffles due to the way he constantly sneezed. Amazingly, the day continued on following this unprecedented trajectory upwards. Her mother laid on cake and ice cream and invited most of the children in the surrounding villages to the farm. She also managed to convince Gerry to remain completely sober for the occasion. It was little short of a miracle. Mrs Sincope would remember practically every little detail of this day for the rest of her life. She would cherish it as her greatest memory. She would think about it in times of grief or strife, the recall of any portion of the day being enough to pluck her spirits back up from almost any injury they had sustained.

Her mother committed suicide four and a half years later by going into the kitchen of their tiny house in Manchester, turning on the gas, waiting about half an hour and then lighting a match. She managed to blow to smithereens not only herself but also the whole of the one side of the house. One of the most unsettling details around the manner in which her mother had killed herself for Mrs Sincope was the fact that her bedroom was directly above the kitchen. It was blown to bits as well. The day of the suicide was a Saturday and was done early in the morning. The only reason the twelve-year-old Mrs Sincope wasn't asleep in her bed at the time was because she'd felt overly hot and did what she usually did when she felt that way, which was to go into the cellar to sleep with Snuffles. This meant that Mrs Sincope's mother must have been either hoping to kill her daughter at the same time as herself or simply didn't care one way or another. Either way, Snuffles saved her life.

Gerry's drinking became even worse after Mrs Sincope's mother's death, and within six months she and Snuffles went to live with her aunt, Gerry's sister. Part of the reason they had moved to Manchester was because she was there already, a connection to build on should times get tough – and they most certainly did. As for the dog, Snuffles lived to a ripe old age. Mrs Sincope took him with her to university and then, after graduation, to London.

Mrs Sincope puts together for the first time the connection between her mother's suicide, the loneliness she felt immediately after Snuffles' death, and how her desperation for marriage went up after her dog died. This revelation feels to her like a huge psychological breakthrough, one she celebrates by swallowing one of her gigantic pink pills. Due to this action, the stimulation of her intellect is short-lived.

Dr Abelman does not make an appearance the following morning as he had said he would. He does not show up the day following that either. Or the one following that, or the one following that. In fact, Mrs Sincope never sees Dr Abelman ever again.

As a result, she never gets the same sort of stimulation ever again. The fading of her personality and intellect takes a further sharp downward turn in the weeks that follow.

Chapter Sixteen

Head Office

Two further months go by. There is no change in Mrs Sincope's pregnancy over this period. The only thing that happens to her overall condition is that she retreats further into herself, becoming more and more addicted to the pink pills. Her mental deterioration continues alongside this, with it becoming ever more difficult for her to concentrate on anything for more than a few seconds at a time. This is partly a psychological side-effect of the trauma she has lived through; most of it is the result of the pink pills.

It is very near the end of this two-month period, bringing Mrs Sincope's time in the hospital to three months in total, when she receives a surprise visitor. It is Dr Sharp. Mrs Sincope hasn't seen her since Sharp's last call, which was during the first week after she'd been admitted. It was the consultation that had ended with Mrs Sincope accusing her husband of trading eyes with the attractive blonde doctor. Mrs Sincope can barely relate to the woman she was at that time now; remembering it vaguely as Dr Sharp enters, it feels like something that happened in a different lifetime. Recalling the incident causes Mrs Sincope to instantly regret anew having spoken to her husband the way that she did on that occasion. Maybe if she hadn't, she thinks to herself, he would still be here, at her side. Her mind, inactive for so long, is now flooded with enough of these thoughts to cause her to panic a little.

Dr Sharp makes her sudden appearance in a strange fashion – she sneaks into the cubicle as if expecting a reprimand from the overly pregnant woman who is lodged there, as if the two had had a particularly bad argument last time they spoke and Dr Sharp was coming now to complaisantly lay down a peace offering. When she sees Mrs Sincope start to panic, Sharp worries that she is the cause.

'Please, Mrs Sincope, don't be frightened. I'm not here to hurt you in any way. I come as a friend, I promise.'

This entreaty calms the patient down immediately. She looks into Dr Sharp's eyes and feels very soothed, for reasons she can't understand. It is actually down to the fact that no one has looked at her with friendliness in months, and in fact, no one had looked her in the eye for about the same length of time. This is her first moment of genuine emotional contact with another human being in a long while.

'I believe you,' Mrs Sincope says. She notices that she herself is crying, several seconds after the tears had begun.

'Are you ready for some fairly heavy information about what's been happening to you?' Sharp asks in a hushed voice she uses for the rest of the conversation.

Mrs Sincope nods her head. Dr Sharp continues.

'You've become Blots' guinea pig. I don't know exactly what it's all about. When head office found out about what he was doing, they thought he was being sloppy. They took him off your case.'

'Head office?'

Mrs Sincope has no idea what 'head office' is even supposed

to mean. She vaguely recalls Blots having used the phrase before and had for some reason never questioned it. Sharp avoids Mrs Sincope's query and continues talking.

'I'm in the process of trying to wrestle your case away from Blots so that I can finally free you from your burdens. I think I'm close now. Give me a week or so and I'll get your case transferred over and Blots off of it for good. Then we can work on your daughter being born.'

This final sentence causes Mrs Sincope to begin crying hard.

'Thank you for this,' she just manages to say.

'I'm sorry you've had to suffer what you have already. Take care, Mrs Sincope.'

Dr Sharp then departs the cloth cubicle.

Mrs Sincope now feels truly optimistic for the first time in what feels to her like forever. There is light at the end of the tunnel at last. As she sits back and smiles, Faith picks an opportune time to have a kick for the first time in weeks, reminding Mrs Sincope that she has a living creature inside of her that is soon going to be free.

'Not long now, dear,' she says to her uterus. 'You and Mummy will be together soon enough.'

This is of course an ironic comment given that she and her daughter are as together as they ever would or could be at that moment, with Faith living inside of her, a perspective completely lost on Mrs Sincope by that stage.

She then takes another pink pill as the effects of the last one started to wear off right around the time Dr Sharp had visited her. Within half an hour, the uptick in her reasoning has disappeared, her consciousness settling into the fog again, as the effect of the pill kicks in fully.

The day after Dr Sharp's visit, Dr Blots makes his first

appearance for two months. He enters dramatically, his eyes wild with rage.

'Have you been consorting with that Sharp woman?' he asks in a semi-bark. Mrs Sincope is smack in the middle of a pink pill high and thus has trouble even figuring out the basics of what is going on. She barely even recognises Blots.

'What, no. I'm here. Just here. Every day,' Mrs Sincope mumbles.

'I know she was here. I know she was. And I know what's going on. I know you are *conspiring* with that woman to have me removed from your care!'

Blots is shouting now, having worked his way up into a lather. Mrs Sincope is still barely there.

'I don't conspi-conspit . . . I don't do that thing.'

She falls asleep, unable to even remain conscious. This causes Blots to completely lose the plot. He runs up to Mrs Sincope and grabs her arms, shaking her awake. This gets her attention; she is suddenly fully conscious again as she realises that she may be in some real danger here. Blots begins to shout into her face, growling like a wild animal.

'You listen to me! I own you! Got that? If I get taken off this case, head office could decide to have you killed and dissected! I'm the only friend you've got in this whole world, Mrs Sincope!'

He pauses for a moment, looking like he might do something physically violent. Mrs Sincope blinks in horror, terrified.

'Do you understand me?' he shouts at her. 'Do you?'

She nods as furiously as she can. This thankfully causes him to back up a little, all the while still glowering at Mrs Sincope.

'If I hear about that Sharp woman coming back here, well . . . you don't want to know what I might do then.'

183

Blots mercifully departs. Mrs Sincope is incredibly upset for a few minutes, shocked at the doctor's use of actual physical force in shaking her awake, followed by the distinct threat of something worse to come. But then, the pink pill's effects overwhelm her again and she is back in an ignorant haze, knowing there is something she should be upset about but not being able to quite remember what that is.

Chapter Seventeen

Alien Life

Two further months pass following Dr Sharp's visit, the one which had brought with it the promise to have Mrs Sincope's case turned over to the female doctor, without Mrs Sincope seeing her again. The only thing that keeps Mrs Sincope going through this period is a request to Dr Blots to have her dosage of pink pills increased, which is approved. By the day of her sixth-month anniversary of having first entered the antenatal ward, Mrs Sincope is taking twelve of the pills every single day. Dr Blots' visits remain infrequent but regular, settling into a pattern of being roughly weekly. Whenever he shows up, he says nothing whatsoever to his patient, simply examining her quickly and then departing.

Throughout this time span, Mrs Sincope thinks about almost nothing whatsoever, so doped up has her brain become. The only genuine thought she experiences from time to time is a recurring dream in which she is an alien from a planet in a galaxy far removed from the Milky Way. The inhabitants of this place have scaly green skin, huge eyes, and large, long tails that they use for a variety of purposes. Within the dream and while taking the form of this green alien, Mrs Sincope dreams about her life as the human version of herself. She often arises from the dream within the dream to discover that she not only feels completely natural being a green, scaly-skinned alien, but also relieved. Her existence as a person had been such a nightmare, she would reflect to her alien husband, who might have been handsome or ugly as far as alien life forms go, it was difficult to objectively say.

On the actual day of Mrs Sincope's six-month anniversary on the ward – although this is unknown to Mrs Sincope, who has long since lost track of how long she'd been in the hospital – Dr Blots storms into the cubicle with a head full of steam.

'Sharp was here again, wasn't she?'

'No. No, she wasn't,' Mrs Sincope replies in honesty.

'Stop lying to me!' Blots shouts. He begins pacing back and forth inside the cubicle. This snaps Mrs Sincope out of her fog, sobering her up as it were, as she worries about a repeat of the time when Blots had shouted in her face after having shaken her awake.

'I promise you, I'm not lying,' she says tentatively, now unsure of what's real. Was Dr Sharp here recently and she'd forgotten about it? Dr Blots stops pacing and snaps his fingers.

'I know what I need to do to teach you a lesson. To make you understand that I'm the only one in this world looking out for you and so you need to tell me the truth. I'm taking away the pills, starting immediately.'

On Mrs Sincope's dinner tray sits around eighty of the pink pills. While food service and any visit from a health visitor had become erratic over the last two months, the steady supply of pink pills has never ceased. Whenever she has come to having less than twenty in her possession at any one time, a new batch of a hundred, sometimes even a hundred and fifty, of them have been dumped onto her dinner tray by some faceless orderly. It is the one thing that Mrs Sincope has long since ceased worrying about in any way whatsoever.

Blots dashes over to the side of Mrs Sincope's bed and in one quick motion, sweeps all of the pills on her dinner table into the pocket of his white jacket. Seeing her medication disappear like this causes her to fly into an instant panic.

'No! Please! You can't do this!'

'The withdrawal symptoms can be brutal, just to warn you. But they should subside within seventy-two hours. Good luck until then.'

As Blots leaves, Mrs Sincope screams after him, begging him to bring her pills back. She stops a few seconds later, mostly as her throat now hurts from all the screeching. She looks round to find some water only to find there isn't any. Usually there is a jug sitting behind her that is refilled every day, but it looks like they inconveniently forgot. She tries to shout out that she needs water, but her voice fails her.

The next hour is a living nightmare. As her last pink pill's effects wear off, withdrawal kicks in extremely hard, right away. The symptoms are thirst, a pounding headache, auditory and visual hallucinations, shaky extremities, and an overpowering sense of anxiety. Mrs Sincope keeps trying to get up out of bed to exit the cubicle and retreat down the ward's main hall in order to get to reception to beg for water, but all that happens is she continuously hallucinates that she has got up and charged towards her goal, only to face some nightmarish vision from the depths of her mind. One that happens several times is she manages to get out of her cubicle only to find that it is surrounded by a sort of moat, sometimes filled with water, other times filled with substances much more unpleasant; on a few occasions it is completely empty, causing Mrs Sincope to fall what feels like several storeys until finding herself back in her bed again.

The worst hallucination involves a demonic version of her husband suddenly appearing beside her. He has blood all over his face; it doesn't appear to be coming from him but rather seems to be the residue of an animal or even possibly a human he had recently killed in a gruesome manner.

'You drove me away,' the hallucination of Mr Sincope tells her. 'It was all your fault. Deep down inside you know this. It was all your fault. I would have stayed if you just hadn't been so hard to live with. It was all your fault.'

He speaks like this for what seems to be hours, all the while standing beside her, blood dripping all over her sheets. Mrs Sincope knows it isn't real – that her husband is not really there with her and it is just a mirage – yet the vision is still deeply horrifying in the moment to experience.

As Blots had predicted, the withdrawal symptoms subside after seventy-two hours, becoming much less powerful until they fade altogether. At the end of this horrifying ordeal, Mrs Sincope feels freed from the cloud that the pink pills had created in her brain. Yet what has replaced it is a hyperconsciousness; a deeply held sense of dread, anxiety and paranoia that is all-encompassing. She barely sleeps for the few days following the last pink pill. Her mind, for so many weeks a complete vacuum, is now filled with the same thoughts, rubbing up against one another over and over again. Why is she still pregnant months after her due date? How is her condition even medically possible? Is Blots behind her condition? If so, why? What's in it for him? What is this 'head office' he and Dr Sharp refer and defer to? Will Dr Sharp ever come back?

That final question is answered about a week after the end of her pink pill withdrawal when the blonde doctor appears from nowhere at the precipice of the cubicle.

'Hello, Mrs Sincope. How are we feeling today?' she asks.

At first, the pregnant woman thinks she must be hallucinating again. It soon occurs to her that she is not.

'That's a very difficult question to answer, Doctor,' she says after a pause. Dr Sharp instinctively looks round herself conspiratorially. She puts her finger to her lips to shush Mrs Sincope. She then moves in close to the patient, bends down to move her mouth in front of the now fifteen and a half months pregnant woman's ear in order to whisper.

'You and your child are in terrible danger. It goes beyond Blots. Right to the most senior ranks in head office. I tried to work round them to help you but the conspiracy runs too deep. Remain silent. I'm here to save you both. Sorry this has taken so long.'

Mrs Sincope has to stifle a sob in her throat. This feels like the real breakthrough at long last. After months of false dawns, someone is finally coming to her rescue. The fact that it is a fellow woman helping her is not lost on Mrs Sincope either.

'I'll be back later, around four in the morning,' the doctor whispers. 'From there, we will sneak out of the hospital and into a waiting ambulance. I have arranged a surgical procedure for you at a hospital in central London. I'll have Faith in your arms by sunrise.'

Dr Sharp backs away from the heavily pregnant woman, waving in a strangely passive way. And then, she is gone.

During the long wait for four in the morning, Mrs Sincope feels the closest to joyful she has for a very long time. She has been given hope of a happy ending to her horrible ordeal. With her newfound positivity, she imagines what Faith will be like at various stages during her life. She used to do this a lot when she was first admitted to the hospital but had found herself thinking about it less and less over time; this is the first interlude of considering what Faith would be like as a fully functioning human being Mrs Sincope had engaged in for months. She fantasises about a daughter that is a verbose and opinionated toddler, banging about, demanding her way constantly. Mrs Sincope plans to be outwardly strict towards this behaviour yet inwardly proud of her assertive daughter. By the time she gets to school age, Faith will be cute and girly, loving her dolls and her dresses, while also being bookish and intellectually curious. She will take to reading quickly and then move onto science and maths, becoming the smartest child in all of her classes. As an adolescent, she will be rebellious – having an older boyfriend, for instance – yet not too wayward. Faith will avoid the pitfalls of drugs and teenage pregnancy and graduate top of her class. She will go to Oxford or Cambridge and become one of the great female thinkers of her age. Being able to make her own means in the world will result in Faith being able to marry for love purely, perhaps even snagging a sort of 'toy boy' whom she will have on hand for passionate lovemaking and to stay at home looking after the children while she's at work. Mrs Sincope smiles broadly as she concocts each of these images of Faith at differing points during this invented life of hers. Then it hits home again that later on that very day she will be holding Faith, still a tiny baby with the whole of her story yet to be told.

Dr Sharp sneaks inside the cloth cubicle silently at four a.m. on the nose. This gives Mrs Sincope an extra boost of optimism; since she'd arrived at the hospital on the day of the induction six months' previous, no one had ever made a time commitment to her that they had subsequently managed to keep. Without a word, Dr Sharp helps Mrs Sincope up out of the bed. This is difficult, as it always is for Mrs Sincope in terms of any sort of mobility these days. Once up and on her feet, Dr Sharp puts her arm round the heavily pregnant woman to support her and the two of them scurry off the ward as fast as they can. Mrs Sincope has one last look at the cubicle which had been her virtual prison for over six months. Euphoria hits her as she takes in the full weight of the fact that she will never be forced to lay eyes on it ever again.

Once they are outside of the antenatal ward, Dr Sharp is practically carrying Mrs Sincope and the effort is extremely draining.

'Like I said, it's all a big conspiracy, everything to do with your case,' Sharp says at one point through deep breaths. 'Someone in head office is behind it all, but I can't discover who exactly. I didn't realise how deep it went until I tried to take it over from Blots. I've been followed everywhere by spies for the last two months.'

'Spies? What do you mean, spies?'

'Head office have had me trailed, everywhere I've gone, even on weekends. It's why it's taken so long to pull together. I had to be extremely careful in putting this escape plan in place at every stage.'

The two women proceed at a slow pace due to Mrs Sincope's size and the limits of Dr Sharp's physical strength. On several occasions the doctor has to stop and lean on the wall for upwards of three minutes, breathing heavily the whole time. Soon enough, however, it is Mrs Sincope who is asking for a breather as staying on her feet becomes more and more difficult.

'You can do it, come on,' Dr Sharp has to say to her when at one point Mrs Sincope announces she doesn't have the strength

191

to go an inch further. 'Think of Faith, that will give you all the strength you need.'

This pep talk works and the two women find themselves again inching towards the hospital's main exit. Mrs Sincope looks up at a moment where again she doesn't think she can possibly continue as the pain in her belly and legs had become totally overwhelming, only to see the exit to the hospital directly in front of her. They had made it! The further proof of the plan's success comes in the form of the back of the ambulance she has now spotted, seemingly waiting for her. She thinks of holding her daughter in her arms, Faith's little hands touching her face, that smell of newborn baby overwhelming her olfactory functioning. These thoughts cause her to burst into tears but also give her a newfound second wind.

This feeling of elation is quickly shattered as Mrs Sincope and Dr Sharp's forward momentum is suddenly halted by a troop of men who appear, seemingly from nowhere, in front of them. Most of the group look like police officers from the Met; some of the others are dressed as hospital orderlies. Standing at the apex of the bunch, arms folded like some sort of conquering Viking, is none other than Dr Blots himself.

'Grab her,' Blots says, pointing at Dr Sharp. With this simple two-word order, several of the male police officers seize the doctor, throw her against the wall and begin pawing her inappropriately. Eventually, after thirty seconds or so of this behaviour, throughout which Dr Sharp shouts and pleads with the officers to stop to no avail, Dr Sharp's hands are cuffed behind her back and she is then frog-marched out through the main exit of the hospital.

'Can someone please help this poor woman?' Dr Blots shouts out to no one in particular while pointing at Mrs Sincope, who has collapsed to the floor. She has also begun to weep profusely after seeing Dr Sharp disappear behind the edge of the ambulance, her last chance of escape having seemingly vanished. The hospital orderlies, all of them men in their early twenties and six foot two at least, run to where Mrs Sincope is lying and pick her up with due diligence and care. Six of them are now gathered all around her, each of them holding a body part.

'Get her back to bed,' Dr Blots says to the orderlies before leaning into Mrs Sincope's face to talk to her directly.

'Do not worry further, Mrs Sincope. The nightmare is over. We are returning you at once to the safety of the antenatal ward.'

Mrs Sincope continues to bawl wordlessly during the whole of the return journey to the cloth cubicle. She tries to console herself with the thought that somehow the incident that had just occurred, the end result of which seemed to be Dr Sharp's incarceration by unknown forces, would have a positive aftermath. Surely, she thinks, the hospital will be forced to move forward on the birth of Faith after the whole debacle.

It is to this thought that Mrs Sincope clings as she is laid back down inside of the cubicle.

Chapter Eighteen

The George Incident

Another month passes following the failure of Dr Sharp to extract Mrs Sincope from the hospital. During this period, which is the end of October through to November, the weather becomes unseasonably cold, almost arctic. The exterior climate obviously has no direct bearing on Mrs Sincope's entirely interior existence; yet looking out of the tiny window to her right and seeing the snow on the ground at least allows her to have some idea of the passing of the seasons. In the aftermath of the incident with Dr Sharp, Mrs Sincope's arms and legs have now been shackled to her bed on the antenatal ward by means of leather straps. This was instituted the morning after the failed getaway. Dr Blots paid a courtesy visit the afternoon she was placed in the restraints to talk her through the 'new arrangement'.

'It's for your own protection, Mrs Sincope. Much harder for someone to kidnap you like Dr Sharp attempted this morning.'

At the time, off the pink pills and still feeling like something positive might come out of the Dr Sharp led failed escape, if only she was willing to push a little, Mrs Sincope acted with much more aggression than she had for months.

'That's not true! I saw what you did! You're trying to keep me here against my will!'

Blots was visibly annoyed with this rebuttal. He started to pace back and forth in front of Mrs Sincope's bed in his by now usual, menacing manner.

'Do you really want to know why you're still here? Why you're still pregnant?' he shouted at her.

'Yes!' she yelled back, refusing to be cowed, even in the face of the possible violence she thought Blots might be capable of if pushed to the edge.

'Have you ever stopped to think that perhaps this is your fault? Some function of your own, singular biology that means it has fallen on me to try and figure out what's happened to you? Trying to keep your baby alive inside of you all these months! Have you ever stopped to think of the toll that's taken on me?'

The 'it's your fault' line hit a nerve; she found all of her determination leaving her. Yet Mrs Sincope struggled to hang on to her aggression as best she could, somehow knowing that this conversation represented something close to a final stand.

'Just tell me why I'm still here,' she said as directly as possible.

'I want you to go back on the pink pills again,' Blots replied as a diversion.

'I don't want to do that. They are addictive. I don't like what they do to me.'

'I have one here. I'd like you to take it.'

'I refuse to.'

Blots shook his head and then removed from his pocket a large needle. He took a moment to prime it for action before grabbing Mrs Sincope's left arm and then expertly plunging the needle into the largest vein within her cubital fossa. She was furious about this but one, there was nothing she could do to resist given she was in leather restraints and two, the anger didn't last long as the drug took immediate effect. She could soon feel her personality drifting away again, her resolve going with it.

An orderly now comes in once a day to release Mrs Sincope from her cow-skin manacles for an hour or so in order that she may stretch her legs and use the loo. She can mostly time her excretions to conform to this timetable, but there are accidents; sometimes the orderly has to change the bedding as a result. The hour-long windows of freedom are an incredible relief for Mrs Sincope. To be able to move her limbs again after having them restrained is as close to solace as Mrs Sincope gets these days.

Her left arm is hooked up to an IV drip, feeding her the drug found in the pink pills on a continuous basis. Her mind has returned mostly to the state it was in before Blots cut her off from the medication the first time. As a result, she has great difficulty concentrating on anything for even a brief length of time. Only in her sleep are her thoughts at least semi-coherent. She has a recurring dream, one based on something that actually happened to her right around the time she conceived Faith. It transpired one evening after Mrs Sincope and her husband had had a spectacular row, the most explosive of their entire relationship. It was built around Mrs Sincope not yet being pregnant despite the couple having tried for almost a year to obtain this state of affairs.

'Perhaps you need to change your diet,' Mr Sincope said in a manner that he thought was innocent enough. It was this comment that was the spark that started the fire, as it was the first definitive indication that Mr Sincope had given to date that he laid the blame entirely at his wife's door for their efforts at conceiving a child having failed thus far.

'Are you implying that it's my body that's letting us down here?' Mrs Sincope then asked, surprised by her own anger. Her husband had obviously hit a nerve within her she wasn't entirely aware of to that point.

'Isn't that the whole point of this discussion?' he asked, genuinely confused as usual.

'Have you ever thought for a moment that *you're* the one who is the problem?'

Mr Sincope took this comment as a direct assault on his manhood. He dealt with it the only way he knew how, which was to laugh about the whole thing.

'You can't be serious,' he said between chuckles.

'As it happens, I'm deadly serious,' she said, staring at him earnestly. Mr Sincope was running out of places to hide in the conversation.

'Let's get one thing perfectly straight here – there is nothing wrong with my sperm.'

'By definition that means that the problem is that I'm infertile.'

'Who knows what the problem is exactly.'

'You do, apparently. At least be honest and up front about that much.'

'This whole discussion took a rather nasty turn somewhere along the way. Let's talk about something else.'

Mrs Sincope had come too far now to let these previously slumbering dogs rest.

'No. I'm not letting this go until you admit that you think the reason why I'm not pregnant is nothing to do with you; that in your mind it's the fault of me and my body entirely.'

'This is ridiculous.'

'Say it!'

'Fine then. It's the fault of you and your body. Can we have some dinner now, please?'

Mrs Sincope made a promise to herself as she ran out of the flat not to cry. It was a promise she managed to keep. She thought she might she break down into full blown sobs the moment she got on a bus; however, she found herself too numb for any kind of further emotional reaction and the threat of water works retreated completely. Being internally anaesthetised was how she rationalised her non-breakdown at first. The more she thought about it, the further towards an understanding of her current emotional state she possessed. More than anything else, what Mrs Sincope felt was relief. So many things that had been hanging in the air – things left unsaid by her husband – had been unearthed during that row. She made a decision then to abandon the random bus ride and catch a taxi back to Sarah's flat, even if that meant heading very close to home.

When she arrived at Sarah's place, her friend asked her what had happened.

'We had a massive fight. Can I come in and have a drink?'

Sarah giddily allowed her into her flat. Perhaps this was the start of the meltdown in her neighbour's marriage that she had long envisioned and indeed been hoping for. While Mrs Sincope had a seat on the sofa, Sarah fixed the two of them their favourite tipple – an old-fashioned dry gin martini.

'What was it about? Did he make a fixed asset joke and you didn't laugh?'

'He blamed me for us not getting pregnant.'

Sarah was appropriately appalled.

'What, directly? He said, "It's all your fault"?'

'No, no, it came out while we were talking about everything. I challenged something he'd said and demanded clarification. Then he clumsily spit out the notion he clearly held that it was my body that was letting the team down as it were.'

Sarah leaned over and put her arm around her friend.

'Don't worry, sweetie,' Sarah said, stroking Mrs Sincope's hair. 'The man's a bastard, I've always told you so.'

The two girls decided to go into town and hit the pub after having a second martini each. Once they arrived at a little place in the West End, Sarah got the first round in, another couple of glasses of the poison that they'd started with. They had another drink at the same pub after that. Then another. They talked about relationships past and present as they got drunk.

'Remember that guy you were dating before you got married? What was his name?' Sarah asked her drinking companion. She was playing ignorant; Sarah knew what the bloke in question's name was: Juan. He was a devastatingly handsome Spanish man who had moved to England after a messy divorce and lived on the same floor as Mrs Sincope and Sarah at the time. He taught Romance languages at a university of some standing. Problem was, Sarah was the one in love with Juan, from day one. Mrs Sincope never picked up on Sarah's feelings in the slightest, an emotional blind spot that was unusual for her. Perhaps this had to do with her own feelings towards Juan, which despite initially feeling flattered that such a good-looking and worldly man was interested in her, soon developed into disinterest and even dislike of the handsome Spaniard.

Mrs Sincope tried to rationalise her antipathy towards Juan in many different ways, but the real reason for it she kept hidden from herself. She didn't feel good enough for him. She felt deep down that a man as good-looking as Juan had to have an ulterior motive to date someone like her. Her mind unconsciously searched for something to attach this theory to and eventually found comfort in the notion of Juan being a poorly paid teacher, looking to hook up with her for gold-digging purposes. Eventually, this evolved into an idea that Juan was also a chauvinist, despite the fact that not one thing he ever said or did backed this idea up.

'Oh God, not Juan! He was sexist, so sexist, I couldn't handle it,' Mrs Sincope said when her ex was unceremoniously brought up by her neighbour.

'Juan was lovely,' Sarah said and then felt immediately self-conscious that in her slightly sodden state she'd allowed more of her real feelings to shine through than she would have preferred. Mrs Sincope then felt strangely jealous.

'You fancied him, didn't you?' she asked Sarah in a curious, non-loaded way.

'I'm a happily married woman, thank you,' Sarah answered defensively.

'Your marriage has never seemed all that happy to me! What about that time Dave cheated on you?'

This kicked off an argument that quickly got out of hand, with each woman trying to convince the other that their opposite number had the worse marriage. Eventually, Mrs Sincope responded by running out of the pub. Once she had settled down a little, her anger at Sarah calming down, she took stock of her evening. She was in the West End somewhere, north of Soho. She made a snap decision that was completely out of character to continue drinking, all by herself. She would find a pub in Soho and see what happened. She couldn't face her husband yet. Part of the reason she didn't want to go home was that she didn't want to face Mr Sincope while she was drunk. Yet the longer she stayed out, the more pissed she got, making the attractiveness of going home recede ever further into the distance.

Once she was in a pub in Soho, drink in hand, Mrs Sincope felt foolish. Sitting and drinking by herself in the West End seemed sordid all of a sudden. She had made up her mind to have a pee in the ladies and then catch a cab home, when she was approached out of the blue by a man dressed Hollywood smart (nice shoes, black jeans, a button-up shirt and the orphaned jacket from a suit) who was both good-looking and exuded considerable charm.

'Why are you all alone?' he asked her in a way that managed to come off as winsome as opposed to creepy.

'My husband and I had a fight,' she said, both confessionally and as a way of announcing directly to this handsome gentleman that she was already married.

'How sad. Mind if I join you?' he asked. Mrs Sincope found the idea of having another drink, now that she had company, appealing. She had informed the good-looking man that she was married and so if he still wanted to chat with her, she'd done due diligence. His name was George and he charmed her for the next half an hour in that Soho pub Mrs Sincope had chosen at random. He said he worked in medical supplies, doing something technical-sounding that Mrs Sincope would have failed to understand completely sober.

The conversation mostly focused on Mrs Sincope and her woes anyhow. She was grateful to be able to unload all of her pent-up feelings and frustrations on a man for a change, particularly a bloke who was willing to sit and thoughtfully listen as well as offer advice here and there. George told her that she was an attractive, fun woman and that it sounded like she was with the wrong man, an observation he picked up from a particularly blurred recap of the events surrounding their wedding day. George invited Mrs Sincope back to his flat, which against her better judgement she took him up on. What sealed the deal for her was the fact that George's flat was in Soho itself, only a few streets stumbling distance away.

The outside of George's building was uninspiring, and as they walked through the dingy corridor after getting out of the lift, approaching the door to George's flat, Mrs Sincope braced herself for the bachelor pad horrors that now awaited her.

Her first step inside George's abode, however, subverted her expectations wildly. Inside, it looked huge; an almost Tardis-like effect that left Mrs Sincope wondering how the interior looked so voluminous. The ceilings were especially, impossibly high, like something from a grand old country manor. The walls were white and lightly glowing, like the set of a science fiction movie. The flat was also very sparsely furnished, with a table in the middle of the main room and a sofa near the back of an adjacent area being the only items. There didn't seem to be a kitchen, at least one that Mrs Sincope could find on first inspection.

'Welcome to head office,' George said. 'Do you like it?'

Mrs Sincope felt distinctly uncomfortable in that strange flat but didn't want to offend her host.

'It's great. Unusual, but nice, I suppose.'

'Thanks. I live here, I work here; I run my little empire out of this place. Can I get you something to drink?'

'Sure. What do you have?'

'Anything you want.'

'Anything at all? What if I wanted a strawberry daiquiri?'

Mrs Sincope didn't even know what that drink was. She'd heard it mentioned on some American television show once and it stuck in her head. She came up with it on the spot in an effort to puncture George's wild claim that she could have 'anything'.

'Coming right up,' he said before retreating into the adjacent room that had the sofa in it. Exactly five seconds later, he emerged with a strawberry daiquiri in hand, which he handed to Mrs Sincope.

'There you go. Should we have a seat on the sofa?'

She was led into the room where George had just emerged from with a fully prepared cocktail only a few seconds previous. Why he hadn't asked her to sit there while he made the drink was a mystery to Mrs Sincope, one that bothered her as they moved into this room. As they entered, it was even more bizarre to her that he had managed to create an exotic drink for her in mere seconds; there were no facilities or bar ingredients seemingly present. In fact, there was nothing in the room whatsoever apart from the sofa. She looked at the glowing white, sci-fi oriented walls and thought to herself that she should be feeling more weirded out than she in fact did. Instead, she felt oddly soothed by her surroundings.

Mrs Sincope took a seat; George sat down next to her. She had a sip of the daiquiri; pleasantly surprising, it was the most delicious thing she had ever tasted in her life.

'Really good, this,' she said to her host. He chuckled a little.

'I'm a bit of an expert on the making of beverages,' George said, his persona getting cheesier by the minute.

'I want to tell you about my work,' he continued, not waiting for Mrs Sincope to respond to his claim of bartending expertise. 'I'm more than just a supplier of medical equipment. I'm also a scientist. Here at head office, I am trying to find a way of making human life eternal.'

'What, so like, no death, you mean?' she asked, thinking George must be taking the piss. Mrs Sincope said this after another large slug of the daiquiri. She was starting to feel very light-headed and a little dreamy. She suddenly wondered if George had placed something in her drink but the thought of him doing so didn't scare her somehow.

'Yes. How can we extend life well beyond what exists now?' George said. 'Could we have humans that live a thousand years and beyond? How can we eliminate death, at least for human beings, altogether? To answer these questions, I have undertaken a large study. You, Mrs Sincope, I have been watching for a very long time.'

This comment caused something strange to happen in Mrs Sincope's brain. She was conscious that George's claim that he had been 'watching her' should be deeply alarming; beyond this, his use of her surname should have raised questions given she had not told him what it was, having only given out her Christian name when they introduced themselves at the Soho pub. Yet despite being aware of these things, she felt unable to feel scared or even mildly alarmed. The feeling of being soothed deepened, in fact.

'Watching me?' she managed to say, getting dizzier and more spaced out by the second.

'This evening, for instance, I watched you dash out of your flat. Followed you in my car as you took the bus. Then I trailed behind you and your friend as you made your way to the West End. I waited outside the pub in the hope that the two of you might part ways. As soon as you were alone, I stepped in.'

Mrs Sincope felt like she should be terrified by George's claims to have stalked her; instead, the emotion she experienced was feeling flattered, something she could not fight against in the moment.

'Why me?' she asked him, as if she were on automatic pilot.

'Many reasons, Mrs Sincope,' he said. 'You will come to know them in time.'

Despite thinking objectively that he must be slightly insane, Mrs Sincope found herself becoming more and more attracted to George. She also wanted another strawberry daiquiri as she'd managed to slurp her way through the first one, which helped this feeling along.

'I wish I could tell you more,' George continued. 'But it's highly top secret for now. The only people who know anything about it at all are a few doctors in select hospitals around London that I have handpicked to help me with my experiments.'

'Could I have another daiquiri?'

George smiled and took Mrs Sincope's glass from her. She watched him closely this time round to see how he would make the cocktail. Disappointingly for her, George went into the adjacent room, returning five seconds later with a new drink in hand. After giving it to his guest and then allowing her a few seconds to consume a little of the drink, he turned back to Mrs Sincope to ask her a question.

'Will you sleep with me tonight?'

Mrs Sincope's immediate response was to laugh in his face. This is why it came as such a shock to her when she found the next words out of her mouth being, 'Yes, of course'. It was as if she had lost control over her mind completely. She thought again about how the daiquiris must be spiked only to push that away as she leaned over to kiss George.

The following morning, Mrs Sincope woke up with a splitting headache. She could barely recall any portion of the lovemaking with George, but she was sure that they had had sex. She panicked when she tried to recall if they had used a condom or not; she really wasn't sure either way. After looking over at George, who was still fast asleep, and feeling nothing but disgust for him, she got up and hurriedly dressed herself. She then wandered around the flat briefly. It looked very different in the cold light of day, the new age sci-fi set-up now seeming to her like the set of a terrible, low budget movie, the Hollywood mirage having been destroyed by daylight. She became possessed with the overwhelming desire to leave before George woke up.

On the tube ride home, she thought about all the things George had told her about science and creating immortal life. Despite having felt fuzzy and not in control at the time, she could somehow clearly remember every word George had said to her the night before. She was convinced at the time that it was all bollocks; the delusions of some science fiction nerd who thought it might work as a line to get a woman into bed (the fact that it had actually worked on her not being lost on Mrs Sincope). The one thing that still bothered her was how the hell he'd managed to make those strawberry daiquiris so quickly.

When she got home, her husband was sat in the kitchen, reading a newspaper. She gingerly walked past him, trying to anticipate what he might say; how he might respond to her having stayed out all night. Finally, when she couldn't take the tension any longer, it was she who broke the silence.

'I suppose you're wondering where I've been.'

Mr Sincope looked up from his newspaper, confused.

'You've been out this morning?'

'I didn't come home last night.'

'Really? Didn't notice.'

She surmised from his words and demeanour that he obviously wasn't upset about her not returning all evening given he hadn't even been aware of it before she'd told him, so she tried to forget about the whole incident as much as she could. Mrs Sincope impressively managed to repress the memory almost fully.

Until now, at least, sat in a hospital antenatal ward, having been there for more than half a year, the George incident flashing into her sleeping mind again and again.

Whenever she wakes up having had these dreams about that night in Soho, she wonders about two things regarding the whole incident. One, whether it was George, not her husband, who had impregnated her. Although she had never thought about this being a possibility until very recently, she has to admit that the timing would have been pretty much spot on perfect – it was the fact that she was ovulating that had precipitated the fight with her husband about whose fault it was she hadn't yet managed to conceive. Two, whether all of George's seeming hokum about creating eternal life really did have some actual validity to it. Had George impregnated her in some bizarre manner that had created her current situation? Had he set her up as some sort of 'guinea pig' as Dr Sharp might have termed it, involving her in an elaborate experiment? There was, of course, no way to answer these questions. Yet they tortured her still.

Chapter Nineteen

Theatre D

At the start of December, Mrs Sincope, having by then been in the hospital for around nine months, is taken out of the leather shackles that had bound her hands and feet. Having been in them for several weeks makes their removal seem like bliss.

The IV drip is taken out of her arm at the same time and as a result, she reverts back to oral consumption of the pink pills. She quickly finds she needs to take between fifteen and twenty of them of them a day to ward off withdrawal. Yet she manages to come to a brave decision through the haze of all that medication: to try and wean herself off the pink pills, slowly but surely. She manages to get down to ten a day within a week. A few days later, she is only taking five in any twenty-four-hour period. Reducing it further turns out to be more difficult than she had imagined, but she is soon down to taking only one a day. Cutting herself off all together proves more difficult, with the withdrawal symptoms being worse than she had expected, but soon enough she is completely clean.

With this weaning off of the medication, Mrs Sincope begins to get her mind back, at least partially. While her confidence is still gone and her personality is nothing close to what it was on the day she first came into the hospital for the induction, at least she can think about something for more than a minute at a time.

Three days after she had managed to break free of the pink pills entirely, a date which unbeknownst to Mrs Sincope happens to be Christmas Eve, Dr Blots makes an entrance into her cubicle followed by four large male orderlies.

'Dr Blots! How wonderful to see you again!' Mrs Sincope squeals. This is mostly for effect, as she is now completely terrified of the doctor. Being off the pills improves her ability to think but also brings with it a great deal of fear and anxiety. Blots doesn't respond in any way to her compliment and in fact, does not even bother to look in her direction. Instead, he turns back towards the four male orderlies standing behind him.

'Get her on wheels and deliver her to Theatre D as quickly as possible,' he says to them like a captain delivering orders to his unit. They all nod simultaneously like robots. Blots then leaves without another word. Mrs Sincope is not overly distressed by this quasi-military display, however, as she has just learned that she is about to experience freedom from the antenatal ward for the first time in months. Thinking about it further, perhaps she is about to undergo some medical process that will bring about the birth of Faith. Maybe this is the beginning of something that will bring to an end her long imprisonment in the hospital.

Mrs Sincope is lifted by two of the robotic orderlies into a wheelchair that sits to the right of her bed. Once there, she is wheeled from the antenatal ward and into the greater hospital. The buzz of people rushing to and fro as the chair scuffles from one corridor to another makes her head spin a little. She feels a touch agoraphobic due to having become so accustomed to being held prisoner in one bed with the same cotton white walls to stare at day in and day out. What is even more baffling is all of the Christmas decorations she spots. Her head spins thinking that it's this time of year; had she really been in the hospital long enough for the calendar year to be almost at an end?

This dizzy feeling is then replaced by a fear of what exactly lies ahead, waiting for her in 'Theatre D', as the man wheeling her chair pushes her through a narrow doorway and into a completely darkened room where the chair then comes to a halt. The man who had shoved the wheeled device from the antenatal ward immediately departs. This leaves Mrs Sincope completely alone in the pitch-blackness, no idea whatsoever where she is. Her mind reels again as to why she had been brought here and for what purpose. What was about to take place in this Theatre D? Could she really be about to undergo surgery that would see the arrival into the world of Faith?

She hears footsteps nearby. A moment after as she has noticed these sounds she feels her arms and legs being grabbed by unseen hands that lift her out of the wheelchair. She is being sat down in a new bed of some kind. Upon laying down, she has both of her arms and both of her legs strapped to this new implement; feels like leather cuffs, she thinks. While she is disheartened to be in restraints again, she takes it in stride knowing that at least she is one step closer to finding out what Theatre D holds in store. Mrs Sincope is then shocked when the chair she is strapped to begins to move, around to her left and seemingly upwards. She looks up to see the light change significantly – she is assaulted with brightness all of a sudden – as what appears to be a theatrical curtain is raised. She wonders what the attraction is – until she quickly figures out that it is she herself. Mrs Sincope squints to see what is beyond the lights but all that is visible to her is a sea of white coats that look strangely disembodied. She cannot begin to tell how many there are in the audience in front of her due to the lighting. Dr Blots then appears to her right holding a wooden pointer. He holds something else in his other hand – a tiny black object she can't immediately identify. Alarmingly, and without a word to her, Dr Blots takes this object and places it inside of her vagina. It is all quick and painless, thankfully, but it still upsets her greatly, even after everything she has been through already, to not even be consulted before something is put inside of her own body.

'We will start with the complete and utter lack of dilation, which as we all know is almost unheard of, even in cases of this extreme magnitude,' Dr Blots says into a microphone headset that Mrs Sincope had previously not noticed Blots was wearing. She hears a murmur go through the room that informs her of the approximate numbers of spectators; several hundred from what she can gather. An image is then put up on a screen to her right. She can't make out what it is up there at first. Then it comes to her: it is the inside of her own vagina. What Dr Blots had placed inside of her must have been a camera.

'This is a woman who is eighty-two weeks on from conception, bear in mind. The cervix, as you can all clearly see for yourselves, is almost completely intact, the child's head nowhere in sight. In fact, the foetus has been in retreat for several weeks. This is a picture of the same cervix three weeks ago.'

An historic picture of Mrs Sincope's insides replaces the live feed. She breathes a sigh of relief at first that the inside of her vagina was no longer being displayed live in front of an audience. Then she wonders how the picture of her insides from three weeks past that is currently on show was obtained in the first place. She gets a horrible pain in her stomach that won't go away after this realisation: someone must have put something

211

inside of her while she was passed out cold in order to take that picture. Mrs Sincope looks up at the screen again to find that her current insides are back on display.

'Here we are today. The interior of this woman looks so fallow, it is a wonder she was ever able to conceive.'

The full force of how violating all of this is suddenly hits Mrs Sincope. Completely without her permission, her inner body is being broadcast to a room full of doctors while disparaging remarks are made about her. A turning point is reached in her mind, one in which she decides to resist what is happening to her regardless of the consequences. Mrs Sincope commences yelling at the top of her lungs.

'Stop it! Stop it! Stop it!'

As she shouts this, she struggles with all of her might against her restraints. The entire room full of white coats falls completely silent, their susurration ceasing full stop. Blots looks furious and begins gesturing towards someone unseen, all the while twirling his right index finger around and around as fast as he can. The curtain that had been raised at the start of the 'show' then falls again, sheltering Mrs Sincope from the theatre full of men who had been gawking at her. She feels an intense relief at this development that is short lived.

Blots approaches her looking furious. She is worried all of a sudden about what the doctor is going to do for an encore.

'You ruined my presentation, Mrs Sincope. I'm afraid there will have to be repercussions for such behaviour.'

He motions to the orderlies, who after pushing a few levers and pressing a few buttons, begin to wheel the bed that she's strapped to out of Theatre D. She is taken through long corridors and down several flights via an old, scary lift into what seems to be a basement area. It is grey and completely unfinished. She is wheeled into a very bare room which contains no furniture. The table is then turned around a hundred and eighty degrees to face the door through which she entered. Blots approaches her with a maniacal gleam in his eye.

'Now is the time,' he says, an instruction to the orderlies, even though he is staring into Mrs Sincope's eyes as he says it. She is then set upon the robotic men who had escorted her to this horrible basement room, each of them focused on a different part of her body. One of them inserts an IV into her left arm; another fits a catheter into her urethra; the other fits her with an adult-sized nappy.

'Mrs Sincope, I am placing you in solitary confinement for the next week. The IV drip in your arm has a sugar and water solution that will keep you hydrated and provide you and your unborn child with enough energy to survive. Someone will be in briefly once a day to change your undergarment. Other than that, you are on your own. I hope this experience will teach you never to interfere with my work in any way ever again.'

As Blots and his gang depart, they shut the lights out, leaving Mrs Sincope alone, in complete darkness, strapped to the bed by leather constraints.

The trauma that is suffered by Mrs Sincope over the following week, which includes within in it Christmas Day, even when compared with what she had already been through, is impossible to describe. Alone, unable to move and in total blackness, without even the medication to keep her occupied, she slumps further and further into herself.

Chapter Twenty

Lucille

Almost two months after the evening that had started in the pub with him chatting to Gary from Sunderland, the one that he concluded in his flat, sipping brandy, having been advised by his mother over the telephone to end his marriage, Mr Sincope left Britain altogether with the idea of rediscovering lost love. It was Aleida, the Argentinean who had been his girlfriend for a brief time before he had met Mrs Sincope, whom he went in search of. He flew to Buenos Aires to service this mission.

If you will recall, Aleida had been on his mind several times during the week he had spent in the hospital waiting for his daughter to be born. Quite why is difficult to say given his overall nonchalance when they had broken up. One could have been led to speculate that in the wake of what had happened with his wife and the spectacular breakdown of their relationship, Mr Sincope had been left to clutch at the proverbial straws of his past life. All he could actually recall now of Aleida was her wild spirit, her Latin licentiousness, and the tears that filled her eyes as he told her they shouldn't pursue a long-distance relationship. She had loved him, Aleida had, Mr Sincope told himself again and again as he made his travel arrangements. Aleida was reimagined as the one that got away; Mr Sincope's one true kindred spirit in this lonely world.

There was the final obstacle of quitting his job and the contractual notice he was meant to serve out to get round, of course. Mr Sincope dealt with this in a manner that was utterly unlike him. He simply emailed Terry a brief note.

Sorry, mate. I won't be in ever again. Gary should be up to speed with most of what I've been working on. Best of luck with it all.

Unfortunately for Mr Sincope, Aleida had found love herself upon her return to Argentina. After a few months pootling around Buenos Aires, trying to figure out what to do with her life after Great Britain had come and gone, she managed to land herself a teaching position in Patagonia. Within weeks of arrival in that part of the country, she met a gaucho down there named Owain who swept her off her feet. They were married within a few months from that first meeting and Aleida pregnant within the year. They had a son they named Llyr – it was important to Owain that his son have a Welsh name like all of his forebears had. Aleida reluctantly agreed to this, as it was true love.

Mr Sincope found all this out, unfortunately, sat in an internet café in the Almagro district of Buenos Aires. He had not emailed Aleida before leaving the UK for fear of what she might say putting him off his trip. Once he had found out that getting back together with Aleida was not going to be a goer, Mr Sincope had several options. One was returning to Britain straight off, which he ruled out immediately. Another was bumming around South America until his money ran out, which oddly did sort of have its own appeal. But the option he went for in the end was replying to Aleida's email that described her new life with Owain and little Llyr by asking if he could come to her village in Patagonia to meet the family. Thankfully Aleida, who now had nothing but warm feelings towards Mr Sincope due to it being his lack of engagement in their relationship that had led her into the arms of Owain, enthusiastically approved of this idea. And so, Mr Sincope departed from Buenos Aires by walking out of the internet café and boarding the next coach for Aleida and Owain's Patagonian village. Watching the natural beauty of southern Argentina unfold in front of him as the coach made its long and winding way to the village of El Calafate on the shores of Lago Argentino had a profound effect on Mr Sincope. He decided during the trip to spend the rest of his life in Argentina, one way or another. This resolution was further ratified in his mind when he arrived at his destination only to find that the villagers had been convinced by Aleida to lay on a huge banquet in his honour. He was touched beyond belief; no one had ever constructed a large-scale meal dedicated to just him before, ever.

At the feast, he got talking to an attractive woman named Lucille, who was also English.

'It's funny – my ex-wife's sister's name was Lucille.'

'That is funny,' Lucille responded with. Mr Sincope then remarked that it would be even funnier still if Lucille were to have a sister with the same first name as his ex-wife. Lucille, upon hearing Mrs Sincope's Christian name, giggled and said that, oddly enough, she did have a sister with that handle.

'What's interesting is that I never met Lucille as she was off backpacking in South America.'

'Wow, all these coincidences! Where did your ex-wife grow up?'

'Up north, mostly in Manchester.'

'So did I! What was her father's name?'

'Gerry.'

'That was my father's name!'

Now feeling spooked by all of these common threads, Mr Sincope got a picture of Mrs Sincope out of his wallet to show

Lucille. The fact that he had kept it all this time said a lot about his mindset towards the woman he was still legally married to; she haunted him in a sense, his guilt at abandoning her being so heavy he fled the country at least partially in an attempt to escape from it. On several occasions since he last saw her in the hospital in Ealing, he had meant to remove her picture from his wallet. Somehow, he could never manage to do it.

The picture of Mrs Sincope was now proving a most useful prop, however, given as soon as he showed it to Lucille, she squealed at him.

'That's her! That's my sister!'

Now, it goes without saying that Lucille was not in fact Mrs Sincope's sister as, if you will recall, Mrs Sincope was in fact an only child and her Lucille was an entirely fictitious one. As to why this living, breathing Lucille claimed to be the sister of the wife of the man she had just met, it is hard to explain in rational terms. She wasn't given to telling egregious lies as a general rule and this was perhaps the biggest doozy she'd ever laid. Her snap decision was mostly driven by loneliness; Lucille had come to Patagonia hoping to marry a gaucho but found when she got there that the local yokels were actually not to her taste. She'd signed up to teach English for a year, however, and was mostly seeing out her final three months in Argentina when Mr Sincope showed up. He was the first Englishman she'd met since leaving Blighty and she was desperate to land him. Why she figured posing as his wife's sister would help in this task would seem to an objective viewer bizarre, particularly given that it was, by pure random chance, the exact right tactic to have chosen. Mr Sincope had always entertained deep fantasies about Lucille, this wild cat sister who had gone off to South America to discover herself. In fact, although Mr Sincope was completely unaware of it on any conscious level, some part of him had picked South America as a place to run off to not because he wanted to be with Aleida but because deep, deep down he was hoping he'd run into Lucille somewhere along the way.

As it turns out, the real life, English-teaching Lucille and Mr Sincope were perfect for one another. After two months together in El Carafate, spending pretty much every waking hour together when Lucille wasn't teaching English to Patagonian children and Mr Sincope wasn't helping the local *departamento* with its budget – he had learned to speak passable Spanish surprisingly quickly – Mr Sincope proposed marriage. It was almost the exact opposite of the way he had done so with Mrs Sincope. He asked Lucille out to the lakeside for a walk one night, only to surprise her with a table laid out in an exquisite spot, accompanied by an excellent meal and a little mariachi band, made up of local gauchos. It was there, in this most romantic spot, that Mr Sincope asked Lucille to marry him. She cried with delight and said yes, pulling him to his feet from his knees and bouncing into his arms.

Their nuptials took place two weeks later in the village square. Of course, Mr Sincope had never actually divorced his first wife, which technically made him a bigamist. But given he never intended to leave El Carafate ever again, this was unlikely to ever present a genuine legal problem for him. And true enough, there he stayed. Aleida became like the sister he never had – not to mention occasional babysitter to his and Lucille's five children, three girls and two boys. He was content and at peace with himself for the rest of his days in a way he could never have possibly imagined during the whole of his life in England.

Lucille never found out he was still married to someone in England and he never discovered that Mrs Sincope was in fact an only child. They went to their graves with their secrets intact.

Chapter Twenty-one

The Anniversary

Mrs Sincope is released from solitary confinement after her week in the dark basement and taken to an entirely new room. It is on the top floor of the hospital and though it is sparsely furnished, it is pleasant enough. She is also the only tenant of the space, another bonus. It is the one good thing to have come out of her week in solitary confinement from her perspective. The door is locked from the outside, preventing her from leaving the room for any reason, but Mrs Sincope feels this is to be expected by this stage. There is a bay window to the right of her bed that is large as well as thick, with metal bars across it, which overlooks Four Fountains Park.

She spends most of her days gazing out this window, watching the people below. A month into her stay in her new room, she manages to catch what appears at long range to be a lover's quarrel between two gay men who stand in front of the 'patriotic' fountain, the one with the man mounting a horse, holding a bulldog in his lap. Mrs Sincope quickly surmises that they are a couple as opposed to two straight friends quarrelling due to the theatrical mannerisms of what appears to be the more feminine of the two; he waves his hands wildly in the air as his partner sits against the horse's stone front leg, looking at his lover with 'how the hell did I end up with this drama queen?' eyes. The following day, Mrs Sincope spots in the park what she thinks might be the same couple she had seen in the Love Café on what was supposed to have been the Big Day; the ones who had sat silently as their child screamed its head off, the only move on either of their parts being to place a plastic sheet between them and the toddler in order to dampen the noise. Almost a year on, the child is now being left to his own devices – now clearly a he – wandering around the knock-off Parisian fountain, staring at the world in wonder as his joyless parents sit side by side but world's apart, each of them staring blankly ahead.

Her mind has been devoid of pain in the preceding month, either physical or mental. She can recall large chunks of her life before the induction and a lot of what has happened to her during the almost twelve months since she began to stay at the hospital, but all of the difficult emotions surrounding any of it have been deflated. Not because of the pink pills – she is off any medication at present – but because she is now afflicted with a form of Post-Traumatic Stress Disorder. It is as if nothing that has ever happened to her is real; rather, all of reality is like a dream to Mrs Sincope now.

On the one-year anniversary of Mrs Sincope's induction – a year since Mr and Mrs Sincope had climbed into their Skoda Felicia and driven to the hospital, coming as they did with an expectation that they would be cradling Faith in their arms within hours – Dr Blots opens the door to her room and enters for one of his rare visits. Mrs Sincope has no idea she has been in the hospital for a full year until Blots informs her of this fact.

'Really?' she asks when informed, in a manner that is devoid of any emotion, as if she were enquiring about the weather as a means of small talk.

'Yes. And I'm sorry to tell you this but there doesn't appear to be any end in sight.'

'Thank you for letting me know, Doctor,' Mrs Sincope says. 'There's something I have been meaning to ask you for some time now.'

Mrs Sincope had thought about George and his flat again for the first time in months just that morning. A dream she'd had about it spurred these thoughts. She wasn't sure by this point whether the George incident was something that had actually happened to her or if she had just invented the whole thing. Still, she doesn't get to see Blots very much so she decides she wants to see what he'll say when questioned about it.

'All right,' Blots says, noncommittally.

'It's about head office. Is it in a flat in Soho done up with white, glowing walls? Is there a man named George who lives there?'

Blots pauses for a moment before laughing out loud. It takes him almost a minute to calm himself down.

'Where do you get these strange ideas from, Mrs Sincope?'

'I suppose it comes from sitting around in bed all day.'

'Are you in any pain at the moment?'

'No.'

'I don't believe you. I think you're being coy. Or you don't wish to disappoint me. Either way, I want to put you back on the pink pills again.'

Mrs Sincope has no reaction to this news. Being on the pills, being off the pills; what's the difference?

'All right then,' she says.

'Here's a couple to get you started.'

Blots takes a couple of the big pink pills out of his pocket and has them resting on the palm of his right hand for Mrs Sincope to snatch away. She duly does so, swallowing them down without any water despite their massive size, a trick she still has up her sleeve from months of practice.

'I'll have someone come up and give you a healthy supply of medication later on today. Until then, happy one-year anniversary, Mrs Sincope.'

As Blots leaves the room, locking the door behind him, Mrs Sincope thinks briefly about the pink pills and whether taking them again is a good idea. But this is a passing moment of lucidity; soon enough, she is thinking about moments from her life mixed up with figments of her imagination, unable to tell one from the other. She has started to imagine that her mother is still alive; that her father is as well. Perhaps one or both of them would visit her later on that day, wishing her well on her one-year anniversary in the hospital.

A few hours later, Gregory, the northern lad from the antenatal ward reception enters the room bearing a hundred pink pills. He places them on the countertop sat immediately to Mrs Sincope's left. He then walks gingerly up to Mrs Sincope and hands her an arrangement of daffodils.

'The staff on the antenatal ward got you these in light of your anniversary,' he says as he hands them to her.

'Thank you very much,' she says, the high from the pink pills starting to wane. She had been thinking about where her next dose was coming from before Gregory had shown up. 'Sorry, I know I've seen you before but I just can't quite remember where. What's your name, son?'

Gregory is crying now. He didn't think he would, yet somehow standing in front of Mrs Sincope, seeing her strange condition and what it has done to her, he can't hold back.

'Name is Gregory, ma'am,' he says though a sob.

'Come now, why so sad?'

'Don't worry about that. Just take care of yourself, all right?'

Gregory leaves without a further word, still crying furiously.

About an hour after Gregory has been and left, the effect of the pink pills has completely worn off. She had been continuously thinking about taking another dose since shortly after Gregory had left, something inside of her stopping her from doing so each time. She turns away from the pills and looks in the opposite direction; out the window and down at Four Fountains Park. There, by the Lichtenstein rip-off fountain, she sees two nervous young people sat next to each other, one a boy and the other a girl – a pretty one at that, Mrs Sincope notes to herself – both of the young people looking into one another's eyes and having what appears to be an intense conversation. The boy is rubbing his girlfriend's hands intently. It had been a chilly March thus far; at least it looked that way to Mrs Sincope who only had visual data to go by. It initially appears from her viewpoint as if the young couple are discussing a tragedy that had recently collectively befallen them.

This diagnosis begins to seem all wrong the more Mrs Sincope gazes upon the pair, however. There seems now to be almost an anticipation of something or other that is imminently due to take place instead. Perhaps they are waiting for someone to arrive that neither of them particularly cares for, Mrs Sincope thinks, but that too seems incorrect; there is too much positivity between them for something so cynical to be why they had gathered. Then, out of the blue, the boy solves the mystery for Mrs Sincope – he jumps up from where he had been sat milliseconds previous, gets down on one knee, and taking a ring from his coat pocket and rather proudly displaying it for the woman he is now clearly hoping to make his fiancée, proposes marriage. The girl reacts predictably, jumping to her feet, putting her hands to her mouth and shouting 'yes!' so loudly that Mrs Sincope thinks she can hear her from where she sits – it is almost certainly an auditory hallucination given the distance involved. As the newly engaged woman wraps her arms round her now fiancé and the two young people literally cry with joy, Mrs Sincope joins in. She feels an immense, almost overwhelming surge of happiness for them. It is her first experience of any emotion since the first few days of torture in the darkness of the basement room, post-Theatre D.

As the couple walk away from the post-modern fountain and out of Four Fountains Park altogether, hand in hand, Mrs Sincope marvels at the way her mind had suddenly come back to her in a way it hadn't since her time spent in solitary confinement. She wonders if it was the mental challenge of figuring out what was going on in the park; whether it was an effect from having taken the pink pills for the first time in weeks and then not followed up with another dose; if it was a by-product of having released the emotion felt at the young couple's happiness. Perhaps it was combination of all of these factors. Whatever had caused the sharpening of her mind all of a sudden, it is a moment of clarity, bringing with it the most sober thinking she had experienced in a long time.

I have to find a way out of here, she thinks to herself. To this end, she eases her body slowly out of bed, the first time she has been up and on her feet in who knows how long. Though she finds walking even a few feet a tremendous struggle, she manages to haul herself to the room's door. Once there, she tries to examine it for frailties, first turning the handle to make sure that it is definitely locked – it most certainly is. After coming quickly to the conclusion that the door offers no easy means of escape, she searches the walls for any possibilities there. She examines every nook and cranny, marvelling the whole while at how strange it feels to be at least partly in charge of her faculties once again.

However, it soon becomes clear to her that the room is air-tight. Upon making this discovery, she collapses to the floor onto her behind, softly sobbing the whole way.

After a minute spent wallowing in self-pity, Mrs Sincope eyes the pink pills that Gregory had left on the table. For one moment, she considers swallowing all of the ones that he had left for her; she would try and overdose, possibly killing herself in the process. She puts this out of her mind in a hurry; she would be killing Faith at the same time, something she won't contemplate. No, best to take a couple of the pills now to dull the mental anguish that had flared up again from nowhere. With clarity of thought comes deep pain, she notes.

As she swallows the pill, she has a thought: she will not allow herself to get as addicted to them as she had done in the past. She will use them to ease her current pain but look to quit taking the pills within the next week or so. After that, she will plan an escape from the hospital in earnest.

This causes her to try and imagine going out into the wide world again. The thought makes her to freeze in terror. What would she do if she were free? She could look for her husband. She could try and find George's flat, see if he really does have anything to do with her condition. She should probably go to another hospital to try and have Faith be born, but that thought terrifies her in numerous ways as well. In fact, the whole idea of escaping from the hospital suddenly scares her so much, Mrs Sincope finds herself in the middle of a panic attack.

In response, she gets back into her bed and pulls the sheets up over her head. At least she knows she only has to wait a few minutes before the effects of the pink pills will calm her down completely. Yes, she will one day escape from her current situation and free her daughter from the womb, she tells herself again as her brain begins to once again retreat. Some day she will find the will and the way.

Some day.

Someday her baby will be born.

Then, the effect of the pink pills hits her completely and all of her thoughts around these things cease. The worries that had been so troubling only a few seconds previous recede into the distance quickly, before fading away completely.

A few minutes later, Mrs Sincope imagines her husband standing beside her. She hadn't thought about him in a long while. This vision of Mr Sincope is smiling down at her, love in his eyes, the exact opposite of the demonic, blood-splattered hallucination she had had of him when she first encountered withdrawal from the pink pills.

'Let go, dear,' the mirage says to her. 'If you can do that, I can stay here with you forever.'

Mrs Sincope feels like she is being pushed into a warm, cosy void, a place devoid of pain and suffering. The ghost of her husband is telling her to let go again and again and she feels compelled to obey.

'You, Faith, and I can be together. We can be together forever and ever, just the three of us.'

Finally, she takes the vision's advice, allowing herself to let go fully of the material world. Mrs Sincope grabs hold of her husband's hand and soon they are walking together towards a light that is so bright it's unbelievable, and yet at the same time can be looked at directly with no visual discomfort. The two Sincopes turn and smile at one another. Soon, they meet with the light so that all around them is transformed into whiteness of an unimaginable intensity.

And there, standing a few feet away, is Faith. Mrs Sincope knows it is her on sight. Faith looks to be around seven years old, clothed in a white dress. Her hair is blond, her eyes dark blue. Mrs Sincope walks towards her daughter and then embraces her. As she does, she knows for certain that all of her troubles are over.

Acknowledgements

Great thanks to Katie Sunley and the whole Headline team for seeing something in this story. Thank you to Greg Rees for editing this book as well as my last two novels. Love to my wife, Polly, for all her support. Some credit needs to go to Franz Kafka for all the revelations.

Acknowledgements

Charlotte Heard is one of few women in the male-dominated world of a Westminster think tank. Quick-witted and resourceful she is a senior member of the team and the young women in the organisation look up to her. But she is determined to realize her ambition to become an MP.

Her dream seems within reach when she finds herself in the midst of a shocking murder investigation. Someone is trying to frame her and Charlotte must find out why.

Can she uncover the truth or will it derail everything she has worked for?

'A gripping story of evil in the influential but murky world of think tanks' Sir Oliver Letwin

'A tongue-in-cheek, Tarantino-style tour through the Westminster world of think tanks and parliamentarians' Professor Tim Bale, Queen Mary University of London

ACCENT

In a world of fake news, who can you trust?

Global pop sensation Noah Hastings takes to the stage for
his sold-out concert. After singing his latest hit, Noah
detonates a bomb strapped to his chest, killing himself
and ninety-one of his fans.

Speculation about the pop star's motivation for the crime
runs riot until the authorities pin the blame on fundamentalist
Islam. But what happens when Noah's inspiration turns out to
be another ideology?

Nina Hargreaves, an investigative journalist, travels around
America searching for the real story. She gets close to the
truth – but risks losing everything she has in the process …

ACCENT